FE...

· Christie Ridgway ·

plunges unassuming kindergarten teacher Stacy Banks into a desperate life-or-death situation at sea. Luckily, she has the handsome and mysterious Ryan to keep her merry Christmas from becoming a winter nightmare.

· Katherine Hall Page ·

brings caterer Faith Fairchild into a world of Christmas miracles, when a local woman discovers a precious child left alone in a manger. But when trouble begins to brew around the infant, Faith must step in to save the child and Christmas.

· Judi McCoy ·

creates a delightful Christmas tale of love and magic. Jewelry designer Claire St. Germaine is flabbergasted when frogs start appearing at her doorstep. Just when she thinks her Christmas can't get any stranger, Claire realizes she is about to meet her frog prince.

· Joanne Pence ·

crafts a fantastic mystery as Homicide Inspector Rebecca Mayfield tracks down a van full of missing Santas. Fortunately for her, an attractive stranger pops up to help her solve the case . . . and give her some much-needed Christmas cheer.

CHRISTIE
RIDGWAY

KATHERINE
HALL PAGE

JUDI
McCOY

JOANNE
PENCE

MISTLETOE
and
MAYHEM

AVON BOOKS
An Imprint of HarperCollinsPublishers

AVON BOOKS
An Imprint of HarperCollins*Publishers*
10 East 53rd Street
New York, New York 10022-5299

ISBN 0-06-073205-9
www.avonmystery.com

First Avon Books paperback printing: November 2004

Avon Trademark Reg. U.S. Pat. Off. and in Other Countries, Marca Registrada, Hecho en U.S.A.
HarperCollins® is a registered trademark of HarperCollins Publishers Inc.

Printed in the U.S.A.

10 9 8 7 6 5 4 3 2 1

MISTLETOE
and
MAYHEM

Out on a Limb

Christie Ridgway

Christmas came a day early, but he wasn't complaining. The timing couldn't be better, as a matter of fact. Thanks to the latest terrorism orange alert, every cop and every fed in the county was ass-deep in work—car inspections at the border crossings, shoe checks at the airport, passenger list searches at the cruise ship terminal. While the authorities were busy counting bottles of tequila from Tijuana, sifting through the underwear of a grandpa en route to Grand Forks, or holding up one of the Princess Line from floating off toward Puerto Vallarta, he'd be busy setting up his future.

He hadn't lived in San Diego long, but the situation he'd inherited was perfect for a scheme—a dream, really—that had been brewing in his mind for years. Nothing was going to get in his way.

No one.

Baring his teeth in a smile for his contact, Jaime, he hefted a battered backpack, testing its weight. "Ten grand is lighter than I thought."

Jaime frowned. "It's all there, yes?"

"Didn't I say so?" He unzipped the nylon anyway, eyed the rubber-banded stacks of twenty-dollar bills, and then let Jaime check them out too. The money looked grubby, but who the hell cared? Clean or dirty, money procured whatever a man could want. He transferred his gaze to Jaime, noting the oily sheen of sweat on the man's dark upper lip. His eyes narrowed. "You'll do as we've planned."

"*Sí*. Yes." Jaime swiped at his mouth, and then reseated the ball cap covering his thick shock of hair. "As you said, *señor*. As we planned." More beads of sweat popped, despite the pleasant midsixties temperature.

With his gaze locked on Jaime's, he shoved his hand beneath his wind jacket, his fingertips sliding over the Vuitton leather belt he'd bought himself as an early Christmas present. It wasn't the Rolex or Phillipe watch that he'd really wanted, but an accessory like that would only draw suspicion. Who would notice a belt? True flashiness would have to wait a few years.

His grip found the Beretta tucked in his waistband, and he pulled it out then tossed the handgun to Jaime. "*Feliz Navidad*."

"This has got to be worse than wrapping an inflatable sex doll," Stacy Banks muttered to herself, winding out another length of Christmas paper. Holding her bottom lip between her teeth, she folded, tucked, and taped. Then she took her veed scissors in hand to create a curly-ribbon confection in red and green. With a delicate touch, she placed it on top. Finally, inhaling a cautious breath, she spun toward the mirror to get a new perspective on the package.

"Well," she said to her reflection. "I suppose I look . . . festive."

And not like a kindergarten teacher, which was much more to the point. Miss Banks of Room 2 at Lemoncrest Elementary wore flat-soled shoes and long denim dresses or soft corduroy pants perfect for the chasing, corralling, and educating of thirty-four five-year-olds. Today's get-up—a Betty-and-Wilma-like sarong of heavy-duty Christmas wrap complete with knee-length paper skirt pleated for ease of movement—was designed for interesting, enticing, and well . . . enslaving just one thirty-four-year-old man.

Stacy plucked the cascade of ribbon out of her own blond curls and picked up a bobby pin to anchor it more securely. Ryan Beausoleil—transplanted from El Paso, Texas, to the condo above hers just a few months before—wouldn't know what hit him. He was toast. He was hers.

If she found the guts to ask him to the party, that is.

But a swift glance at the slip of paper lying on her kitchen table was all the swift-kick-in-the-

derriere she needed. Formatted with a cutesy figure in one corner and the words YOUR HOLIDAY
ELF beneath it, the paycheck showed a sizable
number on the "Amount Of" line and her own
name on the "Payable To" line, representing the
last three weeks of wrapping, ribboning, and
tagging. Extra money was good, and would be a
pleasure to spend at the local mall. But it was the
name scrawled on the signature line that was getting Stacy out of the house.

Her younger sister's name. Her younger, freckle-
faced, former Barbie-stealing sister who had, six
months before, come up with a business idea, a
business plan, a business success.

She'd gone out on a limb.

As had Stacy's friend Delia, who'd traveled to
China two months ago and adopted a baby girl.
As had Stacy's yoga-class colleague, who'd
bought a five-hundred-dollar raffle ticket from
the fire department in August and was now on a
year-long cruise around the world.

In those same months, Stacy had burped the
baby, dutifully filled out lesson plans, worked as
her sister's temporary employee, and never
missed a scheduled session at the local Yoga for
You center.

But she'd never gone out on a limb.

To the rustle of her wrapping-paper dress,
Stacy gathered up a lacy shawl and a tiny evening purse, leaving behind her day planner, her

bulky wallet, and her cell phone. Anything else she needed would be at Your Holiday Elf's end-of-the-season party. Everything but her date.

Stacy knew she'd find him at the JMR Sport-fishing Landing on San Diego Bay. Even in the deepening twilight, the driving directions she'd printed off the Internet were simple to follow and a parking space just as easy to find. The lot was nearly empty, but that didn't surprise her. Ryan had inherited a sportfishing boat from his uncle and he'd told her that December was the off-season. He and the other boat operators who used this landing wouldn't have regular trips running again until spring.

The place wasn't entirely deserted, though. Just as she approached, a pair of men was coming through a locked gate leading to the docks. They held it open for her without question, giving her a friendly check-over in the glow from the string of Christmas lights wound through the cyclone fencing. Too excited and nervous to feel the cold, she'd left her shawl behind.

"Nice package," one of the guys murmured with an easy grin. "Is my name on the gift tag?"

Uneasiness fluttered in Stacy's belly. Not that the men appeared threatening, but she always clammed up at come-ons, even benign ones like this. Each year during the first week of school she read her students *Ms. Shy Makes a Friend*, but the same advice she said aloud every September,

"Go the mile, give a smile," never seemed to stick with her.

"I'm, um, here to visit Ryan Beausoleil." Saying it aloud set her stomach to fluttering again. His name was how they'd met, in the condo mailroom where the box marked BEAUSOLEIL was snuggled beside the one marked BANKS.

Bo-so-lay. It sounded exotic, evocative.

Second, third, fourth thoughts flitted through her brain. His very syllables were out of a kindergarten teacher's league. How could she be thinking of going out on a limb with him?

"He's one lucky dude," the grinner said. He didn't seem to think that she and Ryan were an obvious mismatch, and Stacy took heart from that. "His boat, *The Bait*, is the last one on the left."

With a quick breath, Stacy stepped through the doorway. The gate locked behind her as the two men continued toward the parking lot. She made her way down the deck, its rubberized surface muffling the tap-tap-tap of her midheeled, strappy shoes. The only other sound was a gentle slosh of the water. Small security lights illuminated the silent boats and the walkway itself, yet Stacy had the distinct feeling she was alone.

But Ryan was here! He had to be. He'd told her in the mailroom the day before that he planned to spend Christmas Eve on his boat, catching up on the never-ending upkeep. But God, it was spooky with only that eerie slosh-slosh-slosh of the water and the rabbity noise of her heartbeat in her ears. A breeze washed over her bare arms and shoulders, stirring both her real and ribbon curls. Chills pricked her skin.

This is stupid, she suddenly thought, her feet stuttering to a halt.

Not her fear, but the fact that she'd considered coming out here in the first place. What had she been thinking? Hunky, sexy Ryan Beausoleil was bodelicious, but face it, she wasn't bodacious enough to walk onto his boat and invite him to a party. Especially when she was dressed like a Christmas present. What had seemed fun and flirty at the time, something a man named Beausoleil would appreciate—since everyone at Your Holiday Elf was going in costume—now seemed embarrassing. Goofy even.

She was going to turn around and get out of this creepy place and go back—

To her safe, boring, never-go-the-mile-and-smile life.

No way.

Swallowing hard, she set her sights on *The Bait* and forced herself to march onward. Ryan had seemed interested, remember? He lingered in the mailroom when they happened to meet there. He'd helped her brother carry in the new loveseat she'd bought last weekend. After that, when she'd mumbled something about now owing him a favor, he'd wiggled his eyebrows and then laughed when she'd blushed.

She *knew* he was interested, just as she knew when five-year-old Tyler Brown was up to no good. There was that devilish, and devilishly cute little gleam in his eye. The quirk in his smile that promised naughtiness to come.

Well, this Christmas Stacy wanted to be naughty too.

She paused at the steps that led aboard *The Bait*. The boat was better lit than the others nearby, but she didn't see or hear Ryan.

"Hello?" she called out, sliding her palms down her paper skirt. "Ahoy there?"

No one replied. Still on the dock, she paced the length of the boat—it was a sixty-five-footer he'd told her brother. Equipment bristled from its sides and decks, but the only thing she could identify for sure was the little speedboat winched up at the back—or was that the bow? "Ahoy? Ryan?"

Nobody's home. Disappointment flooded through her. But it was the relief that followed that got her moving again. Ignoring the weasely little nervousness in her belly, she walked back to the stairs, grasped the cold handrails, and mounted the metal laddered steps that led onto the boat. *No backing out now, Banks.* Only kindergarten teacher-cowards would be run off so quickly.

Checking her watch, she promised herself she'd wait for his return a decent amount of time. Three minutes, say. *Then* she'd go.

With reprieve two minutes and fifty seconds away, Stacy felt herself relax—and then felt the cold. There was a lighted, windowed room on this level of the deck and through the glass she could see a small cooking area, a bar, and cushioned benches. *The galley,* she thought, and scurried toward its door. If Ryan arrived in the next two minutes and thirty seconds, though it seemed certain that he would not, surely he'd forgive her for finding a spot to stay warm.

He might be surprised to see her, but he wouldn't be angry.

As her fingers touched the slick metal doorknob, she heard his voice.

Her hand jerked away. Her heart jolted in her chest. The cold went away again as embarrassment rushed heat across her skin. He was talking to someone else. Murmuring. *What if he was with another woman?* She knew he was single. She knew he lived alone.

What she didn't know was if some other woman had gotten to him first.

The boards beneath her feet vibrated. Footsteps. Two sets. Thinking to dash past her neighbor and his companion and get away as quickly as possible, Stacy ducked out from beneath the galley's overhang.

And there he was, half-turned to talk to that someone behind him.

Ryan Beausoleil. Lean, dark-haired, Ryan Beausoleil. He had the wide shoulders and the broad back of a man who worked for a living. Not a man who chicken-pecked at a keyboard or who counted beans for a paycheck, but a man who worked with his body. His glorious, manly, made-her-itch-to-go-out-on-a-limb-body. She took another step toward him—or more precisely, toward escape—her heel hitting the deck with a decided clack.

His head whipped toward her. His dark eyes zeroed onto her face. He went still.

She did too, because as Ryan's companion came around from behind him, she saw it wasn't a woman, but another man, wearing a dirty ballcap. And before whatever that made her feel could register, Ryan's friend pulled something from the front of his pants and pointed it straight at Stacy. A scream formed, but her throat clamped tight, holding back its release.

Ryan's friend was pointing a weapon at her. A big, black, scary *gun*.

2

Guns, of course, were not allowed on the grounds of Lemoncrest Elementary School. Not even toy guns. But Stacy had found that didn't stop the boys on the playground from playing Cops or Army Man or Power Ninjas and creating weaponry out of anything from sycamore twigs to licorice sticks. Kindergarten boys ate their sandwiches into the shapes of guns and then took pretend target practice at their SpongeBob SquarePants juice boxes.

But the weapon pointing at her wasn't any peanut-butter-and-jelly pistol. The person holding it wasn't a five-year-old. Beyond that, Stacy couldn't make sense of the situation. This had to be some weird, waking dream.

"Why you here, lady?" the stranger asked, his accent heavy and Spanish.

The black O of the gun's mouth held hypnotic power. Stacy couldn't tear her gaze away from it. "To invite Ryan to a party." It came out a whisper.

"*Qué?*" the man demanded.

"A party. To invite Ryan to a party." Her gaze flickered to her neighbor. Other than a slight narrowing of his eyes, his face didn't show concern or alarm. She noticed that one of his big hands was wrapped around the straps of a battered backpack and she wondered if inside it was a weapon of his own.

In Spanish, Gun-Man said something to Ryan. He responded with a shrug, his gaze trained on her face. "Yeah, I know her." Then he leaned against the galley's outside wall and tilted his head as if considering her assets. "Nice *agar-raderas*, eh?"

His casual pose and casual tone slapped her back to reality. This wasn't a dream. This was *real.*

Adrenaline surged through her veins. *I have to get out of here!*

"This must be a bad time." Her muscles tensed as she prepared to sprint for the steps behind the two men. She shifted forward. "I'll just get out of your way and—"

"*Pare!*" Gun-Man jabbed the weapon in her direction. "Stop!"

Stacy froze, holding everything still, including her breath.

She'd read in one of those worst-case books that if someone pointed a gun at you, you should run. That your chances were bettered by trying to get away rather than sticking around. Well, they couldn't have been writing about this scenario. There was no way for her to escape that wasn't through the two men or over the side of the boat. And there was no way a bullet would miss her if she attempted either route, not when she was less than four feet from the business end of the weapon.

Her gaze lifted to Gun-Man's face. There was a nervous film of sweat on his stubbled upper lip, but it didn't reassure her any. Neither did Ryan, when she transferred her gaze to him. His expression was watchful, but he didn't look any more prepared to assist her than he had before. There was only one thing she could think to do then and, frankly, the action totally suited her inclinations.

She opened her mouth to scream.

A hard palm clapped against her mouth. Her back was jerked against a warm, solid chest. "Keep your mouth shut, damn it," Ryan ground out. Then he spoke to Gun-Man in Spanish.

Don't scare her. Let her go.

Stacy had no idea if that's what he said, but she prayed it was so.

A rough-toned discussion ensued. Ryan kept his hand mashed over her mouth. His heartbeat thumped against her spine. Hers had to be racing against the inside of the forearm he had pressed against her breasts, keeping her body aligned with his. The backpack hanging from the crook of his elbow lay heavily along her ribs.

As the argument continued, Ryan's grip on her tightened, constricting her lungs. Though she took frantic sucks through her nose, Stacy couldn't get enough air. She needed more but she couldn't bring it in. Black spots floated into the edges of her vision. Her legs sagged. Without Ryan's arm she would slide to the deck.

Of course, came the woozy thought, without Ryan's arm she'd be able to breathe.

"Fuck!"

The pressure lifted off her lungs. Just as she'd thought, without Ryan's arm for support, she slid onto the deck.

"Fuck!" he said again. "We need to let her go, Jaime."

"No! No one off before me. Put her in the galley. Then we sail."

Without another protest, Ryan put her in the galley all right, moving her like a rag doll. Gun-Man and his drawn weapon hovered during the entire operation. By the time her breath was back and her thoughts were clear again, she was alone in the galley, propped on one of the cushioned benches.

A hum, then a rumble sounded from below. She jerked straight in her seat, then leaped to her feet and raced to the door leading from the galley to the deck. Her fingers closed over the door handle. As she felt the boat move away from the dock, she also realized the two men had locked her in.

Whirling, she raced to the door on the other side of the galley. But this one was locked too.

I'm not going to cry. Or scream, either. She

didn't want to draw the men to her until she had something that might help her out of this mess.

She almost cried three minutes later, though, when she realized there was nothing in the room she could use. The refrigerator was empty. The pantry cupboards bare. Even the large broom-sized closet was broomless. Then she spotted Ryan's battered backpack half-hidden beneath a bench. She rushed toward it, hope surging. Maybe he'd left it there for her to find. Maybe he was as much a victim of Gun-Man as she was, and this was his way of giving her anonymous aid.

Her fingers fumbled with the zipper. It traveled an inch, stopped. She yanked at it again, it jerked along some more, then slid all the way open.

Stacy stared at what was inside. She'd hoped for something other than this. A key to get her out, maybe.

Instead, the backpack was filled with money. She shoved her hands through it, searching for something more useful. But there was only money. Wads of it. Banded in packs of twenties and fifties.

The engine sound whined higher and the boat accelerated. Stacy's gaze veered toward the window and she saw they'd left the harbor far behind and were now speeding into the inky night and empty ocean. In frustration, she kicked at the backpack. Rubber-banded bundles tumbled out and skittered over the linoleum floor.

Ryan had left her a key, all right. A key to the

mess she'd gotten herself into when she'd had the stupid, stupid idea of going out on a limb.

A boat, a Mexican, a bag full of money. It was drugs. Ryan Beausoleil was involved in the drug trade.

From behind the interior galley door, footsteps thumped. She lunged for the money, stuffing it back into the bag. The zipper stuck again, and she swallowed back another scream of frustration. With a push, she slid the half-closed bag back into place, then collapsed onto her bench just as the door opened.

Ryan stood there, his wide shoulders nearly filling the jamb. Behind him, she glimpsed a set of stairs, and she assumed they led to the smaller room above the galley that contained the navigational and communication equipment. Stacy pretended she wasn't committing every new detail to memory. She tried looking harmless and victimized.

Which, of course, she was.

But the sting in her eyes *wasn't* tears. She wouldn't give this low-life, no-good, drug dealer the satisfaction.

He must have seen something on her face though, because his jaw tightened. "Look, Stacy, you're going to be just fine, I promise."

Said the spider to the fly. Hah! Hadn't she read the story to her classes a dozen times?

He must have detected her skepticism too, because he took a step inside. "Really, honey. I wish this hadn't happened—"

"That makes both of us." Rising to her feet, she moved to block his view of the half-open backpack. It was better he didn't know what she *did* know. She tucked her arms across her chest and glared at him. "And don't you *dare* call me 'honey.' "

He held up his hands. "Okay, okay." Then he blinked. "What the hell are you wearing?"

"I told you, I was going to a party." Inspiration struck. "And my sister knows I came to your boat to invite you along. So you'd better turn around right now and take me back or . . . or . . . she'll worry."

He appeared to miss the point completely. "I've never seen you dressed like . . . that."

"It's party wear."

"It's wrapping paper. What do you have on underneath that stuff?"

As if she'd tell her kidnapper and that scary friend of his—who at this moment was creeping down the stairs behind Ryan. Instead, she lied. "I'll bet my sister has already called the police."

"*Policía*?" Gun-Man echoed, his eyes going wide and panicky.

Ryan turned.

Just in time to catch the blow from his friend's gun against the side of his temple. Ryan toppled to the floor.

3

Stacy acted on instinct. Blame it on her kinder-garten training, blame it on her soft, stupid heart, but something made her fly across the small room toward the fallen man. Her dress ripped near the waist as she dropped to her knees beside him.

Ryan was breathing, but a knot was already swelling on his temple. A small cut at his hairline oozed blood. She dashed to one of the drawers where she'd earlier spied a stack of fast-food napkins, then rushed back to him. Pushing his thick hair away from the wound with one hand, she used the other to press a handful of paper cloths advertising Taco Bell against the wound.

A slap of cold air yanked her attention toward the door leading outside the galley. It was open, and through it she could see Gun-Man. Wearing the backpack, he was climbing over the side of *The Bait* and into the speedboat that had been winched above the deck, but was now bobbing in the ocean. In seconds, he gunned the motor and sped off, his white ballcap turning to a dot, then a speck, and then to nothing.

Relief slowed the trilling beat of her pulse. One gun gone. One man gone. One man down. Her odds were improving.

The boat made a gentle pitch to the side, rolling Ryan's head toward her knee. When it pitched again, Stacy realized the obvious. The boat was no longer accelerating. They were floating in open ocean.

The thought fled as Ryan groaned. She inched backward, wary of what he might do when he came to. He groaned again and his eyelashes fluttered. Stacy lifted the napkins to see that the bleeding from the cut on his head was slowing.

She pressed them against it again, then looked at his face to find him watching her through half-closed eyes.

"Like the way you smell," he said, his words slurring a little.

"What?"

"Like the way you smell. Perfume. Smell it in the mailroom and know I've missed you. Hate it when I've missed you."

He tried to catch her in the mailroom? That was *her* ploy! She frowned at him. "I don't know what you're talking about. Be quiet. You've been hit on the head."

"Thas' what I thought firs' time I saw you. Hit on the head. Pretty, pretty girl hit me on the head." His head lolled with another soft pitch of the boat, and his eyelids fluttered shut.

Still, she made herself frown at him again. This wasn't one of her naughty little bad boys, she reminded herself. There was one or two in her class every year, good-natured scamps whose mischief, she hated to admit, more often charmed than annoyed her. They were always the devil to control. As was the way they tugged at her heart.

But Ryan Beausoleil wasn't a scamp, he was a criminal.

A criminal who had taken her out into the middle of the ocean and then lost consciousness on her. The boat rocked again. He'd gone and lost consciousness on Stacy Banks, a woman whose sum total of nautical skill amounted to knowing all the words of "Row, Row, Row Your Boat."

"But we gotta get out of here," she said aloud. Ryan didn't stir at the sound of her voice, so she left him on the floor, and moved to close the open door to the deck. Then she hurried to the interior stairway, and headed upward.

It was called a wheelhouse, she recalled, as she surveyed the smaller room up top. There was a built-in bench and a small table on the right. In front, a deck of equipment, studded with unfamiliar-looking lights, switches, and measuring devices stood beneath wraparound windows—windows that gave a view of an unrelenting dark void.

Fear grabbed again at Stacy's heart.

The middle of the night. The middle of the ocean. Alone with a criminal.

"An unconscious criminal," she said out loud, just to emphasize the fact. "And we can't be *that* far from the shore." Peering down at the instrument panel, she tried to detect which would offer navigational aid. When that wasn't immediately apparent, she searched around for the key to start the boat. That didn't come to light either.

"Okay, okay. Calm down," she told her jangling nerves. Maybe Ryan had the keys. Maybe she could tie him up, slap him awake somehow, and get him to tell her how to drive the boat. She rushed down the stairs.

He hadn't moved. The napkins had slipped from his face to the floor. Blood had trickled halfway toward his jaw, then dried. Still, she approached him with caution. "Ryan, Ryan," she called from a few feet away. "I need help getting the boat going."

He remained still as a corpse.

A corpse? Panic joined hands with the fear inside her to seize, then shake her heart. He couldn't be dead! She couldn't think of anything worse—than being dead herself, that is—than being stuck on this boat with a *corpse*.

"Ryan!" Her voice sounded thin and scared. She took another step closer to him. "Damn you, Ryan Beausoleil, you better not be dead!"

His head rolled her way. His eyes popped open. Though cloudy, they stared at her. "Been meaning to ask you something."

"What?" Now her voice was hoarse with relief. He smiled at her, and despite his hazy gaze, it was one of those bad-boy, roguish smiles that got five-year-old Tyler Brown out of trouble three times a week. "Wanna go out sometime, Stacy?"

"*What?*"

"When'm not so tired, that is," he muttered, his eyes closing again. "Gotta be on my toes when'm with you, Stacy."

"I'm going to *hang* you by your toes," she declared, rushing to him. "Don't pass out on me again. I need help."

But she couldn't rouse him. She shook his shoulder, she patted his cheek, she did everything short of whacking him on the head again, which sounded more tempting by the second. The boat seesawed, steeper now. Wherever it was that they were drifting, the seas were rougher.

Swallowing hard, Stacy ran back up the stairs. If she couldn't get the boat going somewhere, she could try to get someone to the boat. But though she flipped switches and turned dials, none of the equipment remotely resembled the elementary school intercom system. Not one of her actions appeared to alert a living soul.

Which made her think of dead people again. Which made her think of Ryan.

Still trying to make outside contact via the instrument panel, she yelled down the stairs. "Ryan! Wake up, Ryan! Wake up!"

The only answer was silence, and then another steep dive-and-roll of the boat. Her stomach clutched and then movement outside the windows caught her eye.

"Oh, thank God," she whispered. Lights. Another boat, big, like this one. Heading straight for *The Bait*.

She was rescued! Or . . .

Was she?

Maybe these were more of Ryan's friends. If they were, she didn't want to meet them, that was sure, because at worst, he was a criminal. At best, he was a lousy judge of character. And the other boat was drawing nearer.

She ran back down the stairs that led to the galley. Ryan still looked to be out cold. Stepping over him, she grabbed the handle to the broom closet. It was bare inside, and big enough to hide her if she scrunched down. The boat pitched again, but she managed to wedge herself inside and pull the door shut behind her. There were metal vents in the door, and they allowed her air and a squint-eyed view of the room.

It wasn't long before their company arrived. And it only took her seconds more to be grateful for her own caution. Three men walked into the galley, carting a bound-and-gagged Gun-Man between them. They dropped him on the floor, then they turned their attention to Ryan, poking at him with their boots, then kicking at his ribs.

Stacy held one hand against her mouth, her stomach churning with another rush of fear.

Ryan groaned and rolled into a ball, but they kept at him. Finally they hauled him to a sitting position by the collar, and dumped him back against one of the benches. He opened his eyes, blinking at the men. Fresh blood ran down his face. "Wha—"

"My line, *amigo*," one of the men said. He wore pointy-toed boots and a black cowboy hat. "What the hell happened? We found Jaime heading toward Baja. He says you tried to steal the money and kill him."

· 4 ·

While the new men on board stood with their backs to Stacy, Ryan was directly in front of her. She could see the confusion on his face as he lowered his head and slowly shook it. Then he lifted his gaze to his questioner. His eyes looked clearer and a scowl turned down his mouth. Even under the circumstances, even with the bruise forming on his temple and blood trickling down his face—or maybe because of them—Stacy thought he appeared dangerous. Reckless.

"Damn it, Ortiz," he said, his voice full of irritation. "You bastards are never going to put a partnership together at this rate. And I thought we were all going to make a shitload of money."

The man he referred to as Ortiz spat out something in Spanish—certainly a curse word. "Just tell me what happened here."

Ryan shrugged. "I'm simply following instructions. You know, trying to get along. Jaime told me the Ortiz, Rodriguez, and Torres clans were meeting on the water tonight. That they wanted me there with the good faith money. Though why I have to pay for a simple meeting with you assholes continues to elude me."

The Ortiz, Rodriguez, and Torres clans. The phrase sounded a warning in Stacy's brain. They were common enough names in the San Diego area . . . her dentist was a Dr. Torres, as a matter of fact, but it was those three names together that set her fingering through her mental index file.

Ortiz, Rodriguez, and Torres.

Then the connection clicked.

Maybe it wouldn't have if Stacy was the type who could ignore the directive to "Read the rest of the story on Page A-27." But even if she didn't study the newspaper from cover to cover, the recent demise of the deadly, long-established Baja drug cartel had been detailed by the new regional DEA head, Doug Parnes, in interviews on every television channel in town. With the top players of that powerful family jailed, it was speculated in the last paragraphs of a newspaper story she'd read, a partnership of some lesser organizations involved in the drug business might grab the opportunity to form a triumvirate to fill the vacuum. A triumvirate of the Ortiz, Rodriguez, and Torres clans.

Stacy pressed her hand harder against her mouth. This wasn't some penny-ante operation. This was big-time drug trafficking.

She thought of her dear, sweet class of kindergarteners. She always advised them that when the people around them were making bad choices they should change their seat. But she had no place else to go. No other seat, no other closet. She was trapped.

Not only that, she had no one to blame but herself. She'd been attracted to Ryan! The poor judge of character was *Stacy*. Once again, she wanted to scream.

"So are we having a meeting tonight, or what?" Ryan asked the black-hatted man, stretching his legs in front of him and crossing them at the ankle. " 'Cause if not, I've got other places to go."

And other people to see. Stacy finished the phrase for him. Now that he appeared recovered from that blow to the head, where did Ryan think *she* was? Would he alert this new group that someone else had been on the boat with him? Her gaze darted to Gun-Man, who was seated on the floor, unmoving, as if he hoped they'd forget all about him. If they removed his gag, surely he would tell these bad guys about her.

At the idea, she drew farther back in the cupboard. Her heels scrambled for purchase on the varnished wood, and one foot slid forward, tapping the cupboard door. The movement, coupled with another pitch of the boat's deck, caused it to swing open a few inches. Swallowing a gasp, Stacy wedged her fingertips into the metal vents and pulled it silently closed again.

But not before Ryan's gaze honed in on hers.

If he'd forgotten about her in the midst of the commotion created by the new arrivals, he remembered now.

If he'd wondered where she'd gone to, he knew now.

Stacy's breath backed up in her lungs.

"So what's it to be, friends?" Ryan asked again, his gaze moving off. "We either get on with this deal or we don't."

The toe of Ortiz's black cowboy boot tapped out an impatient rhythm. "You're a cool one. I don't think I like it."

"You're breakin' my heart," Ryan replied. "Except I don't want to win a congeniality contest. I want to make money like my uncle did. I figure you guys owe me that for killing him."

Ortiz spit out one of those ugly Spanish curses again. "That was a mistake. A *Rodriguez* mistake, not someone from my family. And thanks to it you inherited his boat, didn't you?"

Ryan shrugged. "I'm saying you owe me. I want more."

When he hadn't immediately announced her presence, Stacy had been able to breathe once more, but what was the stupid man doing now? Now was not the time to be needling the ones in control. There were three of them, not counting the tied-up guy. Not that she cared a whit about what happened to Ryan—he was a criminal!— but at least he was a familiar face.

And he hadn't ratted her out.

Hope swelled at the thought. Maybe he could still prove some sort of ally, but only if they decided not to throw him overboard or outright kill him as they seemed to have killed his uncle. Her stomach started to roil again.

She wanted Ryan alive, she did.

If only because he might prove useful to her, of course. If only because she didn't want to be on this horrid boat with a corpse.

"I can't decide if you're worth the trouble," the Ortiz man told Ryan.

"Of course I am." His confident grin was made more raffish by the trail of blood along his jaw. "You've got the drugs, but I've got the boat, the sportfishing business, and the false bottoms built into the tanks that hold the clients' catch."

"Jaime, here," Ortiz said, jabbing the bound man with his foot, "claims he has something even better. He claims he knows someone who can get the U.S. authorities to look the other way while we run our *own* boats. Then we can cut out the middleman. That means we can cut out *you*."

A strange expression flashed across Ryan's face, but then he shrugged again. "Don't know why you'd listen to Jaime. Isn't he the one who claimed I tried to steal the ten grand and kill him?"

Ortiz nodded. "Yes. And what do you have to say to that?"

"The obvious. The ten grand was a show of good faith. From me to your partnership, once I attended the meeting. If I was trying to steal the money and kill Jaime, how come *he's* the one with the money and *I'm* the one out cold on the floor?"

There was a moment of silence. "You're right," Ortiz said, then he nodded to his two henchmen. "Get him up."

With their hands under Jaime's arms, they pulled the bound man to his feet. Stacy tensed again, her body prepping for fight or flight. If they let Jaime tell his side of the story, would he speak about the woman who'd been on the boat? Would they start looking for her?

Ortiz lifted his hand to pull the bandanna away from the other man's mouth.

Or so she thought. Instead, a gun appeared, and Ortiz shot Jaime point-blank in the forehead.

She was on the horrid boat with a corpse. Holding back her scream with both hands, Stacy stared through the vents, straight into Jaime's unseeing eyes. The hole between them was black. The smell in the room was caustic.

Her stomach heaved.

From far away, between the ringing echoes of the gunshot, she heard Ryan sigh. He clambered to his feet, and she focused on his tall body to keep her attention off the dead one lying just a few inches away. His jeans were washed to pale blue. There was a rip in one knee. His running shoes appeared new and the black T-shirt he wore was stretched across his impressive shoulders.

That's what she'd first noticed about him, that mass of him, that pure male mass that took the condo complex's mailroom from comfortable to cozy with his first step inside. Her reaction, her attraction, was the consequence, she supposed, of hanging out with five-year-olds all day long. But obviously she should have looked further than a wide chest and six-plus feet of height when she decided upon going out on a limb.

Ryan stepped closer to her hiding place, looking down at Jaime with an air of casual interest.

"He's dead, all right." Stacy watched his legs draw closer, then he turned. At the little *clunk* of her closet door, she realized he was leaning against it.

"I hate the smell of blood," Ryan complained, sounding more bored than bothered. "What do you say we move to your boat, Ortiz?"

Yes. Go aboard a different boat. Go aboard a different boat and take the corpse with you. Surely someone would happen along and save her. With a little more time, maybe she could get the communications equipment working. Warm feelings toward Ryan sparked inside her again. Surely he was trying to help her out!

Maybe he wasn't all bad. In that mailroom, maybe she'd sensed the good inside him as well as the sexy, handsome outside. He'd helped her brother Mitch with her new furniture, hadn't he? Mitch had even given her the ol' Banks wink of approval—which had been so embarrassingly obvious, that she'd given Ryan bonus points for pretending not to notice.

Ortiz turned to face Ryan. Stacy caught a glimpse of the man between the backs of her neighbor's jean-covered knees. Under the black hat, his face was thin and weathered and if she had to draw a picture of a sociopath, it would look just like him.

Chills rushed over her skin. He wouldn't hesitate to kill her any more than he would hesitate to kill Jaime, she knew it.

"Your boat?" Ryan prompted again.

Ortiz displayed a flash of hard, yellowed teeth. "For now, *this* is my boat. My men dropped us off here and went on to the meeting point."

Ryan's legs shifted as the boat took another roll. "Well, then, *capitán*, can we head up to the bridge and start the engines? I want to get this meeting over with. I have big plans for later tonight that include more than dumping dead bodies and bleaching blood from the floor."

Gratitude waved over Stacy again. It was obvious as could be that Ryan was trying to get her out of the line of fire. So she'd be stuck down here with a corpse. Compared to Ortiz, she decided, she might find Jaime's company comforting. If she didn't think too hard about him being dead, that is.

"All right," Ortiz said. "*Vámanos.*"

As Ryan immediately pushed away from the closet door, Ortiz chuckled. "Eager to set out milk and cookies for Santa Claus, my friend?"

"Well, sure, because I've been very good this year," Ryan replied. "Let me show you."

The door concealing Stacy swung wide. Stunned by the betrayal, she stared straight into the mean little eyes of the man named Ortiz. Her body, her heart, her brain froze, a mouse caught in a snake's hole.

"*Quién es ella?*" Ortiz demanded. "Who?"

The two men flanking him took a step forward.

Ryan pivoted to stand between her and them. Then he reached down to grab her arms and haul her out of the hiding place. They stood together, his arm firmly around her. It probably looked chummy, loverlike even, but she knew it was to prevent her from escaping. As if her cramped muscles and scared-into-paralysis mind could make such a thing happen.

"This is Stacy," Ryan said. "The best Christmas present a guy could have—and my girlfriend."

· 6 ·

If she got out of this alive, Stacy vowed, she was going to hole up in her safe, secure condo and only venture out in daylight hours—and then only to school, where the most dangerous males she encountered stopped her heart with their gap-toothed grins. Where the most dangerous things they did was eat paste and run with scissors.

The wheelhouse was cramped for Stacy and the four men. She was ordered to sit on the small cushioned bench. Hunching, she made herself as small as possible, and tried developing a coherent plan. But she was a *kindergarten teacher*, damn it, not some kick-ass special agent. She didn't have the experience or temperament for this kind of work.

Still, she kept her eyes open and her wits on alert as the men gathered around the bridge. Ryan did something to get the boat humming, but when he put his hands on the wheel, Ortiz tried shouldering him aside.

Ryan didn't budge. "Hey!"

"I'm *capitán*, remember?"

The dried blood on Ryan's face only made his scowl look more lethal. "Only I drive *The Bait*, Ortiz."

The sociopath whipped out his weapon and rammed its nose against Ryan's heart. "Only I have the gun, *sí*?"

Ryan backed away, his hands half-raised, then jerked his head toward Stacy. "Shit, Ortiz, there's no need to frighten the lady."

Ortiz flicked her a dismissing glance. "Comfort her then, *amigo*. Leave the navigation to us."

Stacy scooted down the seat as Ryan wedged himself beside her. She didn't want to talk to him, let alone touch him. But he kept on coming, until his thigh was pressing against hers and his arm was wrapped around her shoulders.

"Howya doing, baby?" he asked, bringing his face close.

She turned her head away and tried squirming out of his reach, but his hand tightened on her outside shoulder to keep them sandwiched together. " 'Baby' is just terrif," she muttered, wishing for something sharp to stab into his criminal, duplicitous hide. "I've always longed to take part in illegal activities."

"Good." He caught her chin with his free hand and brought it around. Then he pressed his lips to hers.

Her heart made a wild surge, but her body had been buffeted by so much adrenaline in the last hours that the latest infusion drained instead of electrified her. Inside, she wanted to struggle away, she wanted to slap at him, she wanted to wail in dismay at what her attraction for him had led her to, but her muscles wouldn't follow her mental orders.

He tilted his head, pressing harder with this better fit. Against the pressure, Stacy's mouth softened. Her stomach clenched, dipped, then a flash of heat incinerated her earlier outrage. Without thinking, she turned into his body.

"Just follow my lead," he whispered against her mouth. Then he lifted his head.

Stacy stared at him. What had happened? What had he said? She blinked, trying to bring the last moments into focus. He'd kissed her, she'd been angry. He'd continued to kiss her, and she'd . . . responded.

God! How could this be? Was she becoming one of those women who sought out prisoners and parolees? Had her circumspect, staid, kindergarten-teacher life been corrupted by just one kiss?

He laughed, soft and low. "I knew you'd look like that once I kissed you."

Outrage flooded back. "What?" she said from between her teeth. "Disgusted? Repulsed? Nauseated?"

He glanced over his shoulder at the men at the helm. "Hold that thought," he whispered, then raised his voice. "You're looking green, sweetheart. You getting seasick?"

She crossed her arms over her chest. "If I am, I hope I puke all over you."

He looked back at her, whispering again, his voice urgent. "Say you're sick and need the head. It's at the bottom of the stairs, right before the galley. When you open the door, scream."

Before she could reply, he was off the bench and pulling her up. "I don't like the smell of barf any more than I like the smell of blood. Stacy needs the head, Ortiz."

The other three men turned to look at her. Their scrutinizing gazes and the mention of blood made her stomach heave. She pressed a hand against it. "I . . . I need the restroom." Maybe this was the plan she needed. It was action, at least, action away from Ryan and the others.

Ortiz grunted and waved toward the stairs. "*Vete!* Hector, you watch her."

Running her hand along the cold, slick wall of the stairway, Stacy made her way down the narrow steps. The door to the galley was open in front of her, and she could see Jaime's body sprawled along the floor. Swallowing hard, she turned her gaze to the narrow door on the right. Then she glanced back, seeing the man named Hector hovering halfway down. Maybe he didn't like the smell of someone being sick either.

Reaching for the handle of the bathroom door, she hesitated. Why was she doing what Ryan ordered? Wasn't her best bet to come up with her own plan? Her neighbor had no allegiance to the law, why would she imagine he might have some sort of allegiance to her? She looked over her shoulder again, and saw that Ryan was standing a few paces behind Hector.

She tried to read his expression.

His eyes were steady, his gaze as solid as his shoulders. This is what she'd liked about him from the start, that sense of confident strength that surrounded him. When he'd picked up one end of her loveseat, his biceps had bulged, but more than that she'd admired how he'd automatically turned, without fanfare or argument choosing to be the one to walk backward from the truck to her front steps. Maybe it seemed like a small thing, but the kindness, the sign of goodness, had opened her ordinarily shy heart.

But she'd been wrong about him then.

Yes, but what other opportunities for action were presenting themselves now? *She* didn't have any good ideas.

Making a swift decision, she inhaled a deep breath and turned the handle. She pulled. From the depths of the dark bathroom, something large and furry leaped for her throat with an unearthly growl.

Forgetting she was supposed to scream, she did anyway, a shriek that was both girly and ghoulish.

Its authentic appeal set off an explosion of activity.

The beast lunging for her throat with outstretched claws dropped to the ground. From above, someone shouted her name. Stacy looked up to see Hector tumbling down the stairs. The Mexican landed at her feet, where the beast scrambled across his body. Screeching at the contact with its claws, Hector batted at it with the gun in his hand. It slipped from his fingers to clatter to the floor.

Stacy scooped it up, heard her name again, looked upward at Ryan. On instinct she tossed the gun to him, just as if she were playing a rainy-day game of Hot Potato in Room 2 at Lemoncrest Elementary. Crouching, he took another step down, then spun toward the wheelhouse.

At the first exchange of gunfire, she leaped into the bathroom and slammed shut the door.

The space wasn't much bigger than the broom closet. And it was darker than her other hiding place, but she didn't want light. She wanted safety. The best she could do was huddle in the space between the toilet and the wall, putting her face to her knees and covering her head with her hands.

Footsteps clattered down the stairs, into the galley, back up the stairs. The sound of gunfire persisted—bullets spitting, ricocheting—but the noise of her pounding heartbeat was louder, filling her head, filling her soul. It was the rhythm of the prayer running through her blood.

Godletmelive Godletmelive Godletmelive Godletmelive

Some time later—Minutes? Hours? Days?—the boat went quiet.

The fact took a while to sink in between her fervent prayers and fevered pulse.

What had happened? Who had survived? Or were all dead?

I'll stay right here, Stacy decided. Right here she could pretend to be part of the wall or the floor and not a trembling, quivering mass of terrified humanity. There was no good reason to venture out. Hadn't she learned how dangerous it was to go out on a limb? With her eyes closed, with the silence continuing, this was as secure as she'd been since the whole nightmare began.

Her head still bent over her knees, she inhaled a slow, calming breath.

That exhaled in a strangled shriek as razors dug into the bare skin at her nape.

Stacy jack-in-boxed to her feet. The razor blades dug into her shoulders as a furry weight latched onto her back. She screeched again and leaped around the toilet to push open the bathroom door.

It swung a mere half-inch. With the beast still clinging to her, Stacy thrust against it with both hands. Her desperation shoved aside whatever on the other side had pinned it closed, and then she jumped into the dim space at the bottom of the stairs.

The thing on her back dropped, and she took in several things at once. The furry beast was a huge, tattered cat. The object that had pinned her in the bathroom was Hector's lifeless body. And the boat was dark. Everywhere. The light fixture over the stairs had been shattered, and she figured the same thing had happened to the others on the boat.

It wasn't a great leap of logic. Because even in the darkness, she could see the blacker holes that bullets had left along the stairwell's white walls and along the linoleum floors in the hallway and galley.

"Stacy." Her name floated through the air in a hoarse, unearthly voice from the direction of the wheelhouse. "Stacy?"

She froze. Maybe she shouldn't acknowledge the voice. Maybe she should go her own way now, whatever way that could possibly be.

"Stacy, it's Ryan."

Of course it was Ryan. And she found she couldn't regret the fact that she wasn't alone on this dark, ghostly boat and that the one who was apparently still alive and talking to her was Ryan.

The man she'd given a gun to.

"Are you all right?" he asked. "Tell me you're all right. And if you are, honey, come on up. I could use some help."

· 7 ·

Stacy crept up the stairs. Grateful as she was that the gunfire had ended, she didn't know what she'd find in the wheelhouse. It seemed better to sneak up on the scene.

But Ryan sensed her approach before she was halfway there. "I need to hear your voice, honey. Tell me you're okay."

She swallowed. "I'm okay." Physically, anyhow. Steeling herself, she stepped into the small room.

Destruction was everywhere. Holes, splintered wood, shattered glass. In the light of a big industrial flashlight propped on the bridge, Stacy saw that the man named Ortiz was sitting froglike among the fragments, his hands bound to his feet with duct tape. Squatting nearby, Ryan tended to the living henchman, duct-taping what appeared to be a folded-up flannel shirt against a wound on his shoulder. The man was bound feet and hands as well, his face grimaced in pain.

Stacy's shoes crunched against broken glass. Ryan took a quick, assessing look at her over his shoulder. "Come over here, then do me a favor and press hard against this pad of shirt while I tape it down."

The cat was pacing back and forth, rubbing its moth-eaten fur sides against Ryan's knees. "Go on, Jack Sparrow," he said to the animal. "You're safe now."

You're safe now. Stacy suppressed a sudden urge to giggle, knowing she was too close to hysteria to start laughing now. But what kind of man took the time to reassure his pet in the middle of all this disaster and death?

"Stacy?" Ryan sent her another swift glance, his tone sharper. "What's the matter? You said you were all right. Can you help over here?"

" 'What's the matter?' " The question was so outrageous, she could only repeat it as she moved forward to assist with duct-taping the injury. Out of the corner of her eye, she kept watch on Ortiz, giving him a wide berth.

"You should be that careful with your boyfriend, *preciosa*," he told her, his eyes glittering. "He's the one acting crazy."

Stacy hunkered down beside Ryan, ignoring the tell-tale sound of wrapping paper ripping again.

Maybe she should borrow the duct tape when he was through with it, she thought. He took her hand and showed her how and how hard to press on the pad of fabric. His calloused palm rasped the back of her hand and she stared at his, fascinated by the smear of blood across his knuckles.

He gave her fingers a reassuring little pat— amazing, it did make her feel better—then glanced over at Ortiz. "I still have hope we can work out our arrangement, but tonight wasn't going how I liked."

"It's not going how *I* like now."

"Yeah, well then you and your partners shouldn't have tried to kill me. And Hector should have stayed away from my woman. Why do you think she screamed? He was getting ready to take out more than his gun."

Stacy stared at Ryan. Was that right? She thought back, remembering Hector on the stairs behind her . . . and then she also remembered Ryan telling her to open the bathroom door and scream. Hector hadn't caused anything to happen. It was Ryan who'd set the whole thing up.

"She's worth all this, your woman?" Ortiz followed that up with a Spanish word that didn't sound the least bit complimentary.

It set a fire beneath Ryan. "Shut up," he said, rising.

Eyes glittering brighter, Ortiz repeated the word.

Ryan lunged for the other man, and Stacy recoiled, glimpsing the gun tucked in his waistband at the small of his back. She squeezed her eyes shut, refusing to witness another murder, but instead of the gunshot she braced for, she heard the distinctive rip of the tape.

He slapped it across Ortiz's mouth. "She's a good woman. You keep your filth to yourself."

Then Ryan strode back to Stacy and drew her to her feet. His big palms covered her shoulders and he looked into her eyes. "You've got guts, sweetheart. Just hang in there a little longer. I'm going to get you home."

The warmth of his hands, the warmth in his eyes started her to trembling. She gritted her back teeth, hoping he wouldn't notice their chatter.

He smiled, and then guided her toward the bench and pushed her down. With gentle hands, he tucked her hair behind her ears, then leaned forward to give her a swift kiss. "Trust me," he breathed against her ear.

"Keep an eye on them," he ordered, straightening. "Let me know if they move."

Ryan himself moved toward the helm of the boat. The almost insolent veneer he'd worn before the shoot-out was gone. He was no longer casual, but he moved with almost-cheerful purpose.

As confusing as the kiss, as the *Trust me*, as the events of the entire night had been, was this new change in him. Who was he? The neighborly upstairs fisherman? The ruthless drug trafficker? Or this man, who appeared to be something in between?

He looked over his shoulder at her, as if he could read her mind. "Cheer up, baby. It's going to be a Merry Christmas after all."

The funny thing was, she wanted to believe him. No, worse, she *did* believe him. What was wrong with her? Had years in kindergarten only provided her with the useless, dangerous ability to naively trust?

"What are you doing to me?" she whispered, then cleared her throat and tried rephrasing the question. "What . . . what happens next?"

"Next?" Ryan played the beam of the flashlight over the instrument panel. "Well, we're not sending out any Maydays, that's for sure. The communications equipment is shot to hell."

It didn't seem to bother him much, which made sense, Stacy supposed. You couldn't call 911 and complain about a drug partnership gone sour. Something thumped to the table in front of her and she jerked, startled, until she realized it was Ryan's big, ugly cat. It paced across the slick surface and then leaped into her lap.

She made a sound, but froze, well remembering its needlelike claws.

"Jack Sparrow likes you," Ryan said.

"Tell that to the scratches on my back," she muttered.

Ryan sent her a grin, then winked. "Later on, maybe I will."

She could only stare at him again as the cat minced in a tightening circle. The man was a chameleon. She was an idiot. All signs pointed to him being a dangerous criminal, but his kiss, his touch, just a suggestive tone could send her blood on an anticipatory race through her body.

The sound of the engines starting up competed with the satisfied purr of the animal curled on her lap. Ryan made a grunt of approval. "I'll have you home in no time."

Time? Stacy checked her wristwatch, squinting at it in the dim light. "Exactly what time—"

"Fuck!" Ryan stared at the instrument panel, then swiftly shut the engines back down. "*Fuck!*"

An icy chill rolled down her back. Jack Sparrow stopped kneading her thighs and lifted its head. Ortiz and his henchman rolled their eyes toward Ryan. "What's wrong?" she asked for all of them.

He muttered a chain of inventive swear words that would have put him on the detention list at Lemoncrest Elementary for the next four years. "Some time during the fight, bullets must have destroyed the cooling hoses to the engines belowdecks. I turned the engines off when I got control up here, but the pumps must have already flooded the engine room. And if I'm not mistaken—and I'm not—the bulkhead isn't holding."

Stacy looked toward the other two men to see if this verbiage meant any more to them than it did to her. From the widened whites of their eyes, apparently it did.

"So that means we're not going anywhere?" she ventured.

"Not quite." Ryan spun toward her and ran his hands through his hair. It betrayed an agitation that he hadn't shown the whole evening, despite everything that had happened before.

Stacy stroked the cat in her lap, trying to calm her nerves at the same time. "What . . . what exactly does it mean, Ryan?"

He took in a deep breath, let it out. "It means, sweetheart, that we're sinking."

· 8 ·

Boats sank a lot faster than Stacy would have imagined. Certainly it didn't take enough screen time to make their plight into a tragic, epic movie. But then, theirs wouldn't end in tragedy. That's what Ryan kept telling her anyway.

She decided to reserve judgment.

As for Ryan, she was reserving judgment about him, too. His actions were as inexplicable as ever. With an economy of movement and minutes, he loaded the living aboard *The Bait* into two inflatable lifeboats he'd tethered together. Ortiz and his wounded companion in one, Stacy, the cat, and himself in the other. They had a set of oars, the other men didn't. Which made sense, Stacy figured, since the two were still bound by the duct tape.

Then, as the top of the wheelhouse disappeared beneath the Pacific, Ryan untied the two inflatable lifeboats, setting Ortiz and his friend adrift.

Appearing semiconscious, the wounded man didn't seem to notice, but Ortiz, still kept silent by the strip of tape, lurched up, sitting as straight as his froglike pose would allow. In the meager moonlight, his eyes telegraphed equal parts rage and panic.

Stacy couldn't stifle her own small sound of distress. The seas weren't rough at the moment, the wind not too biting, and it wasn't as if she had any fondness for the other two, but to cut them loose in open ocean?

Ryan picked up the oars. "We can't afford to tow them after us. Not only do I want to get you back ASAP, but any mischief on their part could jeopardize our safety."

"But . . ." But it made perfect sense, she could see that. Stacy wrapped her arms around her knees and beneath the lifejacket Ryan had insisted she wear, she felt another give in her

Christmas-wrap dress. She couldn't care. Using the duct tape, she'd made a few repairs before they'd left the boat, but it was hard to worry about modesty when her life was at stake.

Life. She looked back to where *The Bait* had gone down. Jaime and Hector were buried at sea. She pressed her cold palms against her eyes.

"They were in a dangerous business," Ryan said, over the slosh of the oars in the water. "You choose it, and you choose knowing you could die like they did."

Her hands dropped. "You're reading minds, now?"

"I don't like it either, Stacy. And I don't like leaving the other two tied up in the lifeboat. But we have to save ourselves first. As soon as I can, I'll get someone out here to retrieve Ortiz and his man."

Stacy looked over her shoulder. Already, the other inflatable was impossible to spot in the darkness. The cat picked its way from its place by Ryan toward her. She reached out for it, needing something warm and furry to hold against her body. "How will you say where they might be?"

"Both the Border Patrol and the Coast Guard have spotter planes and helicopters." Ryan continued working the oars. "I'll give them a general idea and they'll do the rest."

Stacy's fingers dug into the cat, causing it to squirm away. "You're . . . you're going to call in a tip or something to the authorities?" The same one who'd shot at Ortiz and his henchman was also going to try and save them? It was hard to reconcile.

His arms froze midpull. "Of course I'm going to call it in. What kind of man do you think I am?"

A stranger. A drugtrafficker. A chameleon. *A colossal mistake on my part.* "Well, I, um . . . I don't know you very well, do I?"

Something about that answer made him grin and start moving the oars again. "And yet you were willing to offer yourself up as my personal Christmas present."

He said it as a fact, not a question, which might have made her madder if she wasn't so battered by every other emotion she'd experienced that evening. Still, she couldn't let it go unchallenged.

"Just to clarify," she replied, "I did not offer myself up to you as a gift. I came to invite you to a party, a sort-of costume party that my sister is throwing to celebrate her first season in business." Left unsaid was how much she regretted the idea, though she guessed she didn't keep it out of her voice.

Ryan's grin flashed through the darkness again. "Just to clarify—in case you're wondering, that is—I'm with the Coast Guard."

Stacy stilled. "Pardon me?"

"I'm a lieutenant in the Coast Guard. I've been

undercover since coming to San Diego."

"Undercover?" She shook her head to clear it. "Under what covers?"

He laughed. "Not yours, though I've thought a lot about it. I'm part of an undercover *operation*, Stacy, through a temporary assignment I have with EPIC—the El Paso Intelligence Center. It's multiagency—Border Patrol, Coast Guard, DEA, and others. We're trying to keep tabs on the new cartel that's forming to take over the Baja drug trade. When we met in the mailroom at the condo complex, I couldn't tell you, of course. I couldn't tell anyone."

She stared at him. "You couldn't tell me. You couldn't tell me when Jaime pulled a gun on me. You couldn't tell me when Ortiz and his henchman took over the boat. You couldn't tell me when we were within seconds of sinking into the Pacific."

"As you just pointed out, it's been busy. I didn't realize until just a minute ago that you hadn't figured out I was one of the good guys."

"No. I thought you were one of the bad guys!" Her voice edged high and hysterical. "I thought you were like them."

"Yet you let me kiss you. And you followed my directions. And you threw me Hector's gun. Somewhere inside, Stacy, you trusted me. That says a lot."

"It says I was a panicked idiot." For hours

she'd been terrified that she was out on that limb alone. "I should have used Hector's gun to shoot you myself."

"But then you'd be paddling back to San Diego solo."

As if she would have made it this far. She supposed she should be grateful to him, but the whole mess was really his fault. For being so attractive and charming, that he'd lured someone as unsuitable as herself onto this scary, precarious limb. She sighed, then another thought struck. He hadn't hesitated when taking off through the water, and he'd said he was in the Coast Guard, but . . .

"Do you know where we are?" she asked.

He didn't answer. His head was lifted and he let the lifeboat drift for a moment.

"Do you know where we are?" she asked again.

"I'm guessing that we're a lot closer to the drug cartel's designated meeting place than I'd like," he answered, gesturing behind her with his chin.

Stacy's head whipped around. Then her heartbeat whipped into another frenzy as she spied the speedboat bearing down on them. "Does it see us?"

"It sees something," Ryan replied. She turned back toward him, just in time to watch him slip over the side of the inflatable and into the water.

Stacy had only scant moments to consider how to react toward the newcomers. Panicked sounded good. Hysterical, quite natural.

Instead she went for relieved. There didn't seem a chance in hell that she could convince anyone she was out on a pleasure paddle in the middle of the ocean, so she might as well appear to be glad to see them.

"Thank God, thank God! You rescued me," she called to the men as their boat slowed near hers. They looked tough and mean. More of Ortiz's ilk. "I don't know how to get to San Diego and I'm not very good with the oars." When they just stared at her, she kept babbling. "The only company I have is my cat, that's it, just the cat. No one else. Just the cat and me. Just the two of us alone."

Shut up, shut up, Stacy. Just the cat and me, just the two of us alone. She wanted to smack herself on the forehead for overdoing it.

But then her heart jittered. The fact was, her only companion might very well *be* the cat. She forced herself not to scan the water around her, but the question still screamed in her mind. *Where did Ryan go?*

The two men looked at each other, then back at Stacy. "No English," one said. "*No hablamos inglés.*"

"Oh. Well." If they didn't understand her babble, all the better.

Then one of the men gave her a frown and shouted down a question.

She shrugged, smiled, tried to look like everyone's favorite kindergarten teacher, which, of course, she was. "Sorry. *No hablo español,* either."

The two men conferred, and Stacy reached over for the cat, needing the comfort of another friendly being. But it hissed, backing toward the end of the inflatable where Ryan had last been sitting.

"*Senorita!*" one of the men demanded. "*Venga acqui.*"

Stacy looked up to see them gesturing to her with their arms, obviously urging her onto their boat. She eyed the cat. "They want us to board, Jack."

Instinct told her to stall, if not out-and-out refuse—why would she agree to put herself under the control of strangers for the umpteenth time this evening?—but concern for Ryan overruled the feeling. He couldn't last long in the frigid water. The sooner she got in the boat with them, the sooner they would leave and Ryan could return to the inflatable.

After that . . . after that, she supposed she had to believe he'd find some way to save her, because this metaphorical limb she was perched upon didn't feel as if it was going to hold much longer.

"Come along, Jack." Leaning forward, she scooped up the cat, ignoring its struggles. "I don't like this any more than you do, but we've got to do our part."

Still, as hard hands reached down and grabbed her arms to haul her aboard, another scream welled inside her. With the exception of that one shriek by the bathroom, she'd been holding them all in, and its cathartic value was long ago used up.

She looked at the men as they dropped her onto the deck of their boat. "If I let loose and really screamed like I want to, what would happen?" The cat wiggled in her arms again, but she held on. "We need to stick together."

We need a back-up plan, too.

If Ryan couldn't get to her—for reasons she didn't want to think about—then she'd have to find a way out of this by herself. And if she made it back home, she vowed, she'd stick to the safe and mundane for the rest of her life.

One man pointed her toward a seat at the front of the boat while the other man settled on the seat beside it, the one in front of the steering wheel. With the cat held firmly in her lap, Stacy sent out a good-luck prayer for Ryan as the boat throbbed to life. She couldn't stop herself from a quick survey of the ocean around them. Her eyes caught on something at the back of the boat, climbing in.

Something dark and hulking and dripping with water. Her fingers tightened on Jack. The cat yowled, leaping from her arms to land on the driver's back.

The man shrieked. Knowing firsthand the sharpness of the animal's claws, she couldn't blame him. Shouting, he jerked and wiggled this way and that, trying to dislodge the cat. His companion stepped forward to help, Stacy stepped out of the way.

It gave Ryan clear aim at the two men. Though he had to be freezing, both his voice and the gun were rock steady. "*Buenas noches*, my friends. Hold it right there."

· 10 ·

Stacy waved a mental goodbye to the two men they left behind in their inflatable lifeboat. These guys weren't given any oars either, once Ryan determined they were indeed more members of the new drug cartel.

Standing at the wheel, one knee propped on the backless seat, he swung the boat around in a wide curve. Then he idled the engine and looked over at her. "Get ready. They call these 'go-fast' boats for a reason and I want to get back to San Diego as soon as possible."

"You have to be freezing. Isn't there a phone or something on here? Maybe someone could come to us even quicker."

Ryan shook his head. "Did you see them toss a couple of things over the side when I first surprised them with the gun? They dumped a handheld GPS and a cell phone. They want us to know as little as possible about where we are and who they talk to."

Wind whipped her hair across her face and Stacy shivered, knowing Ryan had to feel the cold even more than she. "Let's get going, then."

The boat accelerated smoothly, in two blinks going from zero to bat-out-of-hell. It flew along the surface of the water, piercing the black night. Ryan settled onto the driver's seat, using one hand to control the boat while he drew the other close to his body for warmth.

"Where did you go when you went into the water?" she said, over the high whine of the engine.

"I swam around to the back of their boat while you distracted them. You did great, by the way."

Stacy grimaced. "I wish I'd known that was the plan. Maybe I could have come up with some bigger, better distraction."

He shot her a smile. "Your pretty *agarraderas* worked just fine."

"*Agarraderas*," she repeated. "What does that

mean, exactly? You used it when you talked to Jaime about me."

"Well . . ." His free hand rubbed across his chin. "It's slang, you know?"

"No, I don't know."

He rubbed his chin again, his gaze trained out the windshield. "Literally, it's, uh . . . 'things to grab.'"

"Things to—" Stacy swallowed the rest and felt her face heat despite the cool wind whipping by.

"It's a compliment," Ryan offered, shooting her another quick glance. "No offense meant."

She cleared her throat. "Well . . . um . . ."

"But I'd like the chance to redeem myself for everything said and done tonight, anyway." He reached over and ran a long finger down her arm. "I tried to come up with some excuses for Ortiz, but I'm pretty sure my cover's blown, which means I go back to a real life."

Stacy's skin jittered, whether from his touch or the idea of being involved in Ryan Beausoleil's 'real life,' or both. It was necessary to clear her throat again. "You don't normally work undercover?"

"The Coast Guard doesn't usually get involved in covert drug interdiction. But I was brought in because they suspect a leak in the ranks of the DEA or Border Patrol. They needed a new face."

"Then they should take care of your face a little

better, if you ask me," Stacy said, thinking of all that had gone on. "They send you out, alone and unharmed, and expect you to survive on your own among dangerous criminals?"

"Bad timing. Only a few key people in San Diego know about me and what I'm doing. And it being Christmas, all the Homeland Security agencies are stretched thin . . . which is probably why the cartel chose tonight for their meeting. Less chance of being detected."

"Or of you being rescued," Stacy said.

"We did all right on our own." He ran his finger down her arm again. "Though I appreciate your interest."

She tried to stave off her shiver. "I'm, uh, merely concerned—as any private citizen would be— about the well-being of our military personnel."

His hand wrapped around her upper arm. "You're too cold. Check around and see if there's anything you can put over yourself to keep the heat in."

Besides the cat, wedged beneath her seat, the only item Stacy found was a length of canvas the size of a small quilt. She hurried it over to Ryan and draped it across his shoulders.

"Wha—" he started.

"You're colder than I am."

"But bigger. I'll be all right a little longer."

She shook her finger at him. "Don't argue with a kindergarten teacher."

"I'm scared," he said, smiling. "What'll you do, take away my graham cracker privileges?"

He was irresistible, with that devilish grin on his face. "Worse. No recess. You'll have to stay inside with me when all the other kids are outside playing."

His grin widened, and he scooped his arm about her, pushing her onto his lap and then pulling the tarp around the two of them. "If I'm good, will you play inside games with me, teacher?"

She wiggled against the damp fabric of his pants. "Let me go."

"Only if you keep up that wiggling," he said, his breath tickling her temple. "In these wet jeans that's punishment enough, believe me."

She started to protest again, but he cut her off with what felt like a kiss on her hair. He unfastened the damp lifejacket from around her and let it drop to their feet. "Sharing body heat is better for both of us. Come on, it's what any private citizen—concerned about the well-being of our military personnel, that is—would do."

The boat continued speeding to some destination she hoped Ryan could find, and as warmth kindled between their bodies, Stacy relaxed against his chest.

"Mmm," he said, using his forearm against her waist to snuggle her closer. "This is nice."

"Not being threatened, terrorized, or shot at is like that," she said. "It's very nice."

"Getting to know you better is even nicer. Accidental meetings in the mailroom have been too brief and too undependable."

She swung her head around to stare at him. "Have you really been trying to run into me in the mailroom?"

His eyebrows rose. "Did I say that?" he hedged.

"Yeah, you did. After Jaime hit you on the head."

"Ah." He shrugged. "Well, then, yeah, I have. Do you have a problem with that?"

"No." Despite his earlier warning, she couldn't stop a little wiggle of satisfaction. "No problem at all."

They remained silent a few minutes until Stacy spotted a glow in the distance. "Land?" Her voice rose in excitement. "Land!" Land meant real safety, security, a life beyond this night—this night*mare*.

"Go faster," she urged Ryan. "Let's get there fast."

But instead of agreeing with her, he sat up straighter, tension renewed in the muscles surrounding her. He looked over his shoulder as if he could feel a new pursuer in their wake.

Stacy's heart jerked under another onslaught

of adrenaline. "What now?" she said it calmly, even though the question echoed a protest inside her head. *WhatnowWhatnowWhatnow?*

Ryan's expression was grim, his voice clipped. "Nothing. Just a feeling, is all. I don't want us speeding into a trap."

No trap! There couldn't be any more traps, surprises, or shocks tonight. She wouldn't allow it. She couldn't survive it. The city lights were nearer now, bright and safe-looking. With a *whoosh*, Ryan slowed the boat. A saltwater rooster tail arced behind them, but Stacy couldn't see anything else following them in the blackness.

"What are we going to do?" she asked.

Rolling his shoulders as if there was a new weight on them, he motored onward more slowly. Then he lifted Stacy from his lap and pushed her toward the passenger seat, tossing the canvas after her. "Stay warm," he ordered.

She shivered beneath the tarp as they entered the mouth of the harbor. They were still far from shore, but she could see anchored boats bobbing in the water, and to the left, a well-lit marina. Ryan's gaze snagged on something beyond it, and he made the boat take a sharp turn in that direction.

"What is it?" Stacy asked. "What do you see?"

"Our ticket," Ryan said. "We're going to slip into town unnoticed, I hope."

She bit her lip. She'd tried to remain unnoticed

several times earlier that night, and it had never worked. "Why can't we go straight to the Harbor Police and tell them what happened?"

"Anything going out on police radios could be picked up by a scanner and tip off the mole who's been working with our friends in the cartel. We need to get into the harbor and get to a phone without any of the bad guys picking up on it. Then I'll make a call."

There was considerably more activity ahead. Stacy squinted to make it out, then realized what she was seeing. "It's the Nautical Nativity Parade."

A long line of boats wound about the bay, decorated with everything from Christmas trees to Christmas lights to Rudolph and all his friends. As they drew nearer, she could hear carols being played from some of the boats. She looked over at Ryan. "Are we going to join it? We don't look very festive."

In answer, he leaned over and fiddled with something. A string of red-and-green bulbs lining the outside of the boat burst to life. "Warms my heart to know our drug buddies still have some Christmas spirit," he said wryly, "though it's pretty tame by this parade's standards."

Then he glanced over. "Unless you want to display your Christmas-wrapped self up on the hull."

She drew the tarp closer around her. "I think

I'll pass." The Christmas wrap was all but disintegrated. Beneath it, her flesh-toned, breast-to-midthigh bodyshaper was fairly concealing, but not the least bit festive.

Ryan edged closer to the parade and managed to slide in between a motoring sailboat broadcasting "The Twelve Days of Christmas" and a little outboard piloted by a skinny-looking Santa Claus. "Smile, honey," he said. "We want anyone watching to think we've been up to nothing more than some imbibing of eggnog."

When they'd really been on the run for their lives.

But as she plastered on a smile, the events of the evening swamped down upon her like a freezing wave. Even now, Ryan was scanning their surroundings, braced for yet another threat. Adrenaline punched into her veins again, a potent cocktail that made her stomach churn.

"Sweetheart?" Ryan's voice barely pierced her consciousness. "Sweetheart, what's wrong?"

"I feel sick," she whispered through dry lips. "I feel sick."

His hand clamped over the top of her head and pushed, shoving her ears between her knees. "Breathe, baby. Just breathe."

She was vaguely aware of him maneuvering the boat. The cat came out of its hiding place, apparently disturbed by the new tension in the air.

It wound around her ankles, but when she didn't respond, it walked off, its tail twitching.

Then the boat slowed. She kept her eyes closed, afraid if she opened them that she'd be faced with yet another obstacle to overcome. Ryan put his arms around her and lifted her up. "C'mon, sweetheart. Let's get you inside."

She refused to open her eyes. The ground beneath her feet was still moving, so she knew they weren't on land. "I can't do anymore, Ryan. I can't be brave or clever or even take any orders and follow your lead when you are brave and clever. If one more thing happens to scare me or surprise me, I swear to you, I'm going to scream."

"I know, I know," he soothed. He lifted her and she realized he was moving her from the go-fast to another boat altogether. It was a square, shingled box atop a flat deck. Illuminated by a small security light was a bright yellow door, flanked by terracotta pots of flowers. "Where are we?"

"A houseboat owned by a friend of mine. We can warm up, rest up here. I can even make my phone call."

Stacy's legs were unsteady, so she held on to one of Ryan's belt loops as he touched her feet to the floor then reached down to pull a key from beneath the pot to the right of the door.

Then she was inside a small room that had a

double-wide bunk in one corner and a tiny sink and refrigerator in another. Ryan switched on a lamp, and then, with his hands on her shoulders, he aimed her in the direction of an interior doorway. "Would you like to use the head? It's right through there."

Stacy toddled off, grateful to get away from him for a few minutes to try and get herself together. She sat on the closed lid of the toilet, pulling a fluffy towel free from a rack. Clutching it to her middle like a teddy bear, she tried some slow, deep yoga breathing.

"Stacy?" Ryan tapped on the door. "Just tell me you're okay, sweetheart."

She took a last long breath, then stood up and pushed open the door. "I'm better." He stood on the other side, shirtless. The houseboat must have some sort of heating system, because the main room was warm and getting warmer.

"Good," he answered, pulling her against him. Her bare cheek met his bare chest. Though his pants were still damp, his skin was already hot. She dropped the towel and wrapped her arms around his back. His heart beat against her ear and she burrowed closer.

"Are we safe?" she asked, her lips moving against his chest hair.

She felt the skin beneath it goosebump. "I think so." He combed his fingers through her short, tangled curls. "I made my phone call. Patrols will be sent out to look for the lifeboats."

"And the bodies?" Now that they were warm and safe, she could think about them again. "What about . . . what about Jaime and Hector?"

The fingers combing her hair paused, then he tightened them into a gentle fist and pulled back her head so his gaze could meet hers. "If I could erase that from your memory, I would," he whispered, his voice gruff.

"I wish you could, too," she whispered back, her arms tightening. "But I—"

"Shhh." He bent his head and touched his lips to hers in a light caress. "Shhh."

Stacy hooked one arm around his neck and brought him down for another kiss. She needed more. More contact. More sense that she was alive. More of Ryan.

He groaned against her mouth, then slid his tongue between her lips.

Her body flashed hot.

She went on tiptoe, crowding him. His hands clutched at her hips and she felt pieces of half-disintegrated wrapping paper drop around her feet like rose petals. His tongue pushed harder inside, less soothing and more demanding. She opened wide for him and let the sensation of him possessing her mouth push everything else from her head.

His hand edged from her hip to her ribs. Then it captured her breast, holding it snug.

Ryan groaned again, and lifted his mouth, though he didn't loosen his hold on her. "Stacy, Stacy. I don't know if you want this, or if . . ."

She had to laugh. He was rubbing his thumb over her nipple and they both knew it was hard and aroused. "You can't tell?" She squirmed against him as he copied the movement with his other hand on her other breast.

"Stacy—"

"I want it, Ryan." She wanted it to chase the fears of the night away. And she wanted it because she wanted *him*. "Stop being such a hero. That's not what I need right now."

His thumbs continued flicking her nipples, then he caught the elastic top of her bodyshaper in his fingers and yanked it down. Her naked breasts popped free. He gazed on them. "What *do* you need?" he asked, his voice tight.

His rough palms moved up to cover her flesh.

"I think you've got the idea," she said, closing her eyes. He had great hands, large, with those calluses that added another dimension to the glorious sensation. They were gentle, then firmer as he circled her breasts and brought his mouth down to lick her nipples.

It was almost too much. Standing there, half-dressed, with her undergarment half down, his taut fingers and the light touch of his wicked tongue made her knees melt and heat build between her thighs.

She curled her fingers in his belt loops to hold herself upright, and he laughed softly, exhaling air across her wet nipples. The hard tips tightened more, and so did that swirling heat inside of her.

He lifted her, only to take two steps and drop her again, onto the small bed. She widened her thighs as far as the elasticized bodyshaper would allow, and he crawled between them, bracing his weight on his elbows.

"I have a confession to make." He rubbed the back of his fingers against her cheeks.

She frowned, a little chill taking the edge off the heat. It suddenly occurred to her that she was lying on a bed, about to make love to a man she'd only recently met and barely knew. "What?" she said. "What is it?"

"You know those circulars we get with the pizza coupons from DiLeo's in them?"

"No."

"That's my confession. I've been borrowing the ones that come addressed to you from that little basket beneath your mailbox. I love DiLeo's pizza."

"Hey, that's not borrowing, that's stealing." She tried sounding stern but a smile twitched the corners of her mouth.

"There it is." He swooped down and nuzzled

her cheek with his nose. "You have this one little dimple that has proved my undoing."

Oh, God. This playfulness in him was going to prove *her* undoing. The whole world knew she had no defense against a bad boy with a sweet side.

His mouth trailed down to her neck, his tongue tracing delicate designs against her skin. Her body shivered and he settled deeper against her hips. She could feel his arousal, so hard and so hot that the front of his jeans was already dry.

He found her breasts again, and she arched into his mouth with a small cry. He ground his pelvis against hers, sucking hard on her nipples and heat flashed over her once more. Putting her hands to his shoulders, she shoved. He fell onto his back and she rolled on top of him. Delighted with herself, with him, she grinned.

He grinned back. "You're a feisty one."

"No," she answered, shaking her head. "I'm no such thing." Everyone knew it. Everyone said it. "I'm a kindergarten teacher, remember?"

But she couldn't remember anything when he cupped her breasts again. Rising onto her knees and widening her thighs, her shaper rode up higher. She was free, now, to settle onto him, her panties against his erection. With his kneading fingers stoking the fire inside her, she pressed against him, using his hardness to stroke the spot where she wanted to feel his touch.

Maybe he got the message. One of his hands dropped from her breast and caressed up her thigh, finding its way to the place where they were joined together. His touch was gentle, experienced. Her head dropped back as he tunneled beneath her panties to caress her wet flesh with the rough wonder of a fingertip.

Her inhibitions fled. Moaning, she widened her thighs even more, letting him have more access to her body. She was pure sensation, a flame, a heated thing that shifted and turned to follow his beckoning finger.

She felt something scratchy against her back and realized he'd traded places with her again. She was somehow naked and he was looking down at her as if she were contraband he'd been coveting for years.

Embarrassment washed over her and she put one arm across her breasts and tried closing her thighs to his appreciative gaze. But his knees were between hers and then his hands captured her wrists and held them against the mattress on either side of her head.

"You don't need to be modest," he said. "I love looking at you."

It wasn't that she was modest. She was careful. This was moving too fast, too far, for Stacy Banks, security-minded, heart-cautious kindergarten teacher.

He leaned down to rub his hair-covered chest

against her breasts. "See how good this is," he whispered. "How good it's going to be between you and me?"

His movements set fire to her blood again. It raced through her veins, turning her objections to steam, turning her on more.

It *was* going to be good between them. She'd sensed it in the mailroom. She'd known it, somewhere inside her soul.

Or maybe that was the passion talking. But she didn't care. She just wanted. Now. Now. *Now.*

She struggled to free her hands. "Take off your pants," she said. "I want you naked, too."

He complied, somehow keeping one, arousing hand on her at the same time. When he was naked, she was flushed, she could feel it on her face and see the tinge of pink on her bare breasts.

His jeans plopped to the floor, and then he turned toward her again.

"Oh. Wow," she said. Her hand moved with a will of its own, taking a path down his heavy shoulder to his sinewy forearm to his lean flank. She urged him in position over her again, and rubbed her hands down his back to the high muscles of his butt. "Oh. Wow." It was a repeat, but it didn't feel redundant. She could oh-wow about his long, strong body for the next five years and still not be done with it.

Her hand curled around his hip and brushed

against his condom-covered erection. It jerked, he jerked. Smiling, she was more firm with it this time, and ran her fingers down its length. His groan was gratifying.

But even more gratifying was her own, as he batted her hand away and fitted himself to her body. He pushed. They both gasped.

Her body opened for him, closed on him, drew him in deep.

They both lay still, panting.

"This is good," he choked out. "It might kill me, but it's good."

She was throbbing against his hard flesh, she was throbbing around his hard flesh. The tips of her tight nipples were throbbing, too, pulsing with the rapid beat of her heart. Was it supposed to be like this? She couldn't remember it being like this, with every nerve ending twitching and sparking like a live wire.

He moved, more of a settling instead of a thrusting, and the fit was even better. She lifted her body to his, adding a little rotation of her pelvis. She couldn't help herself.

He couldn't seem to get enough of it. "Do that more," he muttered. "Do that again."

She repeated the movement, and it seemed to unleash something inside him. He pulled back, thrust in, putting his big hands beneath her bottom and lifting her to him.

Pleasure shot through Stacy. She tried to say something about it, but then he made the movement once more and she lost her voice, her breath, her mind.

Surging into her body over and over, he continued to control her, lifting her to him when he wanted it deep, letting her sink back when he wanted it shallow. She was panting with desire, and it was controlling her, too, pulling her along, pulling her out of her safe memories of tepid sex and censored emotions.

Ryan's hands shifted to the inside of her thighs. He pulled them wide and lifted them high, opening her to more sensation, more pleasure. More.

Maybe too much.

Yet desire was as undeniable as Ryan, prodding her along, pushing her past her safety zone and . . . out on a limb.

"Look at me," he ordered.

She opened her eyes, though she thought she should be running, hiding, concealing herself from him.

His gaze burned into hers. "Look at us."

Her muscles tightened, her breath backed up in her lungs. She glanced down, there was no refusing him, and she watched him enter her body, stretching her, opening her, making her into someone new.

Then the pleasure burst and Stacy screamed.

11

Flat on her back, with Ryan in a similar position beside her, Stacy said the first thing that came to her mind. "I never expected the evening to end like this."

His head rolled on the pillow to meet her gaze. His fingers, linked with hers, tightened. "I don't suppose you expected it to start the way it did, either."

"No." That was the trouble with her limb-perch. Since it was new territory for her, she didn't have any maps or lesson-plan books to guide her.

Ryan turned onto his side, his bare knees making contact with the outside of her bare thigh. "Do you regret what we did?"

It would be easy to misconstrue his meaning. To say something offhand about how could she regret that they'd managed to survive all their adventures. To avoid answering the question in regard to their lovemaking. But that would be cowardly.

"Do you?" she countered. Answering a question with a question was only half cowardly.

Tracing her cheek with the fingertips of his free hand, he smiled. "Not for a second. But what about you?"

"I don't even know you." The fear burst out of her.

He caressed her face again. "Not true. What we've been through tonight has showed us a lot about each other, don't you think?"

"Great. Now you know I like to hide in closets and that too much excitement makes me sick to my stomach."

"I'll tell you what I know about you. You're as capable as anyone I've ever worked with. You stay calm, cool, and collected when you need to. You don't hesitate to make important split-second decisions. And you know me better now, too, don't you?"

"I know you've been hiding your identity," she replied.

"My job, maybe, but other than that the only thing I've tried to hide from you, Stacy Banks, is how unbelievably hot I find my sexy, kindergarten-teacher neighbor."

She had to smile at that. "Hot and sexy and kindergarten teacher must be a contradiction in terms."

"Not from where I'm sitting." He leaned in to kiss the tip of her nose. "So give me a chance, Stacy Banks. Give *us* a chance."

Her heart wanted to fly away on the promise of his words. Intuition, instinct, something gut-level inside her wanted to believe this was more than an adrenaline-induced one-night stand and that she'd been right to go out on a limb for him.

But the rational, reasoning part of her brain reminded her he'd duped her from Day One. She'd never suspected he was anything other than the good-natured, good-neighbor sport-fishing boat operator. Now he said he was someone else altogether.

"What if we started over?" she asked.

He groaned. "Do you mean going back to hoping I bump into you in the mailroom? I don't think I can go back to casual, 'coincidental' meetings when all I'll want to do is hold you, kiss you, take you back to my bed, and make you scream again."

That's right, she'd screamed. She'd warned him she would, if something else that night surprised or scared her again. And he did. Or more specifically, the feelings she had for him did. They terrified her.

How could she trust herself? How could she trust him?

She needed a second opinion. There was a digital clock on the microwave across the room. It was only a few minutes after 10 P.M.

"We don't have to go *all* the way back. Just a few hours." She swallowed. "My sister's throwing a Christmas Eve party. Would you like to be my date?"

12

If Ryan wasn't in the partygoing mood, he didn't let on. Instead, he seemed willing, if not downright eager, to accompany Stacy to the Your Holiday Elf party. They'd be late, way late, but she wanted to be with her family and friends tonight. More, she wanted her family and friends to become acquainted with Ryan.

They knew her, and they'd get to know him. If they thought staid, kindergarten teacher Stacy was in over her head with Ryan Beausoleil, they'd let her know. The way she saw it, her heart was better off listening to her family instead of her own hunches. If her instincts were worthy of complete trust, tonight she would have stayed home, or at the very least stayed off *The Bait*.

At the door of her condo, Ryan framed her face with his big hands and gave her a long, lingering kiss. "Are you going to Christmas-wrap yourself for me again? I didn't get to appreciate it properly the first time."

There were stars in her eyes, she was that easy for him to dazzle. "I'm going to slip into something more comfortable than that." She laughed when he groaned and clutched at his heart. Going on tiptoe, she pressed her mouth to his lower lip. "Fifteen minutes?"

"Fifteen minutes." Snapping his fingers, he caught Jack Sparrow's attention.

Jack Sparrow. *Jack Sparrow.* Through a crack in her front door, Stacy found herself smiling as she watched the two of them walk off toward the stairs. Was she crazy? Who could be worried about a man with a cat named after a character played by Johnny Depp?

Her heart lightening, she rushed into the bathroom for a brief hot shower and then gave her hair a briefer scrunch-and-go pass with the blow-dryer. Black pants, a sweater set in soft pink, and a pair of black high heels later, she returned to the bathroom mirror for make-up.

She stared at her reflection. Accustomed to her usual true-blond paleness, the Stacy in the mirror had flushed cheeks and a bright sparkle in her eyes. Her lips were puffy, their color rosy, and for the first time since she was fourteen years old, her make-up routine was whittled down to two steps: dark brown mascara and a swipe of lip gloss.

Maybe Stacy was bringing two strangers to her sister's party tonight.

There was a knock at the door and she hokie-pokied past her twinkling Christmas tree on her way to answer it.

She pulled it open. An unfamiliar man stood on her doorstep, wearing a friendly smile and holding out a small, gift-wrapped package.

"Um, hello," she said. "Are you looking for someone?"

He had sandy hair just beginning to thin and he was well dressed. His tie was red silk with tiny green wreaths, his crisp white shirt was tucked into a pair of dark slacks held up by a simple, yet expensive belt. Having shopped for and wrapped a few like it in the last month, Stacy knew just how expensive.

What was a man wearing an eight-hundred-dollar belt doing on her doorstep?

"Are you looking for someone?" she repeated. A shiver of worry wiggled down her back. If she hadn't assumed it was Ryan knocking, she would have looked through her peephole and dealt with the stranger through the door.

"Stacy Banks, right? I thought I might need this to get you to open up, but . . ." He looked down at the gift in his hand, shrugged, then stuffed it in his pants pocket, never losing that smile. "I'm happy to see you're so cooperative."

Alarm bells rang. As she swung shut the door to lock him out, he inserted his foot in the gap and laid the flat of his palm against the wood surface.

He shoved, hard, and as the door flew open, Ryan stepped up behind the stranger, a gun in his hand. "What the *hell* are you doing here, Parnes?"

13

Parnes, Stacy thought, her mind reeling. *Doug Parnes.* The regional head of the DEA who had been making a splash in the press ever since he'd taken over the job a couple months back. There'd been letters in the newspaper from ordinary citizens praising the way he'd made their city safer. Television station managers had aired minutes-long editorials commending how quickly he'd swept away the remaining vestiges of the old drug cartel.

He was smiling again, looking down at Ryan's gun with mild interest. "What makes you think you need that, Beausoleil?"

Ryan's face had changed. He appeared different to her now, harder, his eyes narrowed and suspicious, his mouth grim. "I don't know. Something about finding you here has my hackles up. When we spoke earlier, you said you didn't need me to come in tonight."

The other man shrugged. "I'm sorry. Plans changed. I tried to get a hold of you by phone, but when that didn't work I came by to pick you up myself."

"Ryan, he knew my name," Stacy said. "He knocked on my door and asked for me by name."

Parnes threw her an offhand smile. "Ryan told me about your little adventure. I thought I'd check on you and give you the DEA's thanks."

Ryan's jaw hardened. "Get away from him, Sta—"

But it was too late. Parnes reached out and pulled Stacy against him, putting her between himself and the gun. Something firm and finger-like pushed against the small of her back. "Don't do anything stupid, Ryan. I have my own weapon kissing this little lady's kidney."

His expression didn't flicker. "So it's you. You're the leak. You're the one helping the new cartel get established."

"Of course not," Parnes replied, his gun still poking into Stacy's skin. "It's not me. You know who the leak is. Now I've got to take you in."

Stacy's head twisted to get a look at the man behind her. What was he implying? That *Ryan* was that bad guy? "No," she whispered.

"Oh, yes," he said, his voice pleasant. "We thought this little undercover op would give us enough intel to shut down the new organization before it had a chance to get started. But no. Instead, thanks to Ryan, they've managed to build an alliance and build a network that looks to bring more drugs into the U.S. than the one before it."

"*Ryan?*" Stacy echoed.

"You're full of shit, Parnes," Ryan replied.

"With the old cartel out, you had the perfect opportunity to become a linchpin, a wealthy, powerful, linchpin of the new one. No one will believe I had anything to do with it."

"I have all the proof I need. Now, come on, Ms. Banks, your country needs your help just once more tonight. I need to take in Beausoleil and you're going to be his incentive to cooperate."

Stacy stared at him. *What*? What was going on? Drugs, leaks, DEA. She was a kindergarten teacher, for God's sake, and had no business mixed up in this. She should be doing something in her own league, like staying safely at home and cutting out construction paper snowmen in preparation for the winter term. Parnes half-turned, keeping her in front of him as he backed one step, two steps, down the path toward the condo parking lot.

"Come along, Ryan," he called out. "I've still got the gun on your lady friend."

"I'm a kindergarten teacher," she said aloud. "Do you understand? A *kindergarten teacher*."

"Who got herself involved with a dangerous criminal," Parnes said. "You should have stayed in the classroom and stayed out of the big bad world. But you'll be safe now, with me."

14

"He's bluffing, Stacy," Ryan warned. "You won't be safe with him."

"Like she was safe with you?" Parnes scoffed. "Ms. Banks has had enough excitement for the evening, don't you think, Beausoleil? The three of us will go to headquarters and calmly straighten everything out."

"We won't make it to headquarters, Stacy." Ryan's voice was hard. "He wants to take us somewhere secluded, because he needs a fall guy, that's me, and he doesn't want any witnesses, that's you. We'll both be dead, just like I'm supposed to be already. You put Jaime up to killing me, didn't you Parnes? He was supposed to shoot me, then steal the good-faith money. For a cheap ten grand, you got your fall guy and he got a merry Christmas. But Jaime didn't like to shoot guns, he was terrified of them, and now he's the one who's dead and I know you're the one aiding and abetting the new cartel. Don't trust him, Stacy."

"Who should she trust?" Parnes asked. "*You?*"

Who should she trust? That was the question.

Parnes started dragged her backward again, and his plan seemed to be working, because Ryan kept pace with them.

"Don't do this," Ryan said.

Stacy didn't know if he was talking to her or Parnes, who continued pulling her backward, the gun pressed to her back. Stacy's feet automatically moved against the pavement. It was a narrow, private pathway they were on, that led only to their four-unit building. There was no reason for anyone else to take it. Besides Ryan, the building's other residents had gone elsewhere for the holidays.

Her head felt muddled, her pulse was thudding thickly, slowly, as if her blood was cold, sticky syrup. Maybe she'd used up her adrenaline. Maybe she was just too tired, too overwrought, too inexperienced to handle one more thing.

The DEA chief could be right and a trip to headquarters would straighten the whole mess out. Perhaps she *could* trust him. After all, he wasn't much more of a stranger to her than Ryan and she was just a kindergarten teacher.

Just a kindergarten teacher.

You're as capable as anyone I've ever worked with. You stay calm, cool, and collected when you need to. You don't hesitate to make important split-second decisions.

At the memory of those words, her blood leaped, bringing new life to her limbs, to her mind. She wasn't "just" a kindergarten teacher. She was a woman who handled a stressful job. She was a woman who faced down crises every day.

But what to do when facing this one?

The solution struck in a flash, her years of teaching experience standing her in good stead. Remembering how the little Brandons, Justins, and the occasional Tiffany made a trip to the principal's office nearly impossible, Stacy sagged, her body slumping against Parnes's controlling arm.

He cursed. "Stand up. Move."

But she'd been taught by tiny masters of the art. She played dead weight.

Cursing again, he tried dragging her along. His feet stumbled, then he caught his balance. He heaved, stumbled again, went down.

She rolled clear, just as Ryan sailed through the air and leaped on top of the other man. Without hesitation, she jumped to her feet and ran for her condo. Then she did what she'd been wanting to do all night long. She locked herself inside and dialed 911.

· 15 ·

Bing was singing through the stereo speakers. Her condo didn't have a fireplace, so the TV was tuned to the blazing Yule Log. Her patio door was open several inches, and the warm, seventy-plus degrees breeze wafted in, bringing along with it the scent of the citrus blossoms on her dwarf lemon.

As it seemed it was every year, Christmas Day in San Diego was too warm for the new flannel pajamas, fuzzy slippers, and cuddly robes that had been under the tree that morning. Next week the temperature would get into the forties at night, and they'd all be complaining about the cost of turning on the heater, but today was the kind of Southern California winter day that tied up phone lines to all points north and east with gloating calls.

Stacy's doorbell rang. She took a last glance at her small dining table, set for brunch with her grandmother's Lenox. On her way out of the kitchen, for luck she ran her fingertips along the string she'd used to hang the holiday cards she'd received. Most of them were handmade, with a liberal use of cotton balls and sparkling glitter.

She checked through the peephole, then opened the door. The pair stood on her doorstep, their expressions unreadable.

"Come in," she said. "I've been expecting you two."

One cleared his throat. "Merry Christmas."

The other made himself comfortable on the new loveseat.

Stacy tried to pretend her heart wasn't jumping. "It's over then?"

"Parnes isn't stupid. He's confessing so he can cut himself a deal. It's over."

But it wasn't for her, Stacy thought. She was changed forever.

Ryan glanced at his companion, as if for support, then looked back at her. "But we're not, Stacy. I hope. Please." He scooped a hand through his thick black hair.

Ryan Beausoleil—nervous?

He cleared his throat again and gazed about the room. "I, uh, thought you mentioned something about inviting your family?"

That was when she had yet to recognize the changes that one night had made in her life. To her self-image. Now she knew that though she loved her family, she didn't need their approval on this. She didn't need them to vet her judgments.

She was strong. Smart. And if the way Ryan was looking at her was any indication, sexy.

He scooped his hand through his hair again. "How can I make it up to you for what happened last night? How can I convince you that I won't be a constant source of danger to you?"

"You said you were going back to regular Coast Guard duty. I think I can take my chances with that." *Go the mile, give a smile,* she told herself. And did.

In a blink, she found herself in his arms, being thoroughly kissed in that made-her-want-to-scream way that he had. Then he lifted his head.

"Did I mention how remarkable you are? I couldn't believe it when you took Parnes down. What made you think of it?"

"All I needed to know I learned in kindergarten." Then she laughed when he swooped in for another scorching kiss. "Well, maybe not *that*."

"Good," Ryan whispered against her mouth. "Because I think it's time for some advanced classes."

They didn't get around to brunch until late afternoon. When they strolled back into the living room, hand in hand, Ryan's companion was missing.

"Damn," he said. "What's Jack Sparrow up to now?"

"Well, in my fantasies, he's—"

Ryan silenced her with another kiss. "Ah. There he is." A long branch of the tree on the patio next door snaked across one corner of hers, and the cat was stretched along it. With a sigh, Ryan strode toward the open door. "I'll get him."

Stacy caught his arm. "No, don't. Let him enjoy it. Believe me, there are all kinds of wonderful adventures to be had out on a limb."

The Two Marys

Katherine Hall Page

The Christmas Eve sky was filled with stars when Mary Bethany found a baby in her barn. They hadn't had a real snow yet; the island never got the kind of accumulation the mainland did, but it was cold. She had pulled an old woolen overcoat that had belonged to her father over her winter jacket and grabbed a shawl her mother had knitted, draping it around her head. Her small herd of goats was letting her know that it was milking time, holiday or no holiday.

Mary wasn't leaving a festive gathering. She wasn't leaving any gathering at all. Just a cup of hot cider, a slice of the fruitcake sent by her cousin Elizabeth, and a few cats for company and to keep the rodent population down. Walking the short distance from the old farmhouse to the small barn she'd built when the herd got too large for the shed, Mary had remembered the legend about animals being able to speak on Christmas Eve. She'd allowed herself to speculate about what her goats would have to say. They were Nubians, pretty, long-eared goats that gave rich milk, containing the highest butter-fat content and protein produced by any breed. Her pretty nannies. Her neurotic nannies. Temperamental, easily miffed divas, they let her know with resounding blats when something was even the slightest bit wrong. She was afraid that given human voices, their conversation would be a litany of slights and sorrows. Or perhaps not. Perhaps they would tell her how much they depended on her, how much they loved her. She had entered the warm barn smiling, and her smile grew broader when she saw the large basket with a big red bow, nestled against a bale of hay. It must be a gift from a neighbor, she thought. She hadn't expected she would be getting any presents. Even her sister Martha's yearly Harry and David cheese log had not arrived. A tag hung from the bow: "For Mary Bethany." She ignored the goats for a moment and knelt down before the gift.

It was an afghan in soft pastel colors. That would be Arlene Marshall, who crocheted so beautifully. The summer people always snapped up her work at the Sewing Circle's annual fair in August. How kind, Mary thought. It would be just the thing to throw across her lap at night when she sat up late reading. But so unexpected. She hadn't seen or spoken to the Marshalls since she'd taken some of her rose-hip jelly over in early September. It had been a wonderful summer for the *Rosa rugosa* bushes that surrounded the house and had seeded in what passed for a lawn and then, beyond it, in the pasture. Mary had gathered the large bulbous bright orange hips and put up jelly, made soup, even dried some for tea. Looking at the gleaming jars on the pantry shelf, she had decided to take some to Arlene and Doug, her nearest neighbors—a mere six acres of fields and woods away.

But this was too much! It must have taken Arlene a long time to make, she realized. The stitch was intricate and the wool so fine. Then she heard a tiny sneeze. The merest whisper of a sneeze. She pulled back the blanket and uncovered—a baby! Eyes squeezed shut, a newborn—tiny—about the size of a kid. She rocked back on her heels in amazement, letting the cover drop from her hands. A baby?

The goats were crying louder, insistently. There was nothing human about their speech, but Mary knew what they were saying. She would have to milk them, or they would wake the child. Whose child? And what was it doing here in her barn? Mary touched the baby's face gently. It was soft and warm. A beautiful child, rosy cheeks—*Rosa rugosa* cheeks—and shiny, fine dark hair, like cormorant feathers, escaping from the hooded snowsuit. A blue snowsuit, new, not a hand-me-down. It must be a boy, she thought. His eyelids fluttered at her touch, but he slept on. Mary stood up shakily. She would milk the goats, then take the baby inside. That was as far ahead as she could think at the moment. In all her forty-seven years, nothing remotely like this had ever happened. Nothing unusual at all, unless you thought an old maid who kept to herself, raised goats, and made cheese was unusual—or odd—as some did. But nothing really *unusual*.

Automatically, she milked the six goats and put out fresh water, more hay, and the grain mixture of oats, corn, and molasses she fed them. They complained at her haste and voiced their irritation. "I don't have time to coddle you tonight," she told them, and something in her tone seemed to chasten them. At least the noise level dropped. "Besides," she added, "if anyone should be upset, it should be me. It's Christmas Eve. You're supposed to be able to tell me what happened here tonight."

She carried the baby into the house, setting the basket down by the woodstove in the kitchen, then ran back for the milk, which went into the shed, where she kept the second refrigerator. She'd had to buy it after she'd started making cheese.

When she closed the barn door and let the latch drop, Mary looked up into the night sky. It was clear and the stars seemed close enough to touch. There was a large one directly overhead.

She blinked and it was gone. Turning at the back door for a last look before she went into the house, she saw the star was back.

In the kitchen, Mary took off her coat and jacket, wrapping the shawl around her shoulders. The baby was awake and making little mewing sounds like a kitten. He must be hungry, she thought, and reached in to pick him up. He settled into the crook of her arm, as if it had been carved just for him.

"You poor thing," she said aloud. "Who are you? And how could anyone bear to give you up?"

Holding him tightly, she pulled the afghan out of the basket. Underneath it lay an envelope with her name on it, some baby clothes, cloth diapers, two bottles, and a package wrapped in brown paper—not the kind you buy on a roll, but cut from a paper bag. The letter wasn't sealed; the flap was tucked in, easy to open with one hand. Mary knew then that the baby's mother had tried to think of everything, even this small detail—that Mary would be holding the baby when she read the letter. It was short and typewritten:

Dear Mary,

Keep him safe and raise him to be a good man. His name is Christopher.

That was it. No signature. No further explanation. Mary picked up the package and peeled the tape from one end. A packet of bills fell out. She shook it, and more followed. Packets of hundred-dollar bills. A lot of hundred-dollar bills.

Faith Fairchild was watching her family. Nine-year-old Ben was in a corner, Lego Technic pieces spread out on the floor. His sister, first grader Amy, was equally involved, but she was at the kitchen counter, perched on a stool, drawing. The elaborate art pack—"Just like a real artist's, I bet"—that her grandparents had sent was reverently placed next to her. Faith drank some of her coffee. She'd made a fresh pot for breakfast—the first pot had disappeared quickly, along with the slices of her cardamom raisin Christmas bread, after the kids woke them at six o'clock to see what Santa had brought. Ben had managed to keep the secret of the jolly old fellow's true identity, whether out of real regard for his sister or to save as a weapon when she did something really outrageous, such as entering his room without permission, Faith didn't care—just let Amy keep believing awhile longer. Last night in a whisper before sleep, her daughter had confessed her fear that Santa might not know they were in Maine. He might think they were in their house in Aleford, Massachusetts, as usual. Faith had reassured her that Saint Nick knew all and would always find them.

Faith's attention strayed to her best present, always her best present—her husband, Tom, the Reverend Thomas P. Fairchild, who was stretched out on the couch, reading Bill Bryson's *A Short History of Nearly Everything.* Tom caught her glance and blew her a kiss. She sent one back to him and wished they could reprise the early Christmas present they had enjoyed upstairs under the eiderdown quilt last night. Children are nature's most effective prophylactics, she thought, looking at her two, awake, alert, and very much around.

They'd put a CD of Handel's *Messiah* on and "We like sheep" filled the air. Faith and her younger sister, Hope, had taken the passage literally as children and created their own version, adding "and goats and chickens and cats and dogs, too." She'd call Hope later and they could sing a few bars together.

Tom still looked pale. Just after Thanksgiving, he'd had a series of stomachaches. He'd eat lightly and they'd pass. Stress, they'd told each other. Early in their marriage, they'd talked about how much they loved the Christmas season, starting with the lighting of the first Advent candle and continuing on to the joys of Christmas Day with its message of hope and peace.

Loved it—and hated it. Having grown up as a preacher's kid, albeit in a parish on Manhattan's Upper East Side, Faith knew all about the stress Christmas brought. It was due not only to the increase in the number of church services—or the lack of private family time (a year-round dilemma)—but also to the problems that surfaced as lonely people compared their lives to the ones they saw on television specials, and as harried parents tried to combine work and assembling Notre Dame in gingerbread with their over-stimulated offspring. Stress, they'd told each other. That was the trouble. Tom swigged Maalox and crunched Tums. They promised each other some time off in January. Then the pains moved to his back, and one bright winter morning complete with blue sky and a dusting of snow like confectioner's sugar, Faith got a call from Emerson Hospital. Her husband was in the emergency ward.

It was pancreatitis, and the sight of him hooked up to an IV, pale as Marley's ghost, was almost more than she could bear. He tried for a grin, but it turned into a grimace. Their doctor was reassuring in that oxymoronic way doctors employ. Lucky to have caught it—but. Sound metabolism—but. So long as he watched for symptoms, he'd be better than ever—probably. They'd have to keep him for a while, and he'd have to take it easy for a bit. So, forget about work for at least a month. Just one of those things.

When he'd said that, Faith had had to stop herself from retorting, Hey, we're not talking about a trip to the moon on gossamer wings! Is my husband going to be all right or not?

Yes, Tom was the best present. She'd been stunned by his illness. He was usually the picture of health, one of those perennially big hungry boys, his tall, rangy frame burning calories as fast as their woodstove consumed logs. At the thought, she got up to add some more to the sturdy Vermont Castings Defiant model—she liked the name: "Take that, Cold!" They didn't really need it, since they'd put in a furnace when they'd remodeled the house several summers ago. But the crackling birch smelled heavenly and filled the room with the kind of warmth no furnace could duplicate. She'd been opposed to putting a furnace in—why spend the money when they would never be on Sanpere Island in the wintertime? She'd suspected it was Tom's idea of the proverbial thin end of the wedge. He'd spend every vacation on Sanpere if he could. While Faith loved the island, too, there were others, like Saint Barts and Mustique, that beckoned more seductively in cold weather.

But here they were. Thank God. It was, of course, where Tom wanted to recuperate, and it had been perfect. The days so far and the days that stretched out ahead, filled with nothing more taxing than the *New York Times* Saturday crossword puzzle and the Audubon Christmas Bird Count, made her slightly giddy with relief. Tom would be fine, better than ever. The words had become a kind of mantra she repeated to herself whenever her husband looked tired or she thought there was a new crease on his forehead.

Outside, Christmas Day was clear and cold. The tide was coming in. It would be high at noon. After stoking the fire, she walked over to the large floor-to-ceiling windows that stretched across the front of the room—living room and kitchen combined. There were Christmas trees of all sizes growing on either side of the shore frontage. The rocks in the cove, exposed at low tide, were glistening like tinsel as the water lapped over them. Inside the house, a small living tree stood in a tub. Twinkling with the tiny white lights they'd brought, it was trimmed with ornaments they'd made from pinecones and clam and mussel shells. The only thing she'd brought from home was the exquisite Gladys Boalt treetop angel figure Tom had given her their first Christmas together. She always put it on the top of the tree even before they put the lights on—that tedious job. The angel had become a kind of talisman, and Faith promised herself that no tree they'd ever have would be without it. The angel's deftly painted smile looked enigmatic this morning—or perhaps that was Faith's interpretation.

Last year had been a particularly hectic one, both at the parish and her catering company. Gazing out at the scene in front of her, she thought what a gift it was to know you could walk away, turn everything over to someone else—her assistant, Niki Constantine; Tom's associate minister; the divinity school intern; and the vestry. She never wanted the reason for all this to happen again; she planned that Tom and she would go gently into that good night someday far in the future, and at the same time. She couldn't bear to think of life without him. But now that he was on the mend, she knew she would always treasure this time, and she was glad of it.

The Christmas season on Sanpere Island was similar only in the barest outlines to Christmas in Aleford, one of Boston's western suburbs, or New York City—the standard by which Faith gauged most things. Holiday decorations, the guy in the red suit, Jesus, Mary, and Joseph, and presents were accounted for in all three places. In Aleford, people put up wreaths, maybe strung a few lights on their bushes; but in Sanpere, yards were filled with snowmen, reindeer, elves, and Santa, of course. Colored lights outlined every house, glowing "icicles" dripped from the roofs, and even more wattage lit up the trees. Faith knew there was a contest each year for "Best Holiday Display," but she'd never suspected the contestants would rival Rockefeller Center.

In Granville, the merchants had given over their windows to the season. The photo studio, a fixture for at least two generations, always featured a gingerbread village made by the island's kindergarten class. A local artist had created a Nativity scene in another store, and a life-size Santa stood on the roof of the bank. But the biggest difference Down East was that in Penobscot Bay, Santa arrived via lobster boat. She'd taken the kids to the town pier in Granville to greet him, along with most of the island—population 3,134 in the winter.

They'd cheered Santa ashore and joined the crowd for cocoa and cookies in the Grange Hall. With no school the next day for the children and all the boats out of the water for the fishermen, the evening took on a leisurely character. It was only the women, Faith had noted, who had that " 'To Do' list" look.

She turned away from the window and thought happily about hers—nonexistent.

"Something smells wonderful, darling," Tom said.

"It will be awhile. I'm steaming a wild-mushroom flan to go with the game hens. Why

don't I heat up some of that potato leek soup
from yesterday to tide you over?" Tom's meals
had progressed from clear liquids to pureed
solids to almost normal fare, but they weren't
sitting down to a goose or any of the other Yule-
tide treats Faith usually made. Much too heavy
for now.

"A cup of the soup sounds great," he said.

"Coming up. I'll have some, too. Kids, Dad
and I are having soup. Do you want some, or a
sandwich?"

Ben's head came slowly up from the intricate
directions. When he was younger, Faith had tried
to help him with the more advanced Legos he'd
received as gifts, but she'd quickly realized she'd
have more luck trying to assemble a cyclotron
from her kitchen implements.

"Sure, PB and J is fine. Thanks, Mom."

"I'll make my own." Amy slid off the stool and
went toward the fridge. She had a more adven-
turesome palate than her brother—she'd eat oys-
ters, for instance—and Faith watched in
amusement as the small towheaded figure pulled
out some sharp cheddar cheese and Major Grey's
chutney.

Faith had just finished delivering lunch and
was about to eat her own, when the phone rang.

"It must be Granny and Grandpa!" Ben was up
like a flash. Tom's parents would be the first to

call. Hers would still be still involved with church obligations.

"Just a minute," she heard him say. It must not be her in-laws, she realized. "I'll get her. Oh, Merry Christmas."

Ben set the phone down and said, "It's for you, Mom." He hunched his shoulders and raised his arms. Not somebody whose voice he recognized.

"I'm so sorry to bother you. You must be in the midst of dinner, or getting it ready. It's Mary Bethany, Faith."

"We're not doing a thing, Mary." As Faith answered, she wondered why Mary was calling. They weren't close friends. In fact, it was her impression that Mary didn't have many—or any— close friends. The older woman lived by herself on her family farm, raising goats, some vegetables, and making superlative goat cheese. The cheese had been their point of contact. Tasting some at a friend's house, Faith had tracked Mary down. Over the last few summers, she'd helped Mary with some new recipes—herbed chèvre, in particular—and encouraged her to market her cheeses more widely. When they'd arrived last week, Faith had stopped by to get some of the plain chèvre for Tom, and Mary had been very sympathetic about his illness—and comforting. "One of the Sanfords had the very same thing and was back lobstering before the season •

ended," Mary had told her. She'd also pressed various rose-hip concoctions on Faith, swearing that they could cure everything from "a sprained ankle to a broken heart." This was the way Mary spoke—slightly quirky and always direct. Mary was a reader. Books were stacked all over the parts of the house Faith had seen, and she was sure the rest looked the same. The two women often exchanged titles and sometimes the books themselves. Faith had become fond of Mary and wondered what *her* story was. Didn't she need something—or rather, someone—besides her books and her goats? Had she had it and lost it? Faith realized that the woman was probably alone today, and so she promptly invited her to join them.

"We're eating lightly, because of Tom, but we'd love to have you with us," she said.

"That's very sweet of you, but I'm afraid I can't get away."

"Oh, Mary, the goats will be all right for a few hours," Faith said. It suddenly seemed important that she join them. Faith didn't like the idea of Mary all by herself in that isolated house on Christmas—or, for that matter, any day. Mary had told Faith that Nubian goats were very needy and got upset if they were left for very long. It apparently affected their milk. "I should really have started with a Swiss breed, something like white Saanens, much more placid," she'd told Faith. "But my first two were Nubians, and here I am."

"It's not the goats," Mary said. "It's . . . well, it's something else. Faith, I know this is a lot to ask, but is there any way you could come over here for a little while?"

Startled, Faith heard herself reply, "Of course. When would you like me?"

"As soon as possible," Mary said, hanging up.

Faith hung up, too, thinking how human the goat in the background had sounded. Almost like a baby crying.

Mary Bethany had not slept since she'd found Christopher in her barn. At first, she'd determinedly blocked out all thoughts of what to do except take care of his immediate needs. She changed his wet diaper and burst out laughing as he sprayed her before she could get the new one on. His skin was softer than any kid's fleece. Soft—everything about him was soft, from the top of his head to the soles of his feet. How could fingernails and toenails be so small, so perfect? He curled his fist around her finger and made that soft mewing sound again. So different from her demanding nannies. So different from the cries of enraged infants she'd occasionally heard in the aisles of the Harborside Market.

Lacking any alternative, she had filled one of the bottles with goat's milk, warmed it, and watched in delight as he greedily sucked it dry. Mary prided herself not only on her cheese but on her milk, too. It was always sweet and fresh. Two lactose-intolerant customers swore they couldn't tell the difference from cow's milk, as if that were the standard. Cow's milk—Mary thought it should be the other way around. She would never have taken up with cows. Much too bovine. No personality.

It was only when Christopher had once again fallen asleep—as she rocked him gently in the chair her mother must have rocked her in—that Mary began to consider her alternatives. Happily, calling the authorities was not a choice. There were no authorities to call. There was no police department on Sanpere, just occasional patrols by the state police. She was happy about this for several reasons, first and foremost being an innate disinclination to "open up a can of worms." They'd bring in social workers, put Christopher in a foster home, everything his mother was clearly trying to avoid by leaving him in Mary's barn. Mary had no idea who the woman could possibly be, but she did know one thing. Christopher's mother had chosen Mary and she had chosen her, because she thought Christopher was in danger. The baby was a trust, a sacred trust, and Mary Bethany was not going to betray that. Let it be according to her wish.

But what to do? Even though she rarely saw other people—only at the bank, the market, or if she happened to be in the shed when they came to buy cheese or milk—there was no way she could pass the baby off as her own. Besides the lack of any physical evidence—Mary had always been as slender as a reed—the notion of Mary with a lover would be greeted not only with skepticism but derision. She could hear them now: "Mary Bethany pregnant? Maybe by one of the goats."

Mary had been born on the island, but the Bethanys were from away. Her parents had come to Sanpere when her father got a job at the shipyard as a welder after the war. Her mother's family had come from Italy, endowing Mary with the dark hair and Mediterranean features that she shared with others on Sanpere. But *their* looks had come down from the Italian stonecutters who had arrived in the late nineteenth and early twentieth centuries to work in the now-abandoned granite quarries. Mary's grandparents had landed in New York and worked in the garment business—the wrong kind of Italians for Sanpere. True, Mary's father's family were Mainers, but from the north, Aroostock County—potato farmers. They weren't fishermen. Her father had learned his trade in the service, met her mother, Anne, at a USO dance, and when the war was over, they'd ended up on Sanpere not for any particular reason, but because people have to end up somewhere. Without the kinship network that was as essential and basic to Sanpere as the aquifer and ledges the entire island rested on, Mary and her older sister, Martha, were always viewed as outsiders. Martha, a bossy big sister, had left as soon as she turned sixteen, married at eighteen, and lived in New Hampshire with what was now a growing brood of grandchildren. Mary had stayed. Someone had had to take care of their elderly parents—the sisters had been late-in-life children. Maybe if she had been more outgoing, more self-confident, like Martha, she would have fit into island life better—or had the guts to leave, parents or no parents. But she had been a shy child, preferring her animals to any human playmates, and books to everything animate or inanimate. Her father had died first, but the farm was paid for by then. They had had enough to get by, especially after Mary started running a small B & B during the summer months to pay the mounting shorefront taxes. Her mother had taken her father's death as a personal affront, and after several years of intense anger, she joined him, presumably to give him what-for. That had been ten years ago.

Mary was alone. There was no lover past, present, or future. When she considered the complications love presented—gleaned from her reading and from observing those around her—she was usually glad to have been spared the bother. But it did mean she couldn't pass the baby off as hers.

Gradually, as the sky lightened, she had come up with a plan. Easy enough to say that Christopher was her grand-nephew, that his mother wasn't well and couldn't take care of him. Although Martha hadn't been on the island since her mother's funeral, it was well known that she had had ten children herself and that those ten had been equally fruitful and multiplied. Mary invented a rich tale of a young niece with three children already, abandoned by her good-for-nothing cheater of a husband, driving through the night to leave the baby, after calling her aunt in desperation. She'd tell her neighbor Arlene, ask her to pick up some clothes and other things the next time she went off island to Ellsworth. "She was so upset, I'm surprised she remembered to bring little Christopher," Mary said now, rehearsing. Arlene had two grandchildren she thought hung the moon. She brought over them to play with the goats when they visited every August. Arlene would be a big help. And since she also had a big mouth, Mary wouldn't have to tell the story to anyone else.

That settled, Mary had turned her thoughts to the rest of the plan. And the rest of the plan had meant calling Faith Fairchild. She watched the sun come up and waited for the right time.

* * *

Faith knocked on Mary's back door. No one used front doors on Sanpere—or anywhere else in New England, to Faith's knowledge. It was a mystery why they bothered putting them on houses at all. Using Mary's front door was also complicated by the tangle of lilac and rosebushes that had grown up over the granite stoop.

Mary opened the door and slipped out. Faith was puzzled. From the urgency in Mary's voice, she had expected to be ushered in immediately and told whatever Mary thought was important enough to pull someone away from hearth and home on Christmas Day. The goats? It had to be the goats. Mary didn't have anything else to worry about. Or, Faith thought with sudden apprehension, it might be Mary herself. That must be it. She's ill. Cancer. She has cancer.

"Faith, I don't know how to put this any other way, but I want to tell you a secret."

Faith felt relief and anticipation in equal measure. She loved secrets.

"But I have to have your absolute word that you won't tell anyone else. Not even your husband."

Husbands were exempt from the secrets rule, but maybe Mary didn't know that, not having one herself.

"Tom's a minister. He'd keep anything you tell me totally confidential. He has to, or they take away his collar or robes or something."

Mary folded her arms across her chest. She was the kind of woman who looks so ordinary that you feel you must know her or at least have seen her before. The gesture and the current expression on her face transformed her. This was a woman you'd remember.

"No Tom. If you can't agree, I can't tell you." She paused. "And I'm sorry I called you out all this way for nothing." Mary's farm backed onto Eggemoggin Reach. By water, or as the gull flies, it wasn't far from the Fairchilds'. By land, it took a good fifteen minutes.

"It's not a crime or anything like that, is it? I mean, of course you haven't murdered anyone." Faith thought she'd better ask. It was no never mind to her, but Tom tended to take a dim view of her involvement in these things.

"No crime has been committed, to my knowledge," Mary said firmly. "But you don't have to agree. Go into the shed. There's some fresh cheese. Take one home with you for your trouble."

"Oh, Mary, of course I agree. You have my word." Instinctively, Faith put out her hand and Mary shook it, opening the door wider.

Faith stepped into the kitchen, thinking they should have mixed spit or pricked their fingers with a safety pin. But she didn't think for long; she simply reacted and was on her knees by the basket instantly. Christopher was wide-awake; his dark eyes shone up at her and his mouth curved in what was definitely a smile. They weren't supposed to do this until they were older, but both of Faith's babies had smiled from birth—and recognized her face, despite what the experts said.

"Where on earth did this beautiful baby come from?"

"I found him in the barn last night when I went to do the milking. His name is Christopher."

"In the barn! Christopher! Was he in the manger? Any visits from angels lately?" It was too much.

Mary grinned, "And I'm a virgin, too. You can hold him if you want. He's a hungry little fellow, and I was just going to warm a bottle."

Faith was only too happy to comply. She adored babies, especially other people's at this point in her life.

"Sit down and I'll tell you everything I know, which is not much. And I'll tell you why I wanted you to come."

Faith called Tom and told him Mary's story— literally Mary's story—the one fabricated for public consumption. She reminded him to take the flan out of the oven, then asked if he'd mind her staying for another thirty minutes or so. Since he was almost asleep, Ben still involved with his Legos, and Amy gathering more pine-cones, Tom thought she could be spared.

Mary was continuing with her explanation.

"I couldn't involve anyone on the island. It would be too dangerous for the baby. His mother obviously brought him here because she knew how isolated it is. Still, there is the bridge, and word could spread to the mainland easy enough."

The Sanpere Bridge across Eggemoggin Reach connecting the island to the mainland had been a WPA project, a graceful suspension bridge that looked from a distance as if a particularly talented child had constructed it from an Erector set. For many on the island, it was still a bone of contention. Joe Sanford, age ninety, had never been across. "Never had a reason. Everything I need is here." But others found it pretty handy, especially before the Island Medical Center was built and the closest health care was in Blue Hill. A new generation of bridge haters had recently grown up as wealthy off islanders began to build second homes similar to Newport's "cottages." These people wanted to preserve Sanpere in aspic—in other words, "The last person across always wants to pull up the bridge behind him."

Mary was right not to involve anyone on Sanpere, even with a blood oath. There were no secrets on the island, and the bridge made sure news traveled.

"But I can't find his mother by myself. Aside from taking care of him, I can't—"

Faith finished for her: "Leave the nannies. So, very fortunately, I'm here for a while."

Mary looked a bit embarrassed. "I'd heard about that business with the real estate man who was found murdered by the lighthouse and how you figured out who did it." Several summers ago, Faith had found a corpse while walking along the shore near Sanpere's lighthouse. The death appeared to be accidental; then more "accidents" occurred, until Faith untangled the threads leading to the killer.

"This isn't like that," Mary said, "but I thought you might be able to help me find out who his mother is and why she left him here."

Faith studied Mary's face. It was a plain, pleasant face, rather flat and with the look of one of those antique Dutch wooden dolls. But today there was something different about it. Faith had never seen Mary look so excited. Not even when one of her does had quintuplets the spring before last.

"But why? Why do you want to find her? To give the baby back?"

Mary was horrified. "Oh no, not to give him back."

"Then why don't you just keep him? Your little grand-nephew."

Mary had been through this the night before many times. Just as she had debated back and forth whether to call Faith. She had changed her mind about the latter so many times that she still wasn't completely sure whether it was the real Faith in front of her or the one she had conjured up and talked to during the wee hours.

"I think she's in trouble. She *must* be in trouble; otherwise, she wouldn't have left him here. And I feel that I have to find her. It's hard to explain. It just doesn't seem fair to Christopher, either. To have her simply disappear. What would I tell him when he was older? I'd have to tell him. Too horrible to find out when he's grown that everything he thought was real wasn't."

"Yes, you'd have to tell him and, yes, we have to find her."

Faith had thought this was what Mary would say. It was what she herself would do. Besides, Mary would be in a precarious legal position. They hadn't mentioned it, but they both knew it. There hadn't been any birth certificate in the basket—or adoption papers.

What Faith didn't ask Mary—and wouldn't ask—was how will you feel if she wants him back. She stood up abruptly.

"Okay, what can we figure out from this stuff?" Faith had spread the contents of the baby's basket on the enamel-topped kitchen table. Mary's circa 1949 style of kitchen was currently back in vogue. To reproduce—unchanged, as if it had been transported intact like Julia Child's to the Smithsonian, what Mary took completely for granted would cost more than all the goat cheese she could sell in her lifetime. Many, many more dollars than those stuck in the Hellmann's mayonnaise jar left so trustingly on top of the refrigerator in the shed.

The basket itself, although a roomy one, was unremarkable. You saw stacks of them at Pier 1— or at rummage sales. Baskets and mugs—that's what future archaeologists will find in our middens, Faith thought.

She picked up the sleepers one at a time. There were three of them. Then she examined the snowsuit.

"Pretty generic. Not Baby Dior or Hanna Anderson—or even Baby Gap. Therefore, we're not talking money here, although"—Faith gestured to the stacks of bills—"there's certainly money here. The clothes are new, but not recognizable brands, so she could have picked them up anywhere. The only thing they tell us is that she didn't buy used baby clothes or get them passed down to her."

"So, no other children and no family involved. And she wanted brand-new clothes for Christopher."

Faith nodded.

"She does have a computer, though—or access to one."

"How can you tell?" Mary asked curiously.

"The printing is a computer printout. Not typed on a typewriter. Much smoother."

"I thought the wording of the note might mean something," Mary said, picking it up. "Not the 'Keep him safe' part, although since she wrote that first, I'm sure it means she thinks or knows he's in danger—but the 'raise him to be a good man' part. Sounds like she hasn't had much luck there—or worse."

"Definitely worse," Faith agreed. "I'd guess Christopher's father is not her idea of a model father figure. Maybe not her own father, either. Or it could be her father who *is* the ideal, but then why wouldn't she have gone to him for help, or her mother, for that matter?"

"Maybe both have passed away?" Mary picked up the note. "She didn't sign it. Just stopped writing. Do you think she was interrupted, or was it that she couldn't think of any way to finish it?"

"Either or neither," said Faith. "But she has to be someone you know, Mary. Your name was on the basket and the letter. Plus, she knew you had a barn and kept goats—knew your routine, that you'd be out to milk them at six. She wasn't taking any chances that the baby wouldn't be found quickly."

"I've been going through all this since I found him, believe me. And I can't think who she could be."

Faith put the clothes down.

"What else? The afghan—exquisitely hand-made. But it doesn't tell us anything except that she's a good crocheter or went to some kind of fair."

"My neighbor Arlene could read it like a book. Tell us where the yarn came from, who does that kind of stitch—at least on the island. Maybe we can think of a way to show it to her without having her get suspicious."

"The cloth diapers suggest she's pretty green."

"You mean inexperienced?" Mary asked.

Faith laughed. "No, as in environmentally friendly, ecoconscious. No disposables, but washable cloth diapers."

"A tree-hugger. Well, I'm with her on that one. Easy enough to wash diapers."

"Wait and see. The jury's still out on whether you use more resources washing the cloth ones than those other diapers consume. And they do cut down on diaper rash. I know how much time you spend tending your herd, but babies are even more work than your nannies."

Mary doubted this, but she was on shaky ground here.

"Computer access, environmentalist, young—that's a logical presumption—and can't keep her baby. This all says *student* to me." Faith was feeling quite Holmesian and wished there had been a bit more evidence, such as cigar ash or mud from a shoe, so she could say that the young woman had been in Morocco recently, purchasing smokes at a stall in the bazaar from Abdul, a dark-haired man with a limp. Hair!

"Are there any strands of hair on the blanket—or on Christopher himself?"

"How stupid. There was one, but I forgot to mention it. It's dark like mine, or like mine used to be." Mary was starting to go gray. "It's not mine, though, because it's long. Not Christopher's, either, but the same color." Mary's hair was sensibly short. She cut the bangs herself and exchanged cheese for a trim from one of her customers who worked over on the mainland at Curl Up and Dye.

"Well, we've certainly narrowed it down. A young female student with long dark hair," Faith said dejectedly.

"It *does* seem impossible," Mary agreed.

But Faith was nowhere near giving up.

"Don't say that. We've barely scratched the surface. What about the money? Where would a student come up with this kind of money? Have you counted it?"

"There's fifty thousand dollars in one-hundred-dollar bills."

"As soon as I leave, you have to hide it. You should have done it already."

Mary nodded in agreement. "I have the perfect place. I'm going to—"

"Don't tell me. I don't know why, but it's better if just one of us knows."

"A student," Mary mused. "Unless she comes from a very rich family with ready access to a trust fund—and then maybe she would have bought more expensive baby clothes—there's only one thing I can think of that brings in that kind of money for someone her age."

"Drugs?" Faith had been thinking the same thing since she'd first seen the stacks of bills.

"There's been a lot in the news about it, and I guess you've heard about all the break-ins on the island. They're pretty sure they're looking for stuff to sell for drugs. Plus, it's not just marijuana but heroin and prescription drugs, too."

Faith had heard about the break-ins. Thirty in September alone, all during the daytime and all summer places closed for the winter. They'd used a crowbar to pry open doors, taking anything of value, as well as canned goods, clothing, and, from one cottage, an iron. It had made her think a woman must be involved either directly or indirectly—"Honey, could you pick up an iron; this one is shot"—or an extremely analretentive male.

"This would explain why she wrote about keeping Christopher safe. If his mother is involved with drug dealers, they wouldn't want a baby around," Mary said.

Or his mother might be dealing herself, Faith thought.

"The paper bag is another clue," Faith said. "It's not from a Hannaford or any other chain. Must be a pretty small mom-and-pop operation. The name looks hand-stamped." Faith studied it—"Sammy's 24-Hour Store— Get your phone books, Mary, and let's see if we can find this place."

Mary put Christopher back in his basket. He had dozed off in her arms. It had amazed her to watch the way he moved from light to deep sleep and then to short periods of consciousness when he was hungry. She'd always thought it must be hard for her kids to leave a doe's nice warm womb, and it was obviously the same for babies.

She handed Faith the Yellow Pages for Hancock and Penobscot counties, the only books she had, and went to check the goats. She'd been so wrapped up in Christopher, she'd been neglecting them. They were such social creatures. Her old dog had died last spring and she hadn't gotten around to getting another. The goats seemed to miss his visits—and the wild goose that had made a nest in their pen, laid her eggs, raised the goslings, and then vanished. The nannies wouldn't be cold. In their own inimitable way, they didn't mind lower temperatures or snow, but they hated rain, and hated drafts even more.

She'd have to make sure no wind was getting through any chinks in the boards.

When she returned, Faith looked smug.

"Bingo! Or I should say 'Orono.' "

"And since that's where the big U. Maine campus is, we're probably right about the student part."

"I wish I could stay longer," Faith said. "But call me if you find out anything more—or if you need help with Christopher." Mary was going to go over the B & B register from last summer.

After giving Christopher's chubby little cheeks one last kiss, Faith left. Back in the rocker, Mary had the baby in her arms again, swaddled tightly in a flannel blanket she'd made by cutting up a larger one. She looked so happy, Faith almost wept. There were other reasons for tears, as well. She hoped Mary would hide the money right away, and not in her freezer or in her underwear drawer, because whoever it belonged to—and Faith had a strong feeling it wasn't the baby's mother—wouldn't waste any time looking for it. Looking for it all over the great state of Maine.

Miriam Carpenter sat staring at the blue book in front of her. When Miriam had called her professor and told her she was too sick to take her exam during the regular schedule, her professor had offered her the chance to come in and take the exam today, the day after Christmas. Having a baby was not an illness, but Miriam's labor pains had coincided with Anthropology 201's final exam. As she looked at the questions again, she wondered if Professor Greene had suspected anything. Miriam was tall and big-boned. It had not been hard to conceal her condition under the many layers of clothing necessary in Maine as the days grew shorter and colder. Yet, during the last few classes, the professor had seemed to be eyeing Miriam in a speculative manner, and twice she had asked in a rather pointed way how she was. But then, Miriam had always been a little paranoid. Or maybe it was only lately. She was definitely a little; make that more than a little paranoid now.

"You can take a makeup exam," Professor Greene had said. "And if you could possibly do it before the first of the year, I won't even have to give you an incomplete. You've done so well this semester. It would be a shame to skip the exam and lower your grade. But you must be going away for the break, home for Christmas."

"No, I'm not going home for Christmas, I'm Jewish, and . . . well, I'm not going home. I live off campus, so I'll be around," Miriam had told her.

The professor had suggested the twenty-sixth, and here she was.

No, Miriam wasn't going home for the holidays, or any other days.

She stared at the first essay question: "Discuss the roots and implications of gender-motivated infanticide past and present. You may select one society or several upon which to focus."

Infanticide. That had never been an option. Male or female. As soon as she discovered she was pregnant, she knew she would have the baby. Knew she would have it, because she was going to stop thinking about it. It wasn't that she was in denial so much as she was simply on a kind of all-encompassing autopilot.

Bruce hadn't found out until last week. They'd stopped having sex in August, when he'd started bringing Tammy around. He was so high most of the time that even before, sex hadn't played a big part in their relationship. What had? The drugs, to start with. She'd never felt so free, so happy. Even coming down, she'd never gotten blue or angry, the way Bruce did. Gradually, it was enough just to be around drugs and the people doing them. Mellow folks, good folks. Folks who smiled when they saw her. Folks who cared about her—at least when they were using. She found she didn't need the drugs, which was a good thing, because somebody had to keep house—and keep the money straight. Somebody had to let kids on campus know where they could go. Somebody had to deal with the suppliers when Bruce was too wasted. She had been the responsible one. "Baby, I don't know what I'd do without you," he told her. She hadn't needed drugs, just Bruce.

She'd gone to a party at his apartment at the end of her freshman year, and stayed. He looked like Kurt Cobain, or that's what somebody had said when he walked into the living room, leaving the group who were shooting up in the kitchen. He'd grinned that big lazy grin and walked straight up to her. "Hey, pretty lady, where have you been all my life?"

It had been good. She was sure it had been good. Then one night, he walked out of the kitchen into the living room and Tammy was there. Miriam heard him say the same words. She'd learned Bruce relied on a few stock phrases in life, and this was one. Another was, "If you're not part of the problem, you're an asshole."

Tammy took over the sex part, and Miriam was left to do everything else, which was mainly cleaning the apartment after the parties, because Bruce was trying to get straight and mostly succeeding. He was straight when she'd told him about the baby.

Her hand automatically went to her neck. She'd wound a long scarf over the turtleneck and would have added a cowl if she'd had one to be sure to hide the necklace of bruise marks his fingers had left. She had thought he would choke her to death, and she'd struggled desperately, pulling at his hands, fighting for breath. They'd crashed to the floor, knocking over a lamp. The bulb had exploded and Tammy had come in. Would he have killed her if Tammy hadn't been there? Tammy had taken in the scene dreamily—she was always pretty wasted—and said, "Leave her alone. She's not worth it."

They'd left her on the floor. She hadn't moved from the protective fetal position she'd rolled into once he'd stood up. She'd assumed he would kick her, but he didn't.

"Get rid of it. If it's here when I get back, I'll kill both of you."

He was leaving for Canada—a major score—and Tammy was going with him. They were going to spend Christmas there.

Miriam started writing. China was the obvious choice, but she didn't want to be obvious.

"The cruel Arctic climate of the aboriginal Inuit reduced the male population significantly as they pursued their traditional hunting and fishing roles, forcing the . . ."

She wrote furiously for a while, then paused. What if her parents had known the sex of the child they were going to have before she'd been born?

She wouldn't be here.

How old was she when she'd first heard her father say to her mother, "You're worthless. Completely worthless. You couldn't even give me a son," saying it in that flat, cold voice he used before he would start the rest? Not caring that Miriam was in the doorway—was she six, or seven?—and could see it all. Could hear it all—especially, her mother's cries.

Miriam shook her head to force the thought to the back of her mind with the rest of the things she didn't want to think about. It was getting pretty crowded.

Her father had answered the phone when she'd called after the baby was born. It had been an easy delivery. She could have done it herself, she realized afterward, but she had been frightened at the thought of being alone and had gotten the name of a woman who believed in home births and said she was a midwife. Maybe she was. But it had been all right. She'd kept Miriam overnight and brought her cups of green tea. During the delivery, she had lighted fragrant candles and played that waterfall kind of New Age music that Miriam's yoga teacher in high school had liked so much. It was something they were trying that year, letting students take yoga instead of field hockey or soccer. There were only three kids in the class. Three kids who didn't have to worry about peer pressure, because they didn't have any peers.

The midwife had given Miriam a beautiful

baby blanket and Miriam had given her a thousand dollars.

Her father had been the only person she could think of to call. She'd just had a baby. Shouldn't she call someone? She'd called him last year to tell him she was in school, and he had told her not to come to him for money. It had been a pretty short conversation. This time when she'd called, she could hear her stepmother in the background, talking rapidly, as usual. Brenda was a high-maintenance lady. Daniel Carpenter made a good living selling real estate in the Portland area, but Brenda, who was some unspecified number of years younger, decorated their house and herself in extravagantly perfect taste—according to her—and went through money almost as fast as she talked.

"Hi, Dad, it's Miriam," she'd said.

"Yes?"

"Well, I just . . . I guess I just wanted to say hi and—"

She'd heard Brenda in the background, "Who is it, Dan?"

"It's Miriam." Her father hadn't bothered to turn away from the receiver.

"What does *she* want?"

"I don't know yet. What do you want, Miriam?"

What she'd wanted at that moment was to hang up, but she hadn't. She'd gotten mad. Why had her mother had to die the way she did, slipping determinedly into a half world of bourbon and despair before Miriam could grow up enough to take care of her—or live without her? And why had her father chosen to marry Brenda, of all people, petite, a perfect size four. Even at age thirteen, Miriam had felt like one of Swift's Brobdingnags whenever they were in the same room, which wasn't often.

"I don't *want* anything. I called to tell you you're a grandfather—a bouncing baby boy—and you can tell Brenda she's a grandmother." Miriam had added the last bit with calculated cruelty. Brenda would not like to be a grandmother.

"I assume your child is a bastard. Like mother, like daughter," her father had said. Then Miriam had heard Brenda's voice closer to the phone, "*Child*, what child? Miriam's had a baby? Boy or girl? Find out where she is."

It had been those last words that had caused a prickle of fear to run down Miriam's spine. Not the ones about her mother. She knew she was the reason for the marriage or, as her father called it, "the entrapment." No, it was Brenda's sudden interest in Miriam's whereabouts that had made her feel more nauseated than any of her bouts of morning sickness.

"Well, good-bye, then. I've got to go."

"Wait. I need to know where—"

Miriam had hung up before he finished the sentence. She had thought she'd keep Christopher with her until New Year's, which was when Bruce had said he'd be back. But anything could change his mind, and she had been foolhardy even to bring the baby back to the apartment. It hadn't taken her long to clear out; she'd been all ready. From the beginning, she'd known what she would do. With her father's words echoing in her ears, she'd decided to head for the coast right then. Bruce didn't want the baby, but for some reason, Brenda did. They'd never had one of their own—was it because they couldn't? Miriam had always assumed they didn't want a child, but maybe they did. Or Brenda did. The ultimate soccer mom. Or a little one as a trendy accessory, a step beyond a bichon frise? In a weird turn of events, she had to keep Christopher away from both his father and grandfather—one because he wanted the baby, one because he didn't. And in their own way, each would murder the child.

Her essay came into focus and the phone conversation faded. Christopher was safe.

It was Boxing Day, and Faith was back in Mary's kitchen. Ben and Amy had been invited to spend the afternoon with friends they'd made at the island day camp they attended during the summer. Tom had urged Faith to go help Màry. He would enjoy the solitude—maybe do some writing—and when she returned, they'd walk to the Point. Every day, he felt stronger.

"There were only three couples who could possibly fill the bill, because of age, proximity—and two mentioned they were expecting a baby," Mary said. "The only single women I had were a young girl from Norway who was 'seeing America' for the summer and a cousin of the Marshalls they didn't have room for. She was in her sixties, so we can cross her off the list. And it would seem unlikely that a Norwegian girl would come all this way to leave me her baby, although the whole thing is so unlikely, perhaps we'd better not eliminate her."

"I think we can for now," Faith said. "But what about these couples, especially the pregnant ones?"

"A first child for each. The Warrens live in Vermont—not that close. But the Tuttles are from Saco and were up here vacationing. They're a possibility, although I can't see them giving their child up. They were looking forward to coming back next summer and every summer after that to watch little whoever play with the goats. The nannies are very sweet playmates, you know."

Faith did know. It occurred to her that someone looking for strong maternal instincts would only have had to watch Mary with her herd and listen to her talk to conclude she was a natural-born nurturer. Not only did Mary keep her goat house clean and dry—it looked like something from Carl Larsson's *On the Farm*—but also she religiously tended to the nannies' every need, both physical and psychological. All her goats had had their horn buds removed, and Mary gently but firmly discouraged butting from the moment they were born. She greeted each one by name, starting with the queen, stroking and petting them several times a day. After the stress of breeding—and delivering—she read to them and even sang to them, as Faith had discovered one day upon hearing a stirring rendition of "Seventy-Six Trombones" with accompanying bleats issuing from the barn. Their play yard was just that, with several cable spools, courtesy of Bangor Hydro, for the nannies to climb on. The pasture had a high electric fence, and Faith was pretty sure the Nubians were better fed than Mary, who seemed to exist on whey sweetened with honey (bartered for cheese), rose hips in various forms, and whatever vegetables—fresh or put up—the garden yielded. Maybe it wasn't such a bad diet; rather, it was the thought of it that repelled Faith's taste buds.

Granted, her charges were ruminants, but if

you were looking for "Mother of the Year," Mary was a contender.

"And the third couple? Who were they?"

"They were young, and I started thinking about them right away last night when you said she might be a student. There was a University of Maine Black Bears bumper sticker on their truck. I don't know how they heard about me. You know I don't advertise, just that card at the market in the summer, so that must have been how they found me. They stayed a week, and he was gone all the time. Said he was helping a friend whose sternman was sick, but he didn't get up early enough for lobstering and he came back late—six or seven o'clock—and then he'd take her off to get something to eat. She helped me with the goats and the garden. So much that I didn't want to charge them full price, but she insisted she'd just been having fun. That it was a vacation for her. Her name was Miriam. His was Bruce. She was the one who wrote in the book. Their last name was Singer and the address was in Calais. I've already checked directory assistance, and there are no Miriam or Bruce Singers in Calais. No street by the name she listed, either."

"How about Orono? Because of the bumper sticker—and the bag the money was in," Faith said.

"Thought of that, too, but same thing. And directory assistance didn't say the phone was unlisted."

"You don't ask for a phone number in the register?"

"I only started asking for a name and address this summer. Before, I'd leave a guest book for people to sign if they wanted to. I'd introduce myself and they would tell me who they were. Nobody ever left without paying, but my cousin Elizabeth told me I should be keeping a record. Said you never know—and she was right, as usual."

"This is the one who lives out west? And gave you her goats when she moved?"

"That's Elizabeth. I was only a teenager. My sister was already gone, and Elizabeth thought her two nannies would be company for me. Dora the First—this Dora is Dora the Second—lived to be twenty, but I lost the other one, Nora, when she was twelve."

Filing away for further thought, the interesting notion of two Nubian goats as a substitute for human contact, Faith mentally thanked Elizabeth for the easier-to-grasp idea of a guest register and got back to work.

"All right. First, let's eliminate the Tuttles from Saco for sure. What could be more natural than for you to call and say you'd like to send some of that jelly of yours to congratulate them on the new baby? You know what I mean. Say how much you're looking forward to seeing them next summer."

"Do I have to? What if something went wrong with the pregnancy? I had a toxemic doe once. Oh, Faith, I don't think I could call up strangers, even strangers who have stayed here."

Mary was tough, but she was also shy. Faith sighed. "Give me the phone."

She dialed the number and a woman answered.

"Hello. May I speak to Mrs. Tuttle, please?"

"Speaking."

"I'm a supporter of the Sanpere Chamber of Commerce, and over the holidays we're trying to reach people who visited our island last summer so that we can plan for next summer. Would you mind answering two quick questions?"

"Not at all. We had a lovely time, and we plan to return next summer."

"Well, that answers both my questions—whether you'd had a positive experience and if you intended to return."

Mrs. Tuttle laughed. "This is the easiest survey I've ever done."

"Could you tell me if you plan to return to the same accommodations as last year?"

"Yes, of course. It was ideal. Bethany Farm Bed-and-Breakfast. I really should have written to Mary. I'm glad you called. It's reminded me to get to it. We had a baby last month, and she said to let her know. Little Cecilia will adore Mary's goats next summer."

"I'm sure she will. Thank you for your time."

Faith hung up. "Cross out the Tuttles."

"I don't know how you do it," Mary said.

After some baby feeding—and baby worship—Faith called the couple from Vermont, just to be sure. After hanging up, she reported that the Warren family now numbered four. Twins. She decided it wasn't necessary to call Norway. Faith reassured Mary that since she hadn't actually said she was from the Sanpere Chamber of Commerce, only a supporter of it, which she was—the Fairchilds contributed every year—no lies had been told or laws broken. Then Faith said good-bye and went back to her own house.

When she got there, Tom was ready for their walk, and Faith almost didn't answer the phone as they were leaving. But what with two small children of her own, plus Mary and Christopher, there was no choice. It was Mary.

"I knew I was leaving something out! Miriam Singer had lovely long dark hair, just like the strand on Christopher's blanket. She wore it in a braid down her back, but one day she washed it and sat out in the sun to let it dry. She looked . . . well, she looked like a Madonna."

The next morning, Faith and Tom were alone in the kitchen.

"I know you want to help Mary, sweetheart, but isn't there someone else who could go? Or maybe she could leave the baby here and take our car. That old truck of hers barely makes it to Granville." The Reverend Thomas Fairchild was feeling better. Emerging from the cocoon of his illness, he wanted to spread his wings—with his wife for company.

"There isn't anyone else. And unless she's taught one of the herd to drive, Mary won't go any farther than Blue Hill. I just want to get her the bare necessities—clothes, a Snugli to use when she's milking, diapers, bottles—you remember. The crib we borrowed from Pix for Amy and never gave back is still in the garage here, and I want to take that over. I'll have to get some sheets, though. I want to do this for Mary. A belated Christmas present from us."

"Come here, gift o'mine," Tom said, reaching for his wife. Outside, Ben and Amy were trying to make a snowman from the two inches of fluffy snow that had fallen earlier that morning. Tom motioned toward the ceiling. "I thought this might be the perfect occasion for some quality adult time upstairs."

Faith hugged him hard. "What's that line about having 'world enough, and time'? I know Marvell was addressing his coy mistress, and I'm not being coy. There will be time—many times."

Tom kissed her, and in a voice suggesting slight regret, but hope for plan B, he said, "Hey, why don't we all go? Maybe see a movie in Ellsworth?"

Faith had been deliberately vague about where she was going. Orono and Ellsworth were in different directions.

"You know you would hate it, and so would the kids. The after-Christmas sales bring out the beast in everyone, and the stores will be packed, especially on a Saturday. I'll be back as soon as I can." She kissed him hard. It was full of promise—promise of plan A.

Tom held her closer. "I swear if I didn't know that Mary *and* her Nubian goats existed, I'd think you made the whole thing up so you could sneak out and meet your secret lover. Mary Bethany. Bethany—the village where that other Mary was born. A baby, Christopher, turning up at Christmas." He settled back, still with his arm around his wife. He was loath to let her go. "I've always felt sorry for Mary—or rather, Miriam, which is the Hebrew. She was as sorely tested as Job. It can't have been easy for her. Some sources put her age as young as thirteen when she became pregnant out of wedlock. The Gospels don't tell us much about her, barely mentioning her by name, but it's not hard to imagine how the good people of Nazareth would have treated her."

Faith agreed. "I always thought it was a little mean of God to leave her on her own for so long while Joseph was off building houses. Here she is betrothed and all, picking out pottery patterns and getting more full with child by the day. *She* knew she was a virgin, but it took awhile before it was all sorted out. I've always imagined her as a feisty lady. She had to be."

"Joseph stuck by her, though."

"Yes, I'll give him that—thanks to one of those convenient dreams people in the Bible always seem to have. But when it came time for the blessed event, why did it take so long for him to find someone to deliver the baby? Mary was on her own again in that stinky barn—or cave, if you want to believe James—having the baby all by herself. But, speaking of Marys, I have to go. The sooner I leave, the sooner I'll—"

"I know, I know, and say hi to your secret lover."

"Hi, lover."

Besides hitting the Bangor malls for baby things and driving to Sammy's 24-Hour Store in Orono, Faith didn't have a plan. If she found Miriam, she'd talk to the girl, make sure she knew what she was doing, but then what? Ask her where the fifty thousand dollars came from? Get her to sign some kind of papers so that Mary could adopt Christopher?

She decided to hit the malls first. Later, with the car loaded, Faith headed north, away from

Bangor and toward Orono. It wasn't far, and once there, she only had to ask twice to find the convenience store.

As she had suspected, the store was a mom-and-pop operation, a cross between a market and a five-and-dime, only they were Dollar Stores now. Sammy's had a little bit of everything—from beef jerky to Rolex rip-offs and dusty plastic poinsettias, still on sale from last Christmas. It was located in a mixed residential/commercial area. There was no Sammy in evidence, unless the tired-looking older woman at the counter was named Samantha. Faith picked up a slightly faded package of colored construction paper for Amy and an ancient balsa-wood model-airplane kit for Ben. At the register, she added a Milky Way for Tom. She'd check the expiration date in the car.

As the sale was rung up, she said, "I wonder if you might help me. I'm supposed to drop off a Christmas gift for a friend of mine. It's for her niece, who lives around here. I've misplaced the address, but the niece's name is Miriam. She's tall and has long dark hair that she usually wears in a braid down her back. Do you know her, by any chance?"

"Sure, I know Miriam. Comes in here a lot. Always polite. Not like some. She lives over there. I'm not sure which apartment, but I saw her this morning, so she's probably home."

Faith looked through the window—obscured by holiday greetings sprayed on by a liberal but unsteady hand—and saw a run-down house that had obviously been carved up into apartments for students fleeing dorm life—or just fleeing.

She thanked the woman and walked slowly across the street. The front door swung open and she stepped onto a pile of junk mail. There were six mailboxes; each card had several names. Some had been crossed out and new ones added above in tiny writing. She studied each as if it were the Rosetta stone. She knew she wouldn't find Miriam or Bruce Singer. But she wasn't finding anything remotely resembling them, either. No initial M. or B. No S's. When people put down false names, she thought, they usually stick to their own initials, even if no monogrammed luggage is involved. A question of human nature. Or they choose a similar name, as in a similar occupation. Singer. No Chanteuses, or Vocalists. What other synonyms were there? Preferably synonyms that made sense. She went back to the cards and searched again. And there it was. Apartment 4B. One name in minuscule writing: Carpenter. The Carpenters. Karen Carpenter. Singers. Miriam Singer; Miriam Carpenter. Faith pushed the buzzer. There was no answer. She pushed all the buzzers until someone let her in. After climbing the dark, narrow stairs, she knocked loudly on 4B's door for what seemed like ages, before concluding that Christopher's mother wasn't home.

Miriam had turned in her exam, avoided Professor Greene's attempts to draw her into conversation, and had spent the evening getting really, really drunk. She hadn't had a drink since she'd discovered she was pregnant, and even before that, all she drank were wine coolers and Cold Duck when Bruce was in a romantic mood. At least I'm in my own bed in my own apartment, she thought when she woke up the next morning with a hangover the size of Texas. She stumbled across the street for some diet Coke and aspirin. She planned to spend the day in bed. She was due. Somehow she had managed to take a full course load, finish all her papers, and even take a final, plus have a baby in the last two weeks.

It wasn't until she was halfway into a *Buffy* rerun when the sickening thought hit her that of course her father knew where she was, because he had caller ID. He'd been one of the first to have it installed and had boasted about what a help it would be for his business. No more "I'll think about its and get back to yous." He'd *know* who you were. Getting a street address from a phone number was a piece of cake for a real estate agent like her father.

She had spoken to him when? Not yesterday. No, the night before. The twenty-fifth. But he hadn't shown up so far—or had he? Groaning, she pulled her jeans back on and went across the hall. Why had she let Bruce convince her to put the phone in her name? No, he hadn't convinced her. She had never questioned it. He had told her to do it and she had.

Ellen the Airhead opened the door. From the way she looked, her night had been even worse than Miriam's. They called her the "Airhead" not because she was spaced-out on drugs, but because she was very, very stupid. But she was usually spaced-out on drugs, too.

"Ellen, think hard. Did a man come looking for me recently? An older man. Tall, with dark hair."

"Dark hair," Ellen repeated obediently.

Resisting the urge to shake her even sillier, Miriam said, "How about some coffee? Why don't I make us some coffee?"

"Okay." Ellen looked around her apartment as if unsure where the kitchen was. Miriam pushed her in the right direction.

With a mug of instant that she had no intention of drinking, Miriam led Ellen back over the previous few days and was rewarded for her patience with a flash of almost total recall on Ellen's part.

"He said he was your father." She hesitated.

"He was—is my father. It's okay. Then what did he say?"

"He was like looking for you, and I go, 'I don't know where she is. Not Canada. Maybe on Sanpere Island with that goat lady.' "

"What?" Miriam screamed. "How do you know about Sanpere?"

"You told me." Ellen stuck out her lower lip. "You didn't say it was a big fuckin' secret. Last summer. You told me all about the nice lady with the goats on Sanpere, the one you and Bruce stayed with. Hey, you didn't drink your coffee."

He had more than twenty-four hours on her, Miriam figured as she frantically tried to find someone with a car she could borrow. It had been easy Christmas Eve. She'd gone to a party on the other side of town and then taken the keys from the drunkest person there.

She debated whether or not to call Mary Bethany, but she didn't want to alarm her. For all she knew, Mary might call the police, the state police. There weren't any police on Sanpere, which was one of the reasons Miriam had picked it. That and Mary. Mary would take care of the baby. She'd raise him to be a good man. Miriam didn't care whether her son went to college, made money, or did anything other than raise goats. All she cared about was that he be as honest and kind as Mary Bethany was. Miriam finally located a car and arranged to go get it from her friend Cindy. Hastily, she threw some things in a knapsack. She was pretty sure Mary wouldn't be fooled by whatever story her father had cooked up, but she needed to give her some sort of letter that would say Christopher was hers. That she was surrendering her parental rights to Mary. That would keep her father away. Mary could use some of the money for a lawyer if she had to.

Stupid, stupid, stupid. She blew a stray strand of hair out of her eyes angrily. How could she ever have called her father!

She was ready to go. Bruce hadn't been back. There was no beer in the fridge—or empties on the counter. Suddenly, she looked at where she had been living for over a year—the stained and sagging couch, a few beanbag chairs, a coffee table scrounged from the trash. It was covered with white rings and cigarette burns. The place stank—stale air and more. The doorknob was greasy. She turned it and pulled the door open. Pulled it open and stepped back into the room.

"Hello, Miss Miriam. Glad to see you're finally home. We've been looking for you."

"For you—and the money."

Duane and Ralph. Bruce's local suppliers. Miriam let the knapsack slip from her shoulder. She let her whole body sag. Then she sprinted past them, slamming the door behind her, and ran out of the house and into the street as fast as she could.

* * *

"I'm sorry, but I don't operate my bed-and-breakfast during the off-season. They should have told you that at the market."

Mary had been startled by the sudden appearance of a big fancy car coming up the long dirt drive that led to her house from the main road, but not so startled that she hadn't quickly erased all evidence that a baby was living in the house. It hadn't been hard. She had prepared herself for the possibility—the eventuality. She'd taken Christopher out through the shed and across into the barn, placing him in one of the mangers, well away from the goats. He was such a good baby, but he might cry, and if he did, the nannies would more than drown him out.

"I must have misunderstood. My name is Dan Carpenter, by the way. I own a real estate agency down in Portland and I'm up here to check out a property."

Mary's eyes narrowed. Skunks, that's what they were. The local agents had given up on her long ago, but there were new ones all the time. Telling her what she could get for waterfront acreage on Eggemoggin Reach, what a genuine Down East saltwater farm would fetch. She knew what it would fetch. More skunks. Skunks who would have the farmhouse down in two minutes and put up some sort of hotel looking place with a tennis court.

"I am not interested in selling my property, Mr. Carpenter. Good day." Mary started to close the door.

"No, wait. Please. I'm sorry. You've misunderstood me. I'm not interested in your property. I mean, of course I'm always interested in property, but that's not why I'm here. I simply need a place to stay for the night."

"They should have sent you to Granville. There's a motel that stays open year-round there, and I can't imagine they'd be full, even with the holidays." Mary started to close the door again.

But Dan Carpenter was very good at what he did. He was used to people trying to close doors in his face—and equally used to getting his foot in them. He'd arrived on the island around noon and headed straight for the market. Other than the post office—which was closed—the market in any small Maine community was the best grapevine. He'd picked up a few snacks and then mentioned at the register that his daughter had stayed at a bed-and-breakfast run by a woman who kept goats. His daughter had recommended it as a place to stay, he'd told the cashier.

"That would be Mary Bethany," the teenager who was minding the till, offered with a singularly repulsive Goth look. Dan had been in luck. Anyone older would either have asked him what his business was that meant he had to stay the night or, more likely, simply grunted, rung up his purchases, and taken his money.

"She won't let you stay, though. Isn't open now. Better go to the motel in Granville." The boy had been a veritable hydrant of information.

But Dan had gone to Mary's after looking her address up in a phone book thoughtfully offered for free by the local island newspaper. A stack of them rested next to the display of motor oil at the entrance to the market. It was one of those typical Maine places that sold everything you needed and nothing you didn't.

He'd cracked tougher nuts than Mary.

"Please, I'm sorry to have troubled you, but could I call the motel? I don't want to drive all the way down there and find they haven't any room at the inn." He gave a little chuckle to show how very, very harmless and how very, very charming he was.

Mary opened the door grudgingly. "I'll call Patty and see. You sit here." She pointed to one of the kitchen chairs, then turned to the phone on the wall.

"Did I hear a baby crying? Are your grandchildren visiting for the holidays?"

Instantly, Mary swung around.

"Those are my goats, mister. I don't have any grandchildren, and there are no babies in this house. Now, why don't you take yourself down to Granville? I don't think I care to call Patty after all."

Dan Carpenter stood up and started walking toward Mary. She grabbed the phone again and he stopped.

"Look, I know Miriam is here with the baby. You are going to be in major trouble for hiding them if you don't get them right now!" He glared at Mary and shouted, into the next room, "Miriam, come here this instant!" There was no answer. He broke the silence. "My daughter, Miriam, is mentally unstable. I don't know what kind of story she's told you, but she's not fit to raise a child. She's a thief, a drug addict, and an alcoholic, just like her mother. A pathological liar, too. I'm only thinking of the baby. My grandson."

Mary listened and watched impassively, her hand still on the phone.

"I don't know anything about your daughter," she said calmly. "She is not here. And, as I told you before, there are no babies in this house. I'd say you were welcome to search the premises, but then I'd be the liar. You're not welcome at all. You came into my home under false pretenses, and now I want you out." She was dialing a number as she spoke the last words. When she had finished dialing, she turned back to face Mr. Carpenter.

"Earl," she said pleasantly into the mouthpiece. "I have a man here bothering me. Could you come over right away? And Earl, bring your gun."

* * *

Ralph and Duane. How could they have connected her to the missing money? Bruce was in Canada and couldn't have known the money was missing from the storage container. And when he did find out, he wouldn't connect her with it. It was one he thought she didn't know about in Brewer.

She'd hidden behind the Dumpster in the parking lot of the convenience store across from the apartment until she'd seen the two thugs leave. They had been to the apartment only once before. Mostly, Bruce met them down in Bucksport or in Bangor. He didn't want them at the apartment. Too risky. She watched them go to both ends of the block and circle the house. Ralph screamed, "Bitch, we know you're out here, so listen up. We *will* find you!" Duane had his cell phone out, but he put it back in his pocket right away. Miriam assumed he was trying to call Bruce, wherever he was, and she blessed Maine's erratic cell service. Her mind was racing. Bruce must have come back, gone to Brewer to stash the prescription drugs he'd brought across the border—that very long border impossible to patrol, just as Maine's very long coast was in better weather. By land or by sea, Maine had always been a smuggler's dream and a law-enforcement nightmare. Obviously, Bruce had found out the money was missing sooner than she'd thought he would—she hadn't taken it all—and had sent Duane and Ralph to grab it, and her.

The two got in their pickup and roared off. It was tricked out with flames airbrushed on the sides. Perennial adolescents: totally amoral, psychopathic ones. But she couldn't think about them—or Bruce—now. She had to get down to Sanpere and make sure her father hadn't taken the baby away.

It didn't take long to walk to Cindy's apartment and pick up the car. Cindy was living with her boyfriend and using Miriam's address for her parents. She stopped by to pick up the mail every week and to score some dope. Miriam figured Cindy owed her. Cindy's parents never called, because, dutiful daughter that she was, Cindy had arranged a weekly time when she would call them, saving them the long-distance fees, since "I'd probably be in the library anyway and you'd just get my roommate, Miriam." Cindy had had Bruce take a picture of Miriam and her on the couch, a stack of books in front of them on the coffee table, to send to her parents. They lived in Duluth, so it was highly unlikely that they'd be dropping by unannounced. Miriam had been impressed by Cindy's thoroughness, but in general college students were a pretty crafty bunch, she'd noticed—or maybe it was that parents just wanted to believe.

Parents! She was driving through Searsport

when she saw her father's car pass. It wasn't hard to miss. There weren't too many silver Mercedes S500's (have to have a killer car to impress the buyers and sellers) around at this time of year. The summer people were going for the SUV version, in the absurd belief that they were blending in ruralwise. To really blend in, they'd have to drive a pickup that was at least ten years old and had vanity plates that combined the husband's name with the wife's or one of the kids'.

Miriam thought fast. Her father had obviously been down to Sanpere if he was coming this way. He might or might not have Christopher. Suddenly, she was furious. She pulled into Hamilton Marine's parking lot, did a quick U-turn, and followed him. He wouldn't recognize Cindy's car, or any other car Miriam might be driving. Her hopes for one as a high school graduation gift—even a used one—had been dashed when neither her father nor stepmother turned up for the ceremony. Returning home, she'd found a note on the front door, telling her to pack her things and be gone by the time they got back from their weekend. There had been a fifty-dollar bill inside. She'd supplemented the money with Brenda's jewelry, some of which had been Miriam's mother's. Because she didn't consider herself a thief, but thought of the whole thing as making up for a lot of years of gifts like tube socks, Miriam had put the pawn tickets in an envelope and left it in Brenda's jewelry box before leaving for good herself.

It was easy to keep the big silver car in sight. If he didn't have Christopher, it would mean the baby was still safe with Mary. If he did, she would take the baby back, and when he resisted, as she was sure he would, she'd grab Christopher and run—or, failing that, make a scene and get somebody to call the police. Christopher was *her* baby, not his.

She was surprised when he didn't turn south toward Portland. What was going on? Where was he heading? He was speeding up, too. Well, so would she. Except she'd have to stop for gas. Damn. She followed for a couple more miles and saw him turn. Okay. She was sure she knew where he was going now. But why?

Her car loaded with baby things, Faith Fairchild passed both Daniel and Miriam Carpenter. She took note of the Mercedes. It was so unusual to see one out of tourist season, but the man driving it meant nothing to her. And Miriam's borrowed Toyota didn't even register. Faith was thinking of how pleased Mary would be. Now they knew the baby's mother's name and address. They'd be in touch with her by phone, meet her—and find out what was going on.

The afternoon light was fading fast. Faith sped up. She hated driving at night in Maine. Even in the summer, the dark was very dark. She wanted to get home before night fell and even your high beams couldn't pick out the twists and turns in front of you.

Mary Bethany had been sure her words would get Dan Carpenter out of the house. Bullies were usually cowards. She was eager to tell Faith what had happened, and she was especially looking forward to telling her all about the call she had put through to the small Granville library, knowing it was closed, and not to Lt. Earl Dickinson of the Maine State Police. Earl did patrol the island—in fact, he lived on Sanpere—but Mary hadn't wanted him around any more than she had wanted Daniel Carpenter.

She went to the barn and decided to stay there until dark, when it would be easy to see headlights, although she wasn't expecting anyone. But she hadn't been expecting Miriam's father, either. "Better to err on the side of caution" had been one of her mother's favorite sayings and in this case, Mary agreed. She'd told Faith to wait until tomorrow to bring the baby things over. The poor woman had had hardly any time with her family these last few days. This meant that any lights Mary saw would not be welcome ones.

Christopher was sleeping so soundly, a warm little bundle against the straw in the manger, that she didn't want to disturb him by moving him to the basket. The nannies were content for once and continued to greet her cheerfully. Christopher didn't move a muscle, so Mary turned her full attention to the herd, starting with Dora, her oldest goat—the queen. Then she spent time with each of the others in order of age. You had to do it this way or they got upset and confused. It was the same order for milking, grooming, everything. Each goat knew her place. No one tried to squeeze ahead. They all got along together and with her. Faith was going to bring her some baby books, which would be a help, but Mary thought raising goats and raising children were much the same. Of course, she wouldn't have to make ear splints for Christopher. Sometimes her Nubians were born with folded ears, which had to be splinted for a few days; otherwise, they'd stay that way. She looked at the herd with pride, noting their shining coats *and* straight ears. Christopher weighed about as much as a newborn kid, too, from the heft of him. Could be he was even a little heavier. She'd made a kind of sling from her shawl and carried the baby close to her body when he wasn't in the basket. She'd once had to do that for one of her kids, which was doing poorly after opening up its muzzle on a nail it'd worried loose. Goats were *very* curious, and child-proofing a house would be child's play— Mary smiled to herself—compared to goat-proofing the barn and pasture. And the nannies were social creatures, like people. Except for me, she thought ruefully, and the enormity of what she was contemplating struck her.

She continued to sit and reflect on the last seventy-two hours, stroking the youngest goat, Sheba, who had a particularly appealing face. Trusting, innocent. Yes, it was in the Bible, but Mary never could understand the Almighty's choice of a goat to bear the sins of the world, abandoning it with all that wickedness in the wilderness—the scapegoat. Why not a scapeox or a scapesheep? Those were around back then, too.

Christopher gave another of those sweet little baby sneezes, and Mary decided it was time to get moving, although the barn was warm as toast and she hated to leave it. Besides the coziness, it was the way the place smelled. Nannies didn't stink the way bucks did at all, just gave off a kind of living things aroma.

The second milking done and the goats fed, Mary went back into the house with the baby. She would have to make cheese tomorrow. The nannies were giving more milk than usual, and even with Christopher's consumption, she had too much.

Mary loved making cheese. Anne Bossi at Sunset Acres Farm over in South Brooksville had given her the recipe years ago, and Mary had taught herself, soon turning out a soft, spreadable chèvre. Every time she added the rennet and returned the next day to her curds and whey, she was as pleased at the way nature worked as she had been the first time. Faith had been the one to suggest adding herbs in addition to salt, and eventually sun-dried tomatoes and mixed peppercorns for two more varieties.

In the kitchen, she stoked the woodstove and settled back in the rocker to feed the baby. The house seemed very quiet. The creaking of the rocker on the old linoleum began to get on her nerves as it never had before. She got up and went into the parlor to finish the feeding, turning on the small television she'd bought for her B & B guests. The early news was on, and she settled into the sofa to watch while the baby drank. His mother must have bottle-fed him, Mary realized. He wasn't missing her teat.

First they tantalized you with the weather, not actually telling you what it was going to be, lest you turn to another station or, heaven forbid, switch the set off. It was going to be—well, something. Then there was more about Iraq. Mary thought about a twenty-year-old Christopher going off to fight some war, and she prayed that by that time the world could come to some sort of truce. Not liking each other. Just a truce.

"This just in. Police are investigating a homicide in Orono and we are live at the scene. Steve, are you there?"

Mary sat up straight, unmindful for the moment of the baby on her lap. A reporter was standing in front of a shabby-looking multifamily dwelling, the sidewalk cordoned off with those yellow crime-scene plastic ribbons. Yellow ribbons for hope; yellow ribbons for despair. She'd never thought about that before.

"Yes, I'm here, Rosemary. Police are not releasing the name of the victim pending notification of next of kin, but according to our sources here, he was a Caucasian male in his twenties and lived with several other people in an apartment on the top floor of the building behind me. Again, the police have not released any information other than they are treating the death as an apparent homicide."

"Do we know anything about how and why this might have happened?"

"Our preliminary sources have indicated that the cause of death was a stab wound in the chest, but police are neither confirming nor denying that. We have also been told that drug paraphernalia and a large quantity of heroin were found in the apartment."

"Thank you, Steve." The picture shifted back to the studio. The anchor, her face carefully composed in a serious expression of regret—and condemnation—said, "A homicide in Orono. We're at the scene and will keep you informed. Now, how about those Bruins, Larry?"

Mary reached for the remote and muted the

sound. It wasn't just that it was in Orono. It was what she had seen as the camera panned past the flashing blue lights and knots of curious—or prurient—onlookers to a small block of stores. Sammy's 24-Hour Store was right on the corner.

She had to call Faith.

Had she waited for the weather report, Mary would not have been surprised at the way the wind picked up an hour later, nor by the snow that began falling in horizontal sheets shortly thereafter. She gathered flashlights, candles, and blankets, setting up camp in the kitchen. There was plenty of stove wood. The house's wiring hadn't been replaced—in her lifetime anyway—and she often lost power just in a stiff breeze, so the possibility was not alarming. Possibility became probability as the howls from the heavens increased in ferocity. She had called Faith right after the news report and left a message with Tom, who *had* heard the weather report and was very worried about his wife.

"How could it take her so long to go to Ellsworth and back?" he'd asked.

"I don't know," Mary had replied honestly.

"This could be a big storm, Mary. I'm going to drive over and get you and your nephew. We're bound to lose power, and you could be snowed in for days."

Although confused for a moment by the reference to her "nephew," Mary quickly realized he meant Christopher. "It's happened before," she told Tom. "We'll be fine. Besides, I don't think you have room for the two of us *and* six goats."

Tom conceded the fact and said he'd have Faith call as soon as she got in. "But it better be soon, or" he added, "I'm calling the state police."

Fortunately, Faith arrived home safe and sound a few minutes later. She called Mary immediately.

"I know you can't leave the goats, but do you want me to come get the baby? There's so much to tell you. I found out his mother's name is—"

"Miriam Carpenter, and I guess I'll keep Christopher here."

"How on earth did you find that out? Is she there?"

That seemed like the only logical explanation, and Faith was momentarily miffed. She had been so clever at putting two and two together—or in this case, many more numbers. And why was it "two and two," anyway? In her experience, things came in double or even triple digits.

Mary told her about Dan Carpenter's visit.

"He wants Christopher. That's obvious, but he doesn't want his daughter. I'm sure she wouldn't have wanted me to give him the baby. I didn't lie, but I took a page from your book and left a lot out. But Faith, he scared me. I'll never let Christopher go to him. When Miriam said a 'good man,' I *know* she wasn't thinking of her father. But I haven't told you what was on the news just a little while ago. There's been a murder in Orono. And I could see that convenience store—Sammy's—when the camera was filming the neighborhood around the house where the police found the body."

"Who was killed?" Faith asked anxiously. Could it have been Miriam? But if it had been, Mary surely would have mentioned it right away. Faith forced herself to calm down.

"They're not releasing the name yet, but he was white and in his twenties—and there were drugs in the apartment."

"Can you describe the building?"

Mary did. Faith could have described it herself. It was Miriam's building, and Faith was pretty sure it was Miriam's apartment. The top floor.

Miriam hadn't been killed, but was she the killer?

Power went out all over the island at 9:45 P.M. Since a good many people were already in bed, this posed no hardship for most. Keeping the fire going might prove a challenge, and trips to the bathroom would definitely be nippy, but this was what winter Down East was all about.

With the storm raging outside, Mary felt a deep sense of peace. She wondered if Christopher was an unusually good baby. He got hungry about every four hours and let her know by slightly increasing the frequency of the little noises he made—noises somewhere between a cry and a bleat to her ears. Sometimes he hiccupped and it was real comical. He was sleeping now, and Mary thought she would nap in the big armchair her father had moved into the kitchen one day, taking the door off to do so. Some summer people had been getting rid of it. Mary had made a slipcover of bright floral chintz that she'd found at the Take It or Leave It at the dump. There hadn't been quite enough, so she'd used some plain blue cotton from the Variety Store for the back. She checked the fire, kissed the baby, and curled up in the chair.

The driving hadn't been too bad until Miriam turned off the main road at Orland, and even then she got lucky. The town plow was lumbering along ahead of her. She could barely see through the windshield, but she kept following the truck's taillights. Her heater was working all right, but the radio had conked out. She was thankful she'd taken the time to fill the gas tank. Once she'd figured out where her father was heading, there was no rush, so she'd stopped at a gas station. No, she wasn't in a hurry. Just the opposite, in fact. She needed time to think. Her father wouldn't have been heading north unless he had been going to her apartment, and that meant he didn't have Christopher. She wished Ralph and Duane had stuck around as a welcoming committee. Torn between her disinclination to return to the apartment ever again and her desire to have it out with her father once and for all, Miriam had found herself driving north, too. She had to make him understand that there was no way he could take her child. He'd taken her childhood. That was enough.

The wiper blades kept freezing. How many hours had passed since she'd seen his car parked on her street, quickly parked herself outside Sammy's, and run upstairs to the apartment? It seemed like days, even weeks, but it had been hours. Only a few hours.

She was tired. More tired than after the baby had been born. More tired than she'd ever been in her whole life. By the time the plow truck turned toward Castine and left her without a guide, Miriam wasn't sure she could make it to Sanpere. But she had no choice. No choice at all.

Don't think about it, she told herself. Don't go there. It never happened. You were never in that apartment. You didn't do a thing.

She made it as far as Sedgwick, getting out every few miles to clear the ice from the blades.

Then, seeing headlights behind her, she pulled over and flagged the 4x4 with its raised plow that was barreling along behind her.

"Pretty rugged night to be out," the teenager commented when she slid into the cab.

"Yeah, well, my mom's sick and I have to get down to Sanpere."

"I don't want to get stuck on the bridge. I'll take you as close as I can."

Miriam closed her eyes. The warmth of the truck enveloped her like a quilt. The radio was working and tuned to an oldies station. It was playing that Tim Hardin song, "If I Were a Carpenter and You Were a Lady." She opened her eyes and listened when he sang, "Would you have my baby?"

She was the Carpenter, she was the lady and she had had the baby. Miriam had heard the song before and was ready for the end of the refrain: "I've given you my onliness, Give me your tomorrow."

Still she cried, hot tears running down her cheeks. Cried silently, looking out the side window into the darkness, her eyes wide open. Exhausted as she was, if she shut them, it would all come back. The room. The blood. No tomorrow.

"Stay with me. I can't let you out here. It's freezing. You'll never make it!" The boy grabbed her arm. He'd slowed near the bridge and now he'd changed his mind. She pulled her arm away.

"I'm not going to mess with you," he said. "Nothing like that. I'll drop you off at my cousin's. She'll be glad to give you a place to stay. You can't get to Sanpere tonight in this storm."

Miriam was tugging at the door.

"I'll be fine. I have really good boots, and this parka is supposed to be what those guys who live down in Antarctica wear. I got it at the L. L. Bean outlet. Don't worry—and thanks a lot."

He wasn't ready to give up. He was only a few years younger than she was. The hood of the gray sweatshirt he was wearing under his jacket was pulled up. He smelled like cigarettes and WD-40, like a million other guys his age in Maine.

"You won't help your mother much if you turn up dead yourself."

She had the door open. He was forced to slow down almost to a stop.

"It's okay. Really. And thanks for the lift."

She was out and away from his headlights before he could say another word. It would have been impossible to explain to him that she didn't care whether she made it through the night or not. She cared only about getting to Mary's. If that wasn't what was going to happen, then that would be it.

Getting across the bridge was surprisingly easy. The high winds had kept the snow from piling up, and there was no danger that Miriam would be blown into the frigid waters below. Unlike other suspension bridges, which allowed for a scenic view, the island bridge had solid five-foot-high walls and was all business. At the top, it was hard to keep from sliding down the other side; because of the snowfall, the roadbed was treacherously slick. The wind blew the falling snow into her face. It felt like grains of sand, sharp and painful. Tiny knife points. She ducked her head down against her chest and pulled her hood more tightly-closed. Knives. She couldn't think about knives.

Back on land, Miriam was sorely tempted to stop at the first house. It was dark, no lights at the window. She'd expected the island, like the mainland, would have lost power. Yet she knew a house was near. She could smell wood burning. A woodstove or a fireplace, maybe both. The pungent aroma meant there would be warmth—a warm room, warm clothes, something warm to drink. But how to explain herself? What was she doing out on a night that wasn't fit for man or beast? And tomorrow, when power was restored and the news came on, what then? She trudged past the smell and all the others that beckoned, until she came to Mary's road, perpendicular to the Reach, parallel to the bridge. It wasn't snowing as hard now, and thankfully she'd recognized the turnoff. Once Miriam started down it, there wouldn't be any more houses. She'd make it—or not.

At first, she thought the knocking at the door was a dream. She struggled to pull herself awake. Conscious, she realized the storm must have torn a branch loose and it was knocking against a window. She hoped the glass wouldn't break.

But it wasn't a dream or a branch. It was real knocking at her kitchen door. She jumped up to look out the window, then quickly pulled the door open. A woman was standing in the snow that was piling up on the top step. She all but fell into Mary's arms.

"It's all right, Miriam. I've been expecting you," Mary said.

"First, we have to get those wet things off. It's all right," she repeated. "Your baby is safe. Hush, don't try to talk."

Mary ran upstairs, pulling a flannel nightgown, sweaters, and socks from her bureau. She'd eased Miriam into the big chair, dragging it closer to the stove. The girl was barely conscious. As she stripped Miriam's wet clothes off, Mary was relieved to see the girl's skin was pale, but not dead white. No frostbite. She rubbed Miriam's feet and put several pairs of socks on them, then wrapped her in a blanket before undoing the frozen braid that hung like a poker down her back. She dried her hair with a towel. The girl had not tried to say a word, but Mary could feel Miriam's eyes following her every move. She heated some whey and honey on the stove, then fed it to the young mother with a soupspoon. After she'd consumed half the cup, Miriam took it herself and drank.

"More," she whispered.

After she finished the second helping, she slept.

Mary had moved Christopher's basket next to Miriam, where she could see him. Now she stationed herself in the old rocker and kept watch over them both through the long, dark night.

The Fairchilds were enjoying the power outage. Two full propane tanks at the back of the house had meant hot chocolate and hot water for baths. Now the kids were snuggled in sleeping bags in front of the woodstove; Tom and Faith claimed the couches. The house was almost too well insulated, and Faith had tossed off her down comforter. Tom was reading Norma Farber's poem, "The Queens Came Late," out loud, as they always did on December 27. It was a tradition they'd started when Ben was two.

The Queens came late, but the Queens were there
With gifts in their hands and crowns on their hair.
They'd come, these three, like the Kings, from far,
following, yes, that guiding star.

They'd left their ladles, linens, looms,
their children playing in nursery rooms
And told their sitters: "Take charge! For this
is a marvelous sight we must not miss!"

The Queens came late, but not too late
To see the animals small and great,
Feathered and furred, domestic and wild . . .

This mention caused Faith's thoughts to drift to Mary's goats—Mary's small, furred, domestic animals—and from there to Christopher, the baby who had appeared on Christmas Eve. In the poem, the Queens bring useful gifts—chicken soup, "a homespun gown of blue," and a cradlesong to sing. Faith's car was loaded with useful gifts, and she'd already brought the baby a few necessities when she'd gone to Mary's yesterday morning. She had gently explained to Mary that, unlike baby kids, kid babies needed more nutrients than goat's milk—superb in every other way—could provide, and Christopher would have to have formula. The Harborside Market had enough in stock to feed him for a while, and Faith had planned to lay in a larger supply on her trip off island. And diapers, "Just as a backup, Mary. You can't keep washing what you have on hand." With the power out, Faith knew Mary must be relieved to have the bag of Huggies. They fit little Christopher better, too.

The cloth diaper had enveloped him almost to his chin.

The Queens came late and stayed not long,
for their thoughts already were straining far—
past manger and mother and guiding star
and child a-glow as a morning sun—
toward home and children and chores undone.

"Read it again, Daddy," Amy begged.

"Absolutely," Tom said. He usually read it at least three times, occasionally four, and they'd be reciting it altogether by then.

The storm was winding down. Faith was sure that Mary was doing fine. She pictured her in the kitchen with Christopher in her arms, next to the woodstove. It wasn't their well-being during the storm that she was worried about. What worried her was the news report Mary had relayed. Faith had heard it for herself on the transistor radio they'd turned on earlier to listen for the latest on the snowstorm. Other than what Mary had described, there had been little more about what had happened in Orono, except for one detail—the name of the victim: Bruce Judd. Miriam and Bruce Singer in the B & B register. That Bruce? Christopher's father?

Murdered.

Faith willed the snow to stop. Their car had four-wheel drive, but it would still be hard to get out in the morning if there was much accumulation. And she had to get to Mary's.

She'd had to wait for John Robbins to plow them out, so it was close to noon before Faith could leave for Bethany Farm. If Tom was puzzled by the intensity of his wife's need to get the baby things over to Mary, he didn't say so. Faith felt slightly guilty at keeping so much from Tom. It wasn't what they did—wasn't what their marriage was about. But she didn't want to upset him when he was coming along so well—or so she rationalized. Still it *was* true. He would be upset— the last thing she wanted, especially now. She felt an almost painful surge of love for him, the kind of feeling you don't have until you're faced with an illness, or worse.

There was no way she was going to drag Tom into this.

The main roads were clear, but when she reached the Bethany Farm road, Faith saw, to her dismay, that it wasn't. She'd have to walk in, carrying a few things, but leaving most behind. She pulled off the road and started out. It was a bright, sunny day—warm enough so the snow that clung to the trees was starting to fall in clumps to the ground. The weighted branches, relieved of their burden, sprang up like jack-in-the-boxes. Ben and Amy had barely stopped for breakfast before racing out to make a fort, or maybe an igloo, or maybe both, with snowmen to stand guard.

By the time she got to Mary's door, Faith had peeled off her outer layer and was imagining her children virtually naked from their exertions. It was hard to get them to wear jackets even when it was actually freezing. Mary opened the door immediately and Faith walked into a storybook picture—Jessie Wilcox Smith or Tasha Tudor. A young woman Faith assumed must be Miriam was sitting in Mary's big chintz easy chair, Christopher cradled in her arms while she fed him. Her long, shining dark hair tumbled over her shoulders, tumbled over the soft blue sweater she was wearing. She glanced up at Faith but finished singing to the baby—"I've given you my onliness / Give me your tomorrow"—before saying, "Hi." It was as soft and melodic as her singing had been.

"Faith, this is Miriam Carpenter. Miriam, Faith Fairchild," Mary said, adding to Faith, "She knows all about you."

But *I* don't know all about *you*, Faith said to herself as she greeted Miriam.

The room was glowing—with the heat from the stove, the smiles of the three women, and the radiant baby. Faith felt enormously relieved. Miriam was here, safe with Mary and Christopher. She wasn't in Orono, couldn't have been in Orono at the time in question and still made it down to the island in the storm.

"I have a lot more stuff in the car, but it will have to wait until you're plowed out. If I try to drive in, I'll get stuck for sure," Faith said. She put down the bags, which contained more sleepers, baby towels, more formula, bottles, and a Snugli. She'd viewed this as a necessity, so Mary could tend the goats with Christopher securely strapped to her chest. She hadn't bought any baby wipes. Mary got them by the carton to keep the goat's udders clean. She had plenty of bag balm, too. Mary's hands were as soft as the finest French leather gloves. Faith had never milked Mary's goats, but she imagined they would feel the same. Christopher's pelt would never suffer.

"I can walk back with you and make another trip," Mary offered.

"No, I'll go," Miriam said.

Mary shook her head firmly. "You're not to stir from where you are. You need to rest up. Besides, Christopher hasn't finished his bottle."

Mary grabbed her jacket and the two women walked out into the sunlight. The air was fresh after the closeness of the kitchen, and Faith felt inexplicably happy.

Mary Bethany looked at Faith's face and wished her own could mirror what she saw

there. She had not questioned Miriam about anything since the young woman had arrived on her
doorstep. Mary had hoped Miriam would open
up without being pushed. She hadn't.

The snow was so soft that small, sparkling ed-
dies swirled about their feet as they made their
way back to Faith's car. The surface caught the afternoon light, turning Mary's pasture into a field
of diamonds.

"Have you listened to any more news?" Faith
asked.

Mary shook her head. "I don't have that kind of
radio. Even if I had, I wouldn't have turned it on
and upset Miriam. She doesn't know about it."

"I heard the victim's name last night and again
this morning. It was Bruce Judd."

Mary stopped walking. "I thought that might
be who it was right from the beginning." She
reached down and shook the snow from a bay-
berry bush, freeing its branches from the ground.

"We'll have to tell Miriam," Faith said. "But
I'm sure she's not involved. She couldn't have
made it all the way here in the storm unless she'd
left Orono early."

Mary started walking slowly. "I don't know
when she left. It was almost three this morning
when she turned up here."

"Oh," said Faith.

"Yes," said Mary. They reached Faith's car,
loaded up, and started back to the farmhouse.

Christopher was back in his basket and Miriam was looking at the things Faith had brought. Faith started to take off her boots and put them next to Miriam's on the boot tray by the door. Miriam's boots were wet. Not still wet from last night, but newly wet. There was a coating of fresh snow on the right toe. She stopped what she was doing. Enough was enough. What had Miriam been doing outside? What possible reason could she have had to go to the barn—the only destination? It was time for the girl to start answering some questions.

"Miriam, your boots, they're—" Faith didn't finish the rest of the sentence.

Miriam was screaming. "It's Duane and Ralph! Look!" She pointed out the window.

A pickup was slowly making its way toward the house, the snow impeding but not stopping its progress.

"They'll kill us! Me anyway! They want the money!"

Mary didn't waste any time.

"Get your boots on and wrap the baby under your jacket. Go straight through the woods to the Marshalls'. Faith knows the way. Go by the shore, just in case you have to use the canoe. The Reach isn't frozen solid. The canoe's under a blue tarp."

As she spoke, she was dialing.

"I can't let you do this!" Miriam said.

"Don't waste time. Just get out of here! You've got to get Christopher away from them!"

Miriam seemed immobilized. Faith grabbed her and pushed her toward her things. "Hurry!"

"You take the baby," Miriam said, pulling on her parka. At the door to the shed, Miriam called to Mary, "Give them the money. Let them have it. Tell them where it is right away! You don't know what they can do!"

As she followed Miriam out the door, Faith could hear Mary telling Sanpere's volunteer fire department—the number you called if anything at all was wrong—"It's Mary at Bethany Farm. Send the truck, and an ambulance, and call the state police as fast as possible!"

Things with sirens. Faith only hoped they would get there in time.

Outside, the sun was almost blinding. They ran toward the woods, crossing the old pasture behind the house. The pickup had stopped and discharged its cargo.

"She's getting away! Both of them!" yelled Ralph. He started to run, calling to Duane, "Come on!"

"There's someone in the house," he said. "I saw the curtains move. She may be trying to trick us. I'm going in!" He started kicking at the door. "Open up, bitch. We know you're there!"

Inside, Mary knew the longer she could keep them out, the farther ahead the others would get. Ralph had stopped running while he waited to see who was in the house.

The door was solid oak, and Mary had hopes it would last until help arrived.

"Son of a bitch!" Duane hopped on one foot, rubbing the toe of his boot, then went back to the truck for something stronger. "What are you waiting for? Follow them, asshole."

Ralph took off again. The two figures were in plain sight, but nearing the woods. Duane shook his head and smacked his fist on the side of the truck before he reached into the bed to get a crowbar. He didn't know what was going on. Mostly, his life was pretty simple. He got what people wanted, gave it to guys to sell, and they handed over a lot more money than he had paid in the first place. No, he didn't like not knowing what was going on. He felt better thinking about what he was going to do to Miriam when he got her—and he would get her.

Lyle Sanford got out of the cab of the pickup. He'd been watching the scene with detached interest. That was some awesome weed these dudes had was his main thought. He'd been at the register at the market when they'd come in looking for "some old lady who has goats." Lyle had paused before answering, a pause Duane and Ralph mistook for reluctance to divulge information. In fact, Lyle was wondering why so many men were looking for Mary Bethany, who was, like, older than his mother and wondering even more where the two in front of him had gotten their cool tatties. Before he'd had a chance to tell them what they wanted to know, they'd offered him some weed and more if he would take them to Mary's farm. Would he! But he had to wait until Darlene came on, so Ralph and Duane helped themselves to some Doritos, pork rinds, and a couple of beers and then went back to sit in the truck.

"Who are they?" Faith managed to gasp as she ran toward the woods and safety.

"Drug dealers. They think I stole some money from them."

There was no mistaking the sound that split the air.

"Oh shit," said Miriam. "Ralph's got a gun."

As soon as Mary saw Duane approach her door with the crowbar, she opened it.

"There's no need to damage my property. What do you want? And what on earth are you doing here, Lyle?" Mary had seen the boy from the window but hadn't recognized him at that distance. She hadn't seen him at the market for a while, so the transformation from white T-shirts to black and the addition of several pieces of metal stuck through various parts of his face was new to her.

"Not sure, ma'am," he mumbled.

"Fer sure we're not here for a fuckin' cup of coffee. Now get Miriam and get the money."

"I don't know what you're talking about," Mary said.

Duane started to go for her.

"That won't work," Lyle said with surprising clarity. "You got to get her goats." He pointed toward the barn.

"No!" Mary cried. "Don't you dare go in there. I'll give you the money. Miriam isn't here. You can see that."

"Well now, this is much better. Ralph will take care of Miriam. Okay, Grandma, let's get the cash—and it had better all be there."

"You stay here; I'll bring it to you." Where was the fire truck? Why hadn't at least one volunteer arrived yet?

"No, I think we'll all stick together."

"It's in the barn." Mary hated to let him anywhere near her nannies. They'd be upset for days, but there was no choice. Lyle tagged along, and, as predicted, the goats bleated in panic. Mary tried to calm them, but Duane told her to hand over the money and hand it over fast.

She walked over to a pile of small square bales

of hay—she bought it like this, rather than in the rolls, because it was easier for her to handle. Easy to handle the other day when she'd hollowed out the middle of one and replaced the straw with the money.

"Here." She shoved the packet at him. "Now get out."

Duane opened it up. "Looks like it's all here, but I think I'll just count it to make sure. Could be you wanted to use some of it for a new billy goat." He laughed. It wasn't a pleasant sound. Mary didn't correct him as to the gender of her nannies. The longer he took, the better. She was straining to hear the sirens, but the only sound in the barn was her goats' piteous racket, louder than ten fire engines.

"Now, now, what's this?" Duane snarled, grabbing Mary's arm. "There's two thousand dollars missing!"

"I don't know anything about that," Mary said firmly, pulling free. "I haven't touched that money since I put it there."

"So I guess you musta taken it out before then." He reached into his pocket and took out a Bowie knife, flicking it open. "Hey, Lyle, get that little goat over there. He needs a haircut."

Faith knew they were close to the shore. There had been a couple more shots, but since Ralph had to look down to follow their tracks, they'd been able to keep ahead of him. Mary's canoe was under a blue tarp. You could find just about anything under a blue tarp in Maine. Miriam tugged at it, freed the canoe, and dragged it to the shore. Mary had been right: The water in the Reach wasn't frozen the way it was in the smaller coves. There were chunks of ice, but they'd be able to get the canoe in. Then what? Faith certainly hoped Miriam knew how to paddle, because otherwise they were sunk.

"Get in! Grab a paddle and go! I'll push us off!"

"I don't know how!" Faith said.

"You'll learn fast. Now go!"

Christopher had started to cry. Faith felt like crying herself, but she saved it for later. The canoe teetered in the water. She didn't even want to think about what would happen if they capsized. A minute, two minutes in water this temperature?

Miriam was moving them along with strong, swift strokes. Faith tried to match the rhythm, but finally she gave up and concentrated on calming the baby.

A bullet hit the water just behind them. Ralph was yelling at them from the shore. He emptied the gun as they pulled farther and farther out of range. Around the corner of one of the points of land that extended like gnarled fingers into the current, Faith could see the Marshalls' dock.

They were safe. And the emergency rescue vehicles must have arrived at the farm by now. Mary would be safe, too.

Mary was fine, but Duane was suffering from a nasty bite on the hand from Dora, the queen, who had been very curious about the bright, shiny object in his hand. She'd slid through the stall's gate, which Lyle hadn't closed properly, and lunged to explore the blade, encountering instead Duane's very fleshy palm. Before he could do more than just shove at the 180-pound pride of Mary's herd, the fire department, rescue corps, and two state police officers all poured through Mary's barn door. They arrested Duane and Lyle immediately and sat down to wait for Ralph and the officers who'd gone after him. One of the volunteers took pity on Duane and poured more than enough iodine on his open wound before bandaging it.

"We can call the farm from the Marshalls', and as soon as we get Mary, they'll drive us back." Faith was nuzzling Christopher's tiny head, which seemed to be keeping him quiet.

Miriam maneuvered the canoe toward the dock, and Faith grabbed a line tied to the end of it, pulling them in alongside.

"Maybe we should put the canoe on the dock. No, it won't be here for long. We can moor it and someone will take it back to Mary." She stepped out and reached to help Miriam. The expression on the girl's face troubled her. They were safe—all of them. Why did Miriam look so sad?

Miriam wondered what it would be like to be Faith Fairchild. Mary *had* told her all about Faith. Her life sounded perfect. She sighed.

"Look, Faith, this is where I get off. Or rather *you* get off."

"*What?*" Faith exclaimed.

"I'm not like you or Mary. I'm not a good girl. And I certainly wouldn't be a good mother."

"It's Bruce, isn't it?" Faith said. The cold dread she'd felt since hearing about the murder gave way to cold certainty.

"Kind of. I didn't kill him, though, if that's what you mean."

"Then who did? Those men? Duane and Ralph?"

"Pretty much. They got their licks in first. But, believe me, you don't need to know about this. Tell Mary that Christopher is hers. I left a letter in the drawer where she keeps her dish towels. If that's not enough to convince the state, I'll sign whatever they want. Help her get a lawyer. She's got plenty of money. It was mine; don't let the cops have it."

By now, Miriam was convinced the money *was* hers—wages for all the housekeeping and accounting she'd done—and certainly Christopher's. His inheritance from his father—all he was ever going to get from him, thank God.

"I thought this was going to be a whole lot easier." She sighed. "I decided last summer that I wanted Mary to be the baby's mother. When he was born, I wanted to give him to her even more. She's the best person I ever met. Tell her that. And also that the week I spent with her was the happiest in my life."

"Then why go?" From the moment Faith had seen the three of them together in Mary's kitchen, she had been picturing a perfect happily ever after. Mary and Miriam—the two Marys—raising Christopher, goats, and vegetables together on into the sunset.

"I'm only twenty-one years old. Even if I was a good person, that's too young to have a child—at least for me. And I have to figure some things out, a lot of things out."

"What about your family? Your father?"

"There isn't any family now, never was much of one. But don't worry, Daniel Carpenter isn't going to try to get Christopher as a trinket for Brenda—that's my stepmother, or rather, his wife—or as a male someone to continue the sainted Carpenter line. Be sure Mary changes his name to hers."

Faith had so many questions, but Miriam was already untying the line.

"How can you be sure that he won't take legal action to get his grandson?"

Miriam hesitated for a moment, then said, "Because, good, kind Mrs. Fairchild, Daddy finished what Duane and Ralph started. I got there just in time to see him go nuts when Bruce managed to pull a knife on him and the knife ended up in Bruce. Self-defense? Helps to have a witness for that."

Miriam had known Bruce was dead. Had known since she opened the apartment door in time to see her father and Bruce struggle, then watch as Daniel Carpenter stood next to the body in shock, holding the bloody knife.

She started to pull away from the dock. The shadows were lengthening; darkness was falling on the picture in her mind, as well. Then she remembered something else.

"I took two thousand dollars from the money I left with the baby. Mary stashed it all in a bale of hay in the barn. She told me last night. I think she knew what I'd do. But I'll pay it back. Be sure to tell her."

Miriam had a lot of things she wanted to be sure Mary knew.

This wasn't the right ending, but it was the ending. There was only one more thing.

"I told you that you can get in touch with me if you need to."

Or you need to, Faith thought.

"The island newspaper is on-line now," Miriam said. "In July, we joked about how high-tech the island was becoming and that Mary would be selling cheese on the Internet soon. We'll use the 'Personals' column—you know, where people put ads saying 'Happy Anniversary' or 'thanks for the cards' when they were in the hospital. I'll call if I see 'Mother Mary come to me.' "

Faith held Christopher up so Miriam could see him. She waved and left them, heading for the bridge, not far away, and a ride to somewhere.

Let it be.

The Twelve Frogs of Christmas

Judi McCoy

Claire St. Germaine peered out her storm door, closed her eyes, and smacked her forehead on the glass.

No! No! No! Not another frog!

Glancing left then right, she squatted and opened the door just far enough to reach out and pluck the dark green amphibian from the porch on her side of the duplex. Cradling the creature to her chest, she stood and drew the bolt home, then walked to her computer desk to retrieve the empty shoebox she now kept at the ready. Carrying the frog in one hand and the box in the other, she made her way to the sofa situated in front of her fireplace, took a seat, and placed the object of her disdain on the coffee table.

The impromptu interloper stared through bulging eyes and croaked, as if reminding her she had a job to do. Claire cringed.

It had taken her a week of debating while the first caller loitered at the front of her house, before she'd done as instructed on the yellow ribbon tied about its stumpy neck. Numbers two through ten had arrived in the same manner. This one—number eleven—wasn't wearing the usual 'kiss me' order, but she assumed it was here for the same reason as the others.

"Hold on to your warts," she muttered, and covered it with the shoebox. Frog number two had hopped beneath the sofa, and number three had bounded across the room and sequestered itself under her computer desk. Hours of crawling on her hands and knees had prompted Claire to come up with the makeshift holding cell for all that had followed, and she had to admit it was one of her brighter ideas.

She removed a pair of generic gray sweats and a snow-white T-shirt she'd purchased specifically for the visitors from her hall closet, and brought them to the sofa. Raising the shoebox, she gave the frog a once-over. With its bumpy, dark green body and tucked-up legs it looked pretty much like all the others, which called to mind a familiar lecture.

A frog is a frog is a frog, she thought with a grimace. And it was time she sent this one packing.

Cupping the fellow in her palms, Claire stood, raised it to chin level, and bent near. The frog closed its buggy eyes, almost as if preparing for what came next.

Ribbit.

Eeuuw! Just her luck she had to lip-lock with a reptilian Romeo that had never heard of mouthwash.

She steeled her resolve, puckered, and leaned in. After planting a quick kiss on its slimy mouth, she set the critter on the floor next to the table and stepped back. No matter how often it happened, it was still difficult coming to grips with what she was certain would next occur. Before she could blink, the amphibian morphed into its proper state.

Claire gazed with what she hoped was an innocent expression at the naked man standing in her living room. Hunched over with his hands covering his male anatomy, his presence annoyed as well as frustrated her. Intent on putting the poor guy at ease, she tossed him the sweats and T-shirt. His confused demeanor matched that of the past ten frogmen who had arrived in the last two months.

He caught the clothing and turned, giving her a clear view of his taut buttocks, long legs, and nicely muscled, albeit hairy back. Aside from the fuzz, she had to admit the guy had a decent body. Hopping on one leg then the other, he eased into the sweats and tugged on the shirt, mussing his thinning brown hair. Moving to face her, he glanced around the duplex with a blank stare, just like each of her past *visitors*.

"Where am I?"

"In Millwood, Maryland, a suburb of Washington D.C.," she answered matter-of-factly. "What's your name?"

"Um . . . Joe . . . Joe Spivey." He frowned. "How did I get here?"

She wasn't surprised by the befuddled look etched on his pleasant face. She'd felt the same the first few times she'd watched the transformation. "I'm not sure. Where do you live?"

"Alexandria, Virginia." He shook his head as if to clear it of cobwebs. "Do I know you?"

"Not really," said Claire, handing him a twenty dollar bill. "Been to New Orleans lately?"

He gazed at the bill, then slipped it in his pocket. "Um . . . yeah . . . last week. But how did you—?"

She shrugged. "Just a guess." The poor man had probably dodged a zillion vehicles on his journey across the country. "Why don't you wait on the porch while I call a cab? I'm sure once you get home and take a nap, you'll wake and remember everything."

Or not.

In truth, the only thing she knew for certain about her visitors was that she was sick to death of kissing them. If it were her choice, she would have each man wake up the next morning as if nothing had happened. It was certainly a lot kinder than having them remember they'd existed on flies and hopped beside a freeway for who knew how long.

Grasping Joe's elbow, she led him to the foyer and hustled him onto the porch. "Have a seat while I make the call. The taxi company has been very responsive these past few weeks. You won't have a long wait."

Claire closed the door and locked it, ignoring his still-blank face. The last thing she needed was more questions, because the only answers she could give made no sense. Even more disturbing, if any of them found out what had been done she might get sued or find herself the principal in an insanity hearing. Definitely an unpleasant thought.

Shivering, she upped her thermostat on the way to the kitchen. Now that it was officially winter, she probably needed to buy heavy socks for her unsuspecting callers' feet. It wasn't their fault they'd been sent here as if they were an installment of the Prince-of-the-Month Club.

She picked up the phone and dialed the cab company, where the dispatcher assured her a taxi would arrive soon. After putting the kettle on for tea, she inhaled a breath and punched in a number she knew as well as her own. Four rings later, the answering machine responded with standard instructions to leave a message at the tone.

Instead, Claire gritted her teeth and dialed a

second number. This time, when she heard the beep, she set her spine and vowed to be forceful. "This has got to stop," she ordered. "Call me as soon as you get this message."

She slammed the phone in its cradle and sighed. Tough situations demanded firm handling, and aside from starting her own jewelry business, this parade of frogs had been one of the most difficult. She ran trembling fingers through her hair, tucking the curly tresses behind her ears. She had a ton of work to do if she planned on making her weekly deadline. She had no time to ponder the perplexing procession of amphibians that had graced her door for the past several months.

Right before Thanksgiving, she'd stopped by an upscale boutique in town and convinced them to take a tray of her unique jewelry designs on consignment. She was also selling at an exclusive store in Tyson's Corner Mall, and had an appointment later that afternoon with the manager of a shop in Alexandria. She didn't want to saturate any one area with her work, and had in fact been thinking of renting a storefront close by, if only to have a reason to speak to other human beings. It wasn't unusual for her to get so engrossed in crafting her creations that three days would pass before she remembered to leave the house.

She had moved to the D.C. area and bought

this duplex in hopes of turning her special hobby into a lucrative career, while at the same time living closer to her older sister Marie, and her best friend Angela. Unfortunately, Marie's free time was stretched thin with the impending arrival of baby number three, and Angela was on her honeymoon, which gave Claire the forced opportunity to devote every waking hour to her business.

Putting together her Web site and launching it on a host of search engines had been a stroke of genius. The orders she'd filled had allowed her to splurge on better quality materials and create even more expensive designs. But she'd had little time to make friends.

So little, in fact, that she'd yet to meet the owner of the other half of her house. Not that it mattered, because the realtor had mentioned him in passing, and from the sound of it, he was an aging college professor mired in a solitary life of academia and research.

Claire heaved a breath. She really did intend to get out and make a few new friends when the jewelry orders slowed. But she hadn't counted on the frogs and their vexing visitations.

If only she could convince the sender to stop the madness.

Dr. Hugh Burton let the living room curtain drop back in place and chided himself for being a snoop. He was entirely too consumed in the habits of his new neighbor, but damned if the activity at her place didn't have him flummoxed. The woman hardly ever left her house, yet she seemed to attract men and frogs like roses did honeybees. Right now, it was difficult to ignore the barefoot fellow sitting on her half of the stoop, wearing barely enough clothing to keep away the December chill.

And just this morning, when he'd stepped outside to collect his newspaper, he'd spotted another *Rana catesbeiana* loitering on her side of the stairs.

He knew little about Claire St. Germaine past her name, and he'd only learned that because he'd received some of her mail by mistake after she'd first moved in. To the best of his knowledge, she'd bought the duplex in September and settled in while he'd been teaching, because the FOR SALE sign was gone one evening when he'd returned from class.

He'd caught sight of her a few times as she'd made her way from the building, and recalled she had thick brown hair streaked with gold and a dimple in her right cheek. He also knew she was approximately five feet eight, with the figure of a goddess, and a laugh like liquid sunshine.

Shocked that his practical brain had generated such a poetic phrase, he had to admit that when he'd first heard Ms. St. Germaine's laughter through the wall dividing their units, he'd been instantly enthralled. Too bad the one time he talked himself into knocking on her door, he'd found her car missing from its parking space.

It wasn't until she'd lived next to him for a few weeks that he'd begun to notice the frogs. And the men. Or was it the men, then the frogs? Hugh scratched his jaw. As far as he could tell the two things had nothing in common, yet they seemed to happen at random and in close succession.

Thinking back, he decided the frogs had definitely come before the men. He would spot one either on the porch or under the bushes, then it would disappear. A short while later, there'd be a man dressed in sweatpants and a T-shirt sitting on the stoop who left soon after. He hadn't even made the nonconnection until the third or fourth time.

As a professor of biology who specialized in herpetology, he soothed his unusual curiosity over Ms. St. Germaine's affairs by reminding himself that amphibians were his life. His interest in them was of a purely scientific nature. Those half-naked men were the real mystery.

Of course, if he found the wherewithal to fire up his courage, the question would be a great icebreaker.

"Hello, Ms. St. Germaine, I'm Dr. Hugh Burton, your neighbor. I teach biology at Georgetown University, and I've come to introduce myself. I don't mean to be nosy, but I was wondering about the frogs."

No, no, no. That sounded way too geekish, even for someone with his exceptionally high geek quotient.

"Miss St. Germaine? I'm your neighbor, Hugh Burton. Sorry it's taken me so long to stop and say hello, but now that I have would you mind telling me why there are so many frogs on your porch?"

If it got him in the door, he'd find a way to turn the conversation to all those men he'd noticed, each one looking as if he'd been zapped by a Taser.

He shook his head, disgusted with his current penchant for minding his neighbor's business. Today was the first day of semester break, and he'd planned to use it by checking the mail on his Web site. Who would have guessed when he'd set up the site six months ago that there were so many amateur herpetologists willing to help in his quest for *Rana sevosa*?

He'd applied for a grant to search for the endangered amphibian, but had no idea when or even if he'd get the money. With his online network of enthusiasts, he hoped to pinpoint the last enclave of *Rana sevosa*. Once he received word on a sighting and photographic verification, he would arrange a leave of absence from the university and embark on his mission.

He heard a door slam and returned to his post in time to see Ms. St. Germaine hurry to her car carrying a large box. Peering to his right, he saw that the man had left, which bolstered his spirits considerably. But he did hope the frog epidemic continued.

Without *Rana catesbeiana*, what would they find to talk about?

· **2** ·

One week after she'd said farewell to her eleventh frog, Claire set out to make her final deliveries of the year. After zipping her hooded jacket, she tugged on her leather gloves, then grabbed her purse and hoisted the three large flat boxes containing her newest jewelry designs into her arms. Though the bulk of her business was conducted over the Internet, sales at the local stores had increased, mostly, she was sure, because of the upcoming holidays. She owed each of the boutiques a final tray of merchandise to display in time for the Christmas rush.

Carefully balancing the load, she stepped onto the porch and found herself in the middle of a winter wonderland. The snow she'd noticed falling gently last night was now coming down in a curtain of gauzy cotton, obliterating the sidewalks and grass. If it continued, the area could look forward to a rare white Christmas. She'd most likely spend the day with her sister, brother-in-law, and their two children, though the thought of staying home, putting her feet up in front of a roaring fire, and getting cozy with a good book and a cup of hot cocoa had merit.

Just to be safe, Claire scanned the porch and stairs, then checked under the bushes for a new *visitor.* If she received a twelfth prospect, she didn't want to leave the poor creature outside to freeze. She knew very little about frogs, but thought she'd read somewhere they were cold-blooded. Did that mean some species hibernated for the winter or that they needed to be kept warm?

Either way, she was relieved she wouldn't have to send a stranger out on a day like today, dressed in nothing but a pair of sweatpants and a thin shirt.

After unlocking her car, she deposited the boxes in the trunk, settled behind the wheel, and turned the key, hoping to coax enough heat from the geriatric engine to run the defroster. While it warmed, she found the long-handled scraper and began cleaning the windows and sideview mirrors. She was certain the snowplows were already out doing their thing, but area traffic was always heavy; one needed to drive with extra caution in this weather.

Back in the car, she concentrated on the most direct route to her customers. Cutting across D.C. would be a nightmare of taxis, buses, cars, and pedestrians, so she decided to take the beltway around the city. If nothing unusual happened, she'd be home well before three o'clock, the time she expected Angie's younger brother to arrive and give her a hand with her twice-weekly chore of boxing her Internet orders.

Shifting the car into reverse, she eased down on the gas pedal and prepared to back from the driveway. Seconds later, she knew that wasn't going to happen.

Frustrated, she revved the engine a few times, then tried something she'd once read in a manual—rocking the car back and forth in order to dislodge it from its rut. When that didn't work, she climbed out and did a check of the tires, dismayed to see worn treads, especially on the ones in the rear.

Claire stared at the snow-laden sky. She belonged to AAA, but the towing services would be too busy with the storm to arrive any time soon. She'd made a friend of the taxi dispatcher, but calling a cab seemed pointless for the same reason, as well as being cost prohibitive. Taking the train was useless, because one of the stores was blocks from a Metro stop, and she had three huge boxes to carry. Angie was still on her honeymoon, and her other friends were probably already at work or stuck in their own parking spaces.

Blowing out a breath, Claire watched it fog the

air. Her hands fisted on her hips, she shook her head to dislodge the snow from her hair. Though wet and cold, she couldn't afford to disappoint her buyers. Maybe one of her neighbors had sand or a shovel, or both . . .

"Ms. St. Germaine!"

Claire turned at the sound of the deep, masculine voice.

"Is there a problem?"

Focusing on her front porch, she spotted a man who was anything but old at the door of the other half of her duplex. Perhaps he was the son of her neighbor. In any case, it seemed her prayers had been answered.

Hugh heard the gunning engine noise before he'd drunk his first cup of coffee. Last night's forecast had warned of snow, so he imagined there was at least a light dusting on the ground. Luckily, he didn't have to drive in the slippery stuff, even though his car had new tires and a fresh supply of winterized windshield fluid.

Dressed in a bathrobe, pajama bottoms, and slippers, he ambled to the foyer, hoping to retrieve his morning paper without having to go outside. Opening the storm door, he was hit by a gust of frigid air and a blast of fluffy flakes. He peered through the curtain of white and blinked, but his glasses were already glazed with the icy precipitation.

Is that who I think it is in the driveway?

After wiping his horn-rims on his robe, he settled the smudged spectacles on his nose. He'd been searching for a clever way to meet his neighbor, and there she stood, a vision shrouded in silver and in need of a hand. Inhaling a breath of courage, he called her name and she spun in his direction.

He shouted again, more forcefully. "Is there a problem? Do you need help?"

"I'm stuck." Ms. St. Germaine shaded her eyes with a gloved hand. "Do you have sand and a shovel I could borrow?"

"Wait inside the car where you'll be warm. I'll be right there," he advised. "It will just take a minute."

Grinning at his good fortune, Hugh raced up the stairs to his bedroom, where he dug through a drawer and found a stack of old clothes. Pulling out jeans—it was much too miserable for a pair of slacks—a T-shirt, and heavy socks, he dressed with lightning speed, wrenched a worn flannel shirt off a hanger and ran back downstairs. At the hall closet, he pulled out a pair of sneakers and jammed his feet inside without untying the laces. Just before he flung open the front door, he remembered to button and tuck in his shirt, and shrug on a fleece-lined leather jacket. After snagging his car keys from the foyer table, he shot outside.

Skittering off the porch, Hugh slid down the

walk like an octopus on roller skates. Too bad he hadn't been smart enough to find a pair of boots instead of athletic shoes. He raised his head in time to see his neighbor jump from the car when she noticed his plight. Before he could warn her of the treacherous conditions, she began the identical slip and slide that had caught him unaware. Lurching toward each other, they collided and crashed to the ground in a heap of arms and legs.

Unfortunately, instead of cushioning her fall as he'd intended, he landed on top of her.

Time seemed to stop as Hugh gazed into her midnight-blue eyes, admired the dimple in her cheek, smelled her minty fresh breath as she exhaled a gasp of air. Despite the snow falling around them, he couldn't stop from nestling between the V of her thighs and succumbing to the warmth of her lush, curvy body. Nuzzling his nose into her neck, he sighed with contentment.

The sound of her voice, so soft and sweet—

"That's a pretty big icicle you're carrying in your pocket. How about you get off me and let it melt?"

Too mortified to speak, Hugh prayed he wasn't blushing as he struggled to stand. Appalled at his caveman reaction to her nearness, he straightened his jacket and searched for a way to redeem himself.

Gazing down, he saw her lying flat on her back with her arms and legs askew. "Good God! Are you all right? Have you broken something?"

The sound of her laughter sent an arrow to his midsection. "I'm fine, and don't be embarrassed. It happens to guys a lot—or so I've been told." Taking the hand he held out to her, she rose to her feet and brushed away the snow. "Besides, I was the one who dragged you down. You're not hurt, are you?"

"No, no . . . it was entirely my fault," Hugh stammered. "I'm Hugh—Hugh Burton—your neighbor. But I guess you already figured that out."

"Claire St. Germaine." Wide-eyed, she gave his hand an impersonal shake. "I really appreciate your help."

Their eyes locked and they stepped apart. Hugh cleared his throat. "Let's see about getting your car out, shall we?"

He offered his arm and she clutched it as they skated to her sedan. "First I tried backing out slowly, then at warp speed, but all that seemed to do was dig the wheels in deeper," she explained, nodding at the ancient compact. "I even rocked it in place, but nothing helped. The only thing left is the sand and shovel route. If that doesn't work, I guess I'll have to call for a tow, but in this storm . . ."

Hugh pulled keys from his jacket pocket and

nodded at his Saab, parked alongside her ill-equipped vehicle. "I think I have what you need." Opening the trunk, he moved his toolbox and sifted through what he deemed a neatly packed store of necessities: a case of bottled water, blankets, flares, a few parking cones, a battery-powered lantern, a first aid kit, and more. Finally, he found the bag of sand and plastic folding shovel he kept specifically for this type of emergency.

Claire arched a perfect brow as she stared into the cavernous hold. "Wow. You must have been some Boy Scout."

"Umm—no—I wasn't. Should I have been?"

She smiled. "I'm joking. I can handle it from here, thanks."

She grabbed the shovel and began digging behind a rear tire. It took a second before he realized the roads were iced over, and there wasn't a plow in sight. By the time he finished his survey, she'd straightened and was zeroing in on the sand.

He held the bag aloft. "You can't mean to drive in this—this blizzard? Do you have to go out? Can't it wait?"

She brushed the snowflakes from her lashes. "I can't afford to disappoint my customers. I don't mind, really."

"Nonsense," he argued, amazed at her determination. "Even if you're the only car on the road, you might skid into an embankment or telephone pole." He eyed her balding rear tires. "I doubt there's enough tread on those to get decent traction. Where are you going?"

She spoke above the muted sounds of the storm. "I have to stop at a few stores. If I don't deliver my merchandise today, I'll lose their business."

Hugh felt like a fool when he realized she'd just about rescued herself while he'd done nothing but fantasize and offer advice. This was a chance to be alone with her and show his manly prowess all at once, sort of like a white knight coming to the aid of a damsel in distress. And if he learned more about his intriguing new neighbor in the process, then all the better.

"Let me drive you. My tires are new, and this car is one of the safest on the road."

She stared at the black, turbo-charged Saab. "I couldn't let you do that."

"I insist." Taking command of the situation, he stowed the shovel and sand and slammed the trunk lid. Then he opened her car door, turned off the engine, and faced her, holding the keys out of her reach. "Your boxes are in the rear?"

"Yes, but—"

He retrieved her items, placed them on his backseat, and opened the passenger door. "Get in. I'll take you wherever you need to go."

* * *

Several hours later, gloved in plush black leather with her fanny snug against a heated backrest and seat, Claire felt as if she were riding in a limo instead of a sedan. Plows had cleared most of the roadway, and the sanding trucks had kept the icy conditions at bay. Now that the snow had slowed to flurries and the sun was shining, the streets were passable and no longer dangerous. It had taken a while, but they were finally on their way to the last boutique.

She gave her chauffeur a sidelong glance as he concentrated on the road. Hugh Burton wasn't the most handsome guy in the world, but he was certainly the most gallant and agreeable. Tall, with a narrow face and square chin, he had curly dark hair and an expressive mouth. Blue eyes hid behind thick horn-rimmed glasses, and she wondered what he would look like with contacts.

With his stubbled jaw, worn jeans, flannel shirt, and leather jacket, he seemed rugged and fit, but it was hard to tell under all those clothes. The only thing she knew for certain was that he had an impressive male . . . package. She'd had her share of experiences with the opposite sex, but never had a man fallen on top of her and shown his interest so quickly.

Her gaze drifted to his large, capable hands with their long, lean fingers and neatly trimmed nails, now gripping the wheel. The memory of those firm yet gentle hands as they'd cradled her in the snow brought a sudden warmth to her cheeks. It was flattering to have elicited such a heated response from a man she believed was a genuinely nice guy. She hadn't meant to make that crude crack about the icicle in his pocket, but it was too good a moment to let pass without comment.

"The store is over there, next to that beauty salon," Claire said when she realized they were approaching the last of her delivery sites. "I'll just be a minute—unless you want to come in?"

Hugh had stayed in the Saab while she'd made the first two drops, and each time she returned, she'd found him assisting another motorist. Since this parking lot had been plowed and the roads were better, she doubted he'd need to be a good Samaritan again.

"I'd like that."

He slipped from behind the wheel, and before she'd gathered her purse, opened her door. Stepping onto the pavement, she saw her box of deliveries resting on the car roof. Impressed by his speed and courtly manners, she led the way into the boutique, where he set the order on top of the counter.

"Why don't you take a look around?" she suggested. "While I let the manager know I'm here."

"Is there a display of your work I might look at?"

Heat rushed to Claire's cheeks. She was proud of her designs; women usually loved them, as did the buyers in high-end stores that specialized in selling one-of-a-kind fashion items. She had no idea what a normal man would think of her creations—semiprecious stones wrapped in gold or sterling wire.

"I'm in the end case on the opposite side, but according to the manager there isn't much left to choose from," she told him. "I'll meet you there."

Elaine Alder, the store's buyer, hurried over, a wide smile on her carefully made-up face. "Claire, thank heavens you're here. When I saw the snow, I was afraid you wouldn't make it."

She lifted the box top and dug through a layer of tissue while Claire mentally crossed her fingers. She'd tried a new technique with this batch, twisting several wires together to form a braid before she wrapped it around the gems. It looked rather unique to her, but it was the sales appeal that counted.

"Oh, these are lovely," said Elaine. "Here's the list of what sold from the last order. Let me take this in the back for pricing and write you a check. I want to get everything in the case this afternoon to be certain it sells."

Claire scanned the list, happily noting that her inventory here was as depleted as it had been at the other two stores. If this kept up, she'd be earning that six figure income in no time. She might even have to hire a full-time employee or two after the first of the year

She walked to her display area, more to see what Hugh thought of her work than to inspect what was left of her designs. Julie, one of the clerks, stood across the counter as he gazed intently into the case.

Hugh pointed to a bracelet. "May I see that one, please?"

Julie slid the glass panel, while Claire protested. "Wait a second—I can't let you—"

He straightened. "I have several women in my life and I've yet to buy their Christmas gifts. Your jewelry would be perfect for the girls."

"But—but—I can't allow you to buy it. If not for you I wouldn't have made it here today. Please, let me give you the pieces you like—as a thank-you."

"Absolutely not." He turned back to the case.

The clerk threw her an are-you-crazy? stare, and removed the item he indicated—a bracelet with chunky turquoise stones dangling from an intricate sterling silver wrap—and placed it on a velvet-lined tray. The piece was one of her most expensive designs, which was probably the reason it still hadn't sold.

"Claire, let the man buy what he wants." Julie rolled her eyes. "Besides, it's already in our inventory."

Claire understood. Technically, the boutique owned the merchandise, so it wasn't hers to give away. She tugged on his elbow, and he glanced at her. "Buy that one if you must, then come back to my place. I have lots more you can choose from. You can have whatever you want."

His brows rose over the top of his glasses. "But not for free."

"For cost, then, but not a penny more." She did a quick tally of how low she could take the prices before he knew she was lying. If she played down the quality of the stones or told him the wire was stainless steel or gold overlay . . .

Elaine approached with her check just as Hugh pulled a credit card from his wallet. "Here's your payment. And call me right after the new year so I can place another order." She eyed the turquoise bracelet Julie was arranging in a box. "Your friend has good taste."

Claire assessed the amount she'd earned and passed the time with Elaine, until Julie handed Hugh a bag with his gift-wrapped package. They exchanged wishes for a happy holiday with the women and headed for the door. On the sidewalk, she scanned the strip mall and spotted a favorite restaurant.

"Do you have to be somewhere important this afternoon?"

"No. Do you need to make another stop?"

Smiling, she tucked her hand in his arm. "No, but I'm buying lunch. And you're not going to talk me out of it."

When Hugh drove Claire home and parked his shiny, black automobile next to her dingy gray compact on their shared driveway, she cringed. Thanks to the brilliant afternoon sunshine, she no longer needed to dig out the car, but she did have to take care of everything that was wrong with it before winter fully set in. Maybe she could use the checks in her purse to purchase new tires, fix the heater, bang out the dents, have it painted, and—

Estimating the cost in her head, she realized she might as well bite the bullet and buy a more current model. She couldn't afford a Saab, of course, but something that didn't inspire pity or need to spend a month in the shop might be nice.

She and her neighbor had spent a pleasant lunch hour; now it was time for her to ready her Internet sales for shipping. Lost in thought, she climbed the porch steps and found a note on her door. Tony, Angela's brother, had an accident and wouldn't be able to come to work until after the holiday.

Poor Tony. Claire heaved a sigh. And poor me. She walked into the foyer and removed her coat. Most of the orders scheduled to be mailed today were Christmas gifts, so sending them next week would be much too late. She'd lose business and future customers if she didn't make the delivery on time, and now she'd have to do the chore by herself when she should be creating new designs. Bummed by the message, she didn't notice that Hugh had followed her inside until he cleared his throat.

"You seem upset. Is something wrong?"

"I'm sorry, I didn't mean to ignore you." She'd promised him a cup of cocoa and a private showing of her work; instead, she was being rude. "It's just a little bad news. Someone I know broke his elbow shoveling snow this morning and—"

Hugh's amicable expression flattened. "Your boyfriend?"

"Hardly. Tony is my best friend's thirteen-year-old brother. His mother dropped off this note on their way back from the emergency room. Tony's been working here after school a couple of days a week, boxing and labeling Internet orders to earn spending money. This is my last delivery before Christmas, and I have about a hundred invoices to fill." She eyed her watch. "The UPS man will be here later to make the pickup."

He opened her closet, removed his jacket, and hung it on a hanger. Grinning, he began rolling up his sleeves. "Then I guess we'd better get started."

Claire sucked in a breath. "Oh, no. I couldn't accept any more of your help. You're supposed to be choosing a few pieces of jewelry for yourself, remember, not coming to my rescue for a second time today."

"Consider lunch payment for the first rescue. Hot chocolate will do for the next few hours." He wandered to her computer station situated in a corner of the living room, and found the list. "I take it you have the items set aside and ready to go?"

She couldn't believe her ears. This guy was too good to be true. "Everything is in the second bedroom upstairs. I turned it into a design studio when I moved in, but I need to keep a big supply of gems and shipping necessities on hand, so there's barely enough space for my worktable. That's why my computer is in here."

"I use that bedroom as my office, and I agree it's on the small side. I have a large amount of books and research materials, and I'm forced to store half of it on shelves I've set up in the same corner you use for your computer. Someday, I'm going to have a house with a huge library that will hold everything."

Claire remembered they had the same floor plan, only in reverse, and knew he understood her need for space. "My dream is to rent some footage in a strip mall, and install a sales area in the front, while I create designs in a back workroom—when I have enough money to pay the exorbitant start-up costs, of course."

She headed toward the kitchen as she spoke. "I'll make the cocoa, then we can check out which of my jewelry is still available. If you don't find anything you like, you can pick out an already sold design and I'll duplicate it." He sat at the table and she raised a brow. "Are you sure you want to help?"

"Absolutely."

Claire found herself grinning like a fool. "Okay, but only if you promise to accept something in exchange for your time." She took a carton of milk from the refrigerator, then measured and poured it into a saucepan, noting he didn't comment on her offer.

"You make hot chocolate from scratch?"

From the tenor of Hugh's voice, it sounded as if she were whipping up duck *à l'orange* or cherries jubilee. "Is there any other way?"

"How about a package mix, water, and a microwave?"

"That is so sad," she said, using a whisk to beat the sugar and cocoa powder into the milk. "I don't make anything from a box, unless it can't be helped."

She lowered the heat under the saucepan, then propped her backside against the counter. Hugh was flipping through a jewelry design magazine she'd read at breakfast. Without his coat, she saw that he was on the big and cuddly side, not over-weight exactly, but not slim. At five eight herself, with size nine feet and generous hips, Claire had dated few men who'd made her feel as protected and safe as Hugh had today. How would it be, she wondered, to snuggle against his broad chest with her head tucked under his chin?

Heat scorched her cheeks at the outrageous mental image, and she walked to the cookie jar at the far end of the counter. After arranging the homemade chocolate chip morsels on a plate, she brought them to the table, then went to the stove and stirred the cocoa. When it began to simmer, she filled two mugs with the steaming brew.

"Can I do anything?" Hugh asked as she served the drink.

"Nope, and help yourself to cookies. You're going to need energy for this afternoon's project. The process involves a dozen trips up and down the stairs to retrieve merchandise."

"Not a problem. And this smells fantastic." He sipped, then smiled. "Tastes just like my mom used to make."

Earlier, when he'd mentioned that he had to buy gifts for his *girls*, Claire had almost asked who they were. She figured he was single, because he didn't wear a ring, and she'd never noticed any women coming in or out of his house. She was also fairly certain he was straight thanks to his reaction to their body lock on the front lawn. They'd talked about weather-related driving hazards all morning, and her business during lunch. Aside from revealing he was a college professor, she didn't know much about him. Maybe he was so involved in his career he wasn't ready to commit to a full-time relationship.

Mentally, she put the brakes on her wayward train of thought. The fact that a nice guy like Hugh didn't have a girlfriend was none of her concern. They were neighbors who'd been thrown together by circumstance, nothing more. But it would be bad manners if she didn't show at least a casual interest in him, as he'd done with her.

"Where is your mom now?" she asked.

"Living the high life in Florida. She sold everything after Dad died two years ago, and bought a condo. She lives near my older sister, because Jeanne is the only sibling with children. My other sisters are married, too, but they live farther away."

"Then the gifts—my jewelry—would be for them?"

"Correct. The bracelet I bought at the boutique is for my youngest sister, Leah. She lives in Colorado and wears lots of turquoise. I'm going to need something for Mom, Jeanne, and Barbara, my sister in Texas."

Ah, that explained it, thought Claire. Any man with three sisters had to learn how to interact with women or suffer the consequences. It was obvious his female relatives had encouraged him to be considerate of the opposite sex, instead of demanding and self-absorbed. A refreshing change from the last two guys she'd dated.

She finished her cocoa, as did Hugh. After clearing the table, she led him upstairs, grateful she'd remembered to make her bed and straighten the second floor before she left the house. "This is my studio," she said proudly.

He stood next to her and Claire inhaled a breath. In the span of a heartbeat, Hugh's proximity had sucked all the oxygen from the room. The space seemed to shrink, as if they were together in a closet. A very small, very intimate closet.

She backed up, but the retreat still wasn't enough. The urge to act on the idea that had plagued her in the kitchen overwhelmed her. If Hugh turned and they each took a step forward, she could rest her head on his chest and . . .

Thankfully, he seemed oblivious to her silly fantasies. He'd sidled to a tray of necklaces she planned to put on sale after the holidays and studied them. Because they were devoid of price tags, he would have no idea of their worth, so she'd be able to fudge her cost and give him a great deal.

He inspected a gold-wrapped necklace studded with pink tourmalines, and Claire smiled inside. The man definitely had an eye for the best of her work. "Have you found something you like?" she asked, moving toward the table.

"This is beautiful. The tourmalines are of excellent color and clarity."

She sighed. So much for trying to squeeze a low price past him. "That one is still available. Do you think it would work for one of your sisters?"

"I think it's perfect for Barbara. How much is it?"

Claire frowned. Either her brain had iced over or her imagined lack of oxygen was causing a meltdown, because for the life of her she couldn't calculate the cost of the stones and wire and make it sound sensible.

"How about we get the orders out first? Every item has to be checked before packing, so you can inspect each one. If you find an already-sold design for your other sister or mother, I can whip up something similar tonight. We can ship everything via second-day air, and your relatives will have their gifts in time for Christmas."

He returned the necklace to the tray. "That sounds like a plan." He glanced at the pile of boxes. "Now show me where the orders are and tell me what to do."

Hugh conceded that Claire had been correct about the job. He'd run the stairs over a dozen times, unfolded and taped boxes, and wrapped like a madman for hours, while his neighbor had printed labels and packing slips, slid them into plastic mailing sleeves and pasted the sleeves on the cartons. The stack next to the front door was so huge it consumed the entryway and inched into the living room, threatening to cover a side table.

He'd found gifts for his mother and both sisters while he'd packed and written the invoice numbers down, so Claire could look up the designs and re-create them. He'd also sneaked a peek at the prices, though he could have gone online at home and seen them firsthand.

Ms. St. Germaine charged a pretty penny for her jewelry.

Not that it wasn't worth it. She used quality stones and her creations were intriguing. While they worked, she'd told him that she tried to vary her pieces so that each one was different from the next. When people bought her products, they believed they were getting one-of-a-kind designs, and she wasn't about to disappoint them.

He admired her determination and integrity, as well as her smiling face and cheerful disposition. He also admired her wit and good humor. But most of all—and Hugh would never admit this to her because he knew from listening to his sisters that women detested being treated as objects—he admired her appearance.

He loved the way her hair caught the last rays of afternoon light as it shone through the window near her computer and turned her curly shoulder-length mass an earthy palette of browns and burnished gold. He enjoyed watching her blue eyes sparkle with mischief when she made a particularly clever comment. And he really liked the way her dimple flirted with her cheek when she smiled.

Then there was her body. The entire time he'd worked, he'd done nothing but think about her curvy hips and how they would feel nestled against him, as they'd been that morning. He'd daydreamed about the silk of her hair and how it would feel when he sifted through it with searching fingers; imagined the weight of her generous breasts filling his palms and swelling to his kiss, the nipples hardening under his tongue.

Hugh frowned. Undoubtedly, that was the reason she had so many men lurking on her doorstep. Lucky for him, Claire was absorbed in the printer as it spewed the last of her packing slips, and didn't notice what his wayward thoughts were doing to his anatomy. He only hoped by the time they were through, he'd be more in control and she wouldn't notice.

"All finished," she said, spinning in her desk chair with the final paperwork in hand.

He shifted the pile of boxes in his arms so they dipped below his waist. "Great, the orders are ready." He heard the familiar rumble of a UPS truck. "I'll slip those in the mailing sleeve and glue them in place if you want to take care of the driver."

She stood and headed for the foyer, chirping out a cheerful "thanks" as she sauntered past, and he hurried to finish with the cartons. Then he waited while she bantered with the delivery man. When the driver teased her about the amount of business she gave his company, Hugh had to stop himself from jumping to his feet and escorting the fellow none-too-gently to his truck.

They said good-bye, and he breathed a sigh of relief. Maybe Claire would agree to have dinner with him, so he could ask her about the frogs that had called her to his attention in the first place. He was just about to issue the invitation when the doorbell rang. She opened it and the UPS man handed her a package.

"I almost forgot this was on the truck. You have to sign for it, so it must be pretty special."

Claire did as he asked, then gazed at the box. That's when her mouth formed an O of surprise. "There are air holes punched in the top."

"Well, so there are," said the driver. "I didn't notice. Maybe it's a plant of some kind."

"Do you have a list that gives the contents?"

"Sorry, no. Guess you'd better open it before it turns brown or does whatever plants do when they bite the dust." He checked the sheet again.

"We got it here in twenty-four hours, as requested, so we're not liable if anything's wrong."

"I understand. Good-bye." She stared at the box as she closed the door. Then she walked slowly into the living room and sat on the sofa, where she continued to gaze at the package as if it were a ticking time bomb.

Soon her complexion paled and her eyes glazed over. For a second, Hugh thought she needed a glass of water or something stronger. He stood and flipped on both table lamps, hoping to brighten her mood as well as the interior of the house.

Then the oddest thing happened. The box moved on her lap.

Claire let out a little scream, but she kept her hold on the package.

Hugh blinked. Plants were living things, but they didn't bounce of their own accord, and whatever was in that box had. He took a step toward her, and the noise stopped him cold. A sound very much like a snore rose from the package.

Claire shrieked a second time, and quickly set the box on her coffee table.

"Maybe you should open it?" His brain was trying to process the sound when he heard it again. Hugh shook his head, because he couldn't believe his ears. People didn't send live frogs through the mail, at least, not ordinary people, but he'd bet a year's pay he'd heard a croak. He sometimes received deliveries of certain species for the school, but those were set up through the university, and involved quite a bit of paperwork and special packing.

After a moment, she raised her eyes. "Um, well. Do you have that list of jewelry you want to buy?" She cleared her throat. "Give it to me, and I'll start work tonight."

The box moved again, sliding six inches farther on the table.

"Claire, there's a frog in that box."

He reached to pick up the package, and she whisked it away. "A frog? Of course it's not a frog. Why would someone send me a frog?"

He raised a brow. "Maybe it's meant to be a companion to those I've noticed hanging out on your steps."

"Frogs? On my steps?" She shot him a glare. "You must be mistaken."

"I know what I've seen, and I've seen frogs. Lots of them. At least ten in the past few months."

She scowled, clutching the box to her midsection. "Have you been spying on me?"

"Of course not. It's just that I couldn't help but notice." From the look in her eyes, he didn't dare mention the men he'd spotted, as well. She'd probably think he was stalking her. "I've merely been wondering about them. It's cold, and they tend to go dormant in this weather."

She chewed on her full lower lip, and Hugh almost lost his train of thought. Questioning her about all he'd observed was going to be more difficult than he'd first thought. It was evident she was angry at the idea that he'd been watching her, but more than that she seemed shocked and confused over the contents of her package.

Why did the topic of frogs upset her so?

He leaned forward, but couldn't read the return address. "If it's from south of here, I'd imagine the poor creature is freezing. And it may need to eat or drink. If you put it outside, it will probably find a few crickets and a nice warm spot to hibernate in until the spring."

She straightened. "Oh, really. And what are you, some kind of frog expert?"

Hugh raised a corner of his mouth in a grin, hoping to gain her confidence. "Actually, I am."

· 4 ·

Tongue-tied by his answer, Claire swallowed her next comment. Hugh knew about frogs—confessed that he'd seen her so-called visitors littering the porch—and wanted to inspect this one! She had to get rid of him.

Right away.

"I think it's time you went home." The box on

the table took another six-inch jump. *Damn!*

Hugh bent to grab the package. "At least let me see the creature, so I can tell you if it's safe to release it here. It might be better suited to a swamp or stream."

"Don't touch that fro—er—box," she ordered.

He raised his hands in surrender. "All right, fine. But you really need to get whatever's inside out of there. It could be injured or dying. You wouldn't want to kill it, would you?"

Claire threaded her fingers through her hair, pushing the heavy mass behind her ears. None of the other frogs had been sent via UPS. Why had the method of delivery changed? What was different about this one? She swiped her upper lip, embarrassed to find herself perspiring. She was probably red in the face, too. She was a terrible liar. How in the heck was she going to get out of this mess—with a frog *expert*, no less?

"How do you know about frogs?"

"I'm a professor of biology at Georgetown, but my specialty is frogs." Hugh gave a smug smile. "To put it in more scientific terms, I'm a herpetologist."

"Herpawhatagist?"

"Herpetologist. I study frogs. They're my passion."

"You have a *passion* for frogs?" Claire could think of a lot more things to be passionate about. Chocolate, lobster, shoes, chocolate—whoops, she'd already listed that one—good books, classic movies . . .

"I can tell by your sour expression that you have a less than stellar appreciation of amphibians." His deep voice took on an injured tone. "But they're actually fascinating creatures."

The *creature* in the box let loose another boisterous burble, almost as if it agreed with Hugh, and an idea shot to the forefront of Claire's brain. One she hadn't considered until the thing in the box burped. What if the frogs could see and feel and think like a human—before she kissed them? What if, inside their slimy froggy bodies, there was still the mind of a man? A man who could be listening to this very conversation, and when he came to his senses would remember every word?

Claire thought about the eleven frogs she'd already received, saw in her mind each man's dazed expression after she'd returned them to their original state with a kiss. None of them had seemed to be aware of what had happened to them, but who knew what they recalled of their experience when they came fully to their senses?

As if reading her mind, the creature belched a third round of croaks, only this time it sounded as if it was snorting underwater.

"For God's sake, open the package," Hugh said, his voice frantic. "I think it's choking."

Claire tamped down a cry of despair. This could not be happening. If the man—er—frog died, she'd have killed a human being. Sort of.

She pulled the package toward her and broke apart the tape on the sides, then peeled the paper from around the carton. Underneath the brown wrapper was a box covered in smiling Santas and beguiling elves, topped by a big red bow. Thank heaven there were punch holes in the lid.

"It's a Christmas present?" Hugh's voice rose a few decibels. "Someone sent you a frog as a gift?"

"Yes." Claire thought it best she stick as close to the truth as possible. It was going to be hard putting anything over on a—a—frogophile.

"If you ask me, that's one peculiar gift. No one I know makes a practice of sending frogs through the mail—and certainly not for Christmas. I don't count the *Rana catesbeiana* Barbara gave me when I graduated college, because that was a joke. Besides, her frog came in an aquarium."

"Your sister gave you a what?" asked Claire, feeling shell-shocked.

"A *Rana catesbeiana*. The scientific name of the common bullfrog. It's the same genus I've seen on your half of the porch." He peered at the package. "If it wasn't impossible, I'd say I recognize this call, but I must be wrong."

The frogman croaked out another guttural grumble.

"I think you'd better hurry," he warned.

Claire inhaled as she made a decision. Perhaps, if she satisfied his curiosity, Hugh would leave. Then she could go about her usual ritual of bestowing a kiss, handing the guy clothes, and sending him on his way.

"Oh, all right. But I really do have to get to work on the designs you chose. I take it you still want them finished in time for Christmas?"

"I do, but this is infinitely more important than a few trinkets. Please . . . hurry."

Trinkets! Claire huffed at the insult as she tore into the paper, then peeled tape from one edge of the box. Raising the lid, she peered inside as Hugh loomed from above. Two bulging but unblinking eyes stared at them through a smelly nest of damp cotton and straw encased in an open plastic bag.

"Oh, my God."

Hugh whispered the words as if in prayer, sending a chill down Claire's spine. "What?" she whispered back.

"It's *Rana sevosa.*"

Dragging bits of cotton and straw, the frog struggled over the edge of the box and sat like a squat, brown Buddha surveying new territory.

"What is a rana—whatever you said?" She wanted to add, and why is it such a big deal, but knew he would tell her if she was patient.

"The Dusky Gopher Frog."

At just under four inches long, with dark spots on its taupe-colored, slightly bumpy skin, this frog was smaller than the others, but aside from the size and color, it was still a frog. "And how is it different from those *Rana casabas* you talked about a minute ago?"

"Casaba is a type of melon," corrected Hugh. "*Rana catesbeiana* is your everyday, garden-variety frog indigenous to most states in the union. *Rana sevosa* is special. Very special."

His voice wavered and she stared at him. Behind his black-rimmed spectacles, his blue eyes were shining, while his face seemed overcome with awe.

Hugh knew the call of *Rana sevosa* so well, he sometimes heard it in his sleep. Moments ago, he hadn't believed his ears. Now he could barely believe his luck. Without taking his gaze off the frog, he pulled a tissue from a box on the coffee table and polished his glasses. Then he knelt and gently cleaned the amphibian of debris. Holding out his palm, he encouraged the specimen to hop aboard.

Cupping his hand over the handsome fellow, he sat at the end of the sofa and raised it to the light. He needed to study a few photographs and drawings to be certain—he wouldn't be a good scientist if he didn't do his research—but he was 99 percent positive that he held in his hand the frog on his Web site. The frog he'd been searching for.

The one thought to be the extinct Dusky Gopher Frog.

"Who did you say sent him to you?" Hugh leaned forward and set the amphibian back in its box, then added the lid.

"I didn't."

"Does this mysterious frog giver live in the South?"

"New Orleans."

"Ah, that explains it."

"Explains what? Why is it so special?"

"The U.S. Fish and Wildlife Service put the Dusky Gopher Frog on the endangered list in 2001. None have been spotted in Louisiana, one of their few stomping grounds, for ages. A small group existed in Mississippi, but there hasn't been a sighting in several years. Their range is narrow, mainly the river delta. Most herpetologists fear they are lost."

"But not you?"

"I kept hoping they were wrong. I have a Web site for serious students, many of whom reside in Louisiana, and they've been on the hunt for me. Once I verified a sighting by a photo or recording of the frog's call, I planned to take a sabbatical and devote all my efforts to finding a pair. After that, I wanted to breed them or investigate cloning. There's no other way to continue the genus."

"That sounds very noble," said Claire. She

stood. "Right now, it's too much for me to absorb." She gave a half smile. "I really appreciate everything you did for me today. Now, if you'll excuse me, I have things to take care of."

"Where do you intend to house him?"

She glanced around the apartment and shrugged. "I'm sure I have an old fish bowl somewhere . . ."

Standing, he folded his arms. "I can't allow you to keep such a valuable creature without the proper habitat."

Striding past her, he took the stairs to the second floor. She heard him rummaging around overhead and realized he was in her utility closet. Before Claire could go after him, he returned with a clear plastic storage box—the kind in which she sometimes kept shoes—and headed for the kitchen.

"What are you doing?"

"Cleaning this out. I'll need a flashlight, a cup, and a plastic bag or two."

Annoyed, she located the items and set them on the counter. "In case you've forgotten, this is my home."

"But I'm the frog expert." He stormed toward the back door. "Come along, if you wish."

She followed him outside and watched as he inspected the withered flowerbed edging the house. Then he squatted and handed her the flashlight. "Shine that in the border so I can find what I need." He picked up a few moss-covered rocks and set them in the cup, as well as a bit of still-green weed. After turning over a couple of flat pieces of rotting wood, he dropped one in a bag.

Inside, he arranged the treasures in the bottom of the box, added a shallow bowl filled with water, and snapped on the lid. Then he used a knife to punch a few air holes, and carried the container to the living room. After setting the box on the coffee table, he removed the lid and placed the frog and a small pile of straw in its new home.

"There," he stated with pride. "That should do it."

"Fine, you can go now." Claire didn't care that she sounded grouchy or rude. Hugh's involvement with her frog was getting out of hand.

He glanced from the makeshift aquarium to her, and back again. "On second thought, I'm commandeering this amphibian for verification. When I'm through certifying that it is indeed the endangered Dusky Gopher Frog, we can discuss how to proceed."

"Wait!" She trotted after him as he carried the box through her living room. "No! You can't just—"

He stopped at the front door. "In the meantime, I suggest you go on my Web site"—he recited the URL—"and take a good look at the posted information. Read about my work and what a find such as this means to the world."

Before she could say goodnight, he was gone.

Now what? Claire stared at her front door, then glanced at her watch. If Hugh didn't return the frog, her dilemma would become a disaster. She had to kiss that frogman. And soon.

It was six o'clock, so the interfering but well-intentioned gift giver should be home having dinner. She rushed into the kitchen and dialed, only to be serenaded by the same annoying message she'd heard earlier.

"I just received your Christmas gift," Claire ranted without a polite greeting. "What were you thinking, sending an amphibian via UPS? And what possessed you to turn someone into an endangered species? Do you realize you—I—we could go to prison for harboring such a valuable specimen? It's a federal offense to keep an animal the government considers endangered, and according to my sources this one hasn't been seen for years. Where did you find a model for it?"

Now that she'd voiced the questions out loud, she was truly curious. If *Rana sevosa* was extinct, how did the sender even know it had existed?

"Call me as soon as you get this message."

Claire set the receiver in its cradle and dropped into a chair. The frog had been sent next-day air, which meant the meddler would know it had arrived today. Claire had no doubt her calls were being ignored on purpose.

She went to her living room and stood in front of her computer. The screen saver changed to a fresh view, one of several island paradises, and she thought maybe, instead of a new car, she should spend the money she'd collected today on a relaxing trip to a spa or Caribbean hideaway for Christmas. Any place would be fine, as long as it didn't have frogs.

I suggest you go to my Web site and take a look at the posted information. Read about my work and what a find such as this means to the world.

Hugh's parting comment sliced through her panic. Claire pinched the bridge of her nose between a thumb and forefinger, acknowledging she was in the midst of a huge mess. If she didn't get the frog back from Hugh, she'd be condemning a human being to a lifelong diet of flies. The poor guy probably had a family, a job—maybe even a girlfriend. She had no idea what criteria was used when the men were chosen, but they must have had lives of their own to live.

From the sound of Hugh's reverent tone, *Rana sevosa* would reside in the lap of luxury. He'd probably spend his days in a fancy aquarium eating the most succulent of insects while he basked in scientific glory. And if Hugh found a female, he'd enjoy the rest of his froggy life making more little *rana-bananas* to repopulate the bayou.

But that didn't justify a human remaining a frog.

She gazed out the window. In the light cast by the glow of a corner streetlamp, she saw fresh snow falling in big fat flakes. Hugh certainly wouldn't hurt the frog, and she couldn't go over there and demand its return without a good reason. At least, not tonight when he was so volatile on the subject.

Would it be terrible if her visitor spent one more night in his present condition? Would twenty-four more hours be such a big deal? Maybe Hugh could learn something about the frog, take a few cell or DNA samples and use them for cloning, whatever he needed to preserve *Rana sevosa*. Surely, he planned to give her the frog tomorrow?

Her mind made up, she figured she'd better go online and check out his website. The more she knew, the better armed she'd be to plead her case. The site responded quickly, and she noted it was concise and professional with the topic on the opening page spelled out in large bold letters: WHERE IS RANA SEVOSA? THE SEARCH FOR THE DUSKY GOPHER FROG.

Beneath the heading was a picture of Dr. Hugh Burton, looking very much like a serious teddy bear as he held up a drawing of what she assumed was *Rana sevosa*. Underneath the photo was a list of Hugh's impressive credentials, ending with his Ph.D. in biology and a roster of the papers he'd published. The length of the list suggested he was a master in his field.

The next page had a close-up colored drawing of *Rana sevosa* in one corner and a grainy photograph in the other. It was obvious from the photo's poor quality that the frog hadn't had its picture taken in a long time. Claire was far from an expert, but had to admit that from what she remembered, her guest closely resembled the specimen in question.

Leaning back in her chair, she took mental stock of her options. There would be ramifications, no matter what she did, but her first course of action was convincing Hugh to return her frog. Then, when it was gone, she'd have to come up with a reason for its disappearance. No way would he believe the truth, even if she told it. And he'd never forgive her if she confessed she'd returned it to Aunt Polly, so the woman could put it back where she'd found it. In fact, he'd probably travel to New Orleans and confront her aunt, which meant he would learn all about Happily Ever After and Polly's unconventional lifestyle.

No matter what she finally decided, he'd have every right to report both of them to the endangered-species police.

She scanned the site and read a few of the reports sent from Hugh's team of amateur frogophiles. Several seemed to be as passionate about amphibians as her neighbor, going so far as to detail sightings of other possibly endangered frogs they'd encountered on their search. Many of them expressed their anticipation at being the first to find the Dusky Gopher Frog so they could meet their idol, the renowned Dr. Burton, in person.

Claire glanced at the clock and realized it was late. She hadn't eaten since the cocoa and cookies that afternoon. She walked to the kitchen and made a second call to Aunt Polly, but received the same message-machine greetings. Sighing, she nuked a Lean Cuisine. After that, she had to get started on Hugh's jewelry order. He had the frog, which guaranteed it would be safe for a little while longer.

Maybe things would look better in the morning.

· 5 ·

Claire woke early and ate a quick breakfast, then phoned Aunt Polly at home and Happily Ever After, prepared to give the woman a stern lecture for ignoring last night's messages. Instead of reaching Polly or an apprentice, she got the standard recording from both machines.

Frustrated, she went to her studio and put the

finishing touches on Hugh's jewelry, intent on delivering the order in person. She'd feel better once she saw for herself that the frogman was alive and croaking. She boxed the items, a rose quartz bracelet and one of jade, and the tourmaline necklace, and smiled in satisfaction. The quartz bracelet was part of a batch she'd planned to advertise on sale after Christmas, which allowed her to pass the savings to her neighbor. The jade was a new design, so she would charge him only for the materials, while the tourmaline necklace would be a thank-you for the previous afternoon's assistance.

She'd wrestled with her conscience throughout the night and vowed to do everything in her power to convince Hugh to return the frog, including stealing the darned thing, even if it meant getting reported to the authorities. Once she did the humane thing—kissed *Rana sevosa* into a man and sent him packing—she'd insist Aunt Polly tell her where she'd found the model for frog number twelve, and give the information to Hugh. What he did with it was his business, and they would be even.

After stacking the boxes in a gift bag, she opened the inside door and surveyed a scene even more tumultuous than yesterday. The storm had returned, blowing fat flakes in a blinding swirl of white, and sending wintry chills up her spine. Stepping back into the foyer, she gazed at the thick blanket of snow in the front yard. So much for her plans.

It would be impossible to get a cab dispatched in this weather, not to mention how insensitive it would be of her to send an unsuspecting stranger away without shoes, socks, or coat. He had to live near Aunt Polly, because he'd been shipped UPS from the store. That meant another bus ticket, but she'd have to drive him to the station, which was not an option given the poor condition of her car. And she couldn't ask her neighbor for any more favors. Who knew where the conversation would lead on the ride?

Without warning, Hugh appeared on the other side of her storm door and smiled through the frosted pane. "Good morning."

"I was just coming to see you," she said over the moaning wind. Suspicious of his cheerful greeting, she opened the door a few inches and stuck out the bag. "Your jewelry is finished. Where's my frog?"

He raised a checkbook. "I want to pay you."

"Not now." Claire shook her head. "First I want to see *Rana sevosa*."

His smile faded. "I'm still studying him, but I promise you, he's quite comfortable. I want to make sure he's thriving, before I consider returning him."

She frowned at the word *consider*, while his concerned expression turned to one of panic.

"You're not thinking of sending him back, are you?" he asked.

"I haven't made up my mind what to do with him, but I think it's important he be with his family."

"Family?"

"You know—his friends—pondmates—whatever you call the group of frogs he lives with." She gave herself a healthy mental kick for sounding like such a dope. "Just don't grow too attached."

"Attached?" He grimaced. "Might I remind you that *Rana sevosa* is not a pet but an endangered species. I'll count myself lucky if I locate one or two others, let alone a group of pondmates. His singular appearance is of great environmental and biological significance. It's your duty as a citizen of our planet to see to it he's preserved and studied. I need to reach the person who gave him to you. I have a dozen questions to ask and I—"

"I'm sorry. I can't let you speak to Aunt Polly. She's—she's frail—and bedridden. You'd only upset her."

"An aging aunt sent you a frog? You must be joking."

Claire pretended she hadn't heard him, and held out the gift bag a second time. "It's freezing. Why don't you take this inside and look over each item to make sure it's what you want. If you're satisfied, you can drop off a check and my frog at the same time. Give me the addresses, and I'll call for a pickup. I'll even put the shipping charges on my account."

As if oblivious of the frigid temperature and falling snow, Hugh wedged a foot onto the jamb. "Are you offering me a bribe?"

"Excuse me?"

"Because it won't work. *Rana sevosa* belongs to the world. I don't want to go to the authorities about this, but—"

Claire thrust the bag into his hands and pulled on the door, hoping to nudge his shoe out of the way. "I resent your accusations, Dr. Burton. If you'll excuse me—"

"I'll buy him from you." His jaw clenched. "I'll give you whatever you ask—money is no object."

"Now who's offering a bribe?" Claire snapped, wounded by his suggestion of attempted amphibian payola.

Snow eddied and whirled around him, the flakes glistened on his dark hair. His blue eyes were pleading behind his glasses, his mouth set in a grim line. "I'm sorry, I don't mean to be insulting. I merely want you to understand how serious this situation is."

"Believe me, I do understand," she muttered. "I'll have to think about it. Come over after supper tonight and we'll talk." She stopped before closing the door. "And bring my frog!"

* * *

Hugh gazed into his bathroom mirror. Freshly shaved and showered, he'd tamed his wavy hair and dressed in his nicest pair of jeans and best sweater. He couldn't remember the last time he'd gone to this much trouble to impress a woman. Then again, this was his first real attempt at seduction, so he wasn't quite sure of the proper steps, but he was going to give it the old college try.

He detested the idea of taking advantage of Claire St. Germaine, but he really didn't have another choice. Not if he wanted to get to the bottom of this little intrigue. He'd posted several alerts on his Web site asking his dedicated scouts to scour every nook and cranny of the last known Louisiana haunt of the Dusky Gopher Frog. Alas, he'd received no positive response. As a scientist, it was his duty to discover the origin of this particular *Rana sevosa*. At the very least, he should be able to convince her to let him *borrow* the frog so he could plot a course to preserve its future.

If he had to whisper sweet nothings and ply her with a bit of alcohol on that journey, so be it.

Not that it would be a chore to lure the lovely Claire to his side. Since the moment he'd seen her, he'd thought the woman perfect. The time they'd spent together yesterday had only confirmed she was his dream girl personified. He loved everything about her, from her sun-streaked curls to her oh-so-kissable mouth, to her captivating female form. He even admired the stubborn loyalty she showed toward her ailing aunt. If the quirky woman—and he meant quirky in the nicest way possible—was dying, the Dusky Gopher Frog might be the last gift she ever sent her niece. He only hoped Claire would return his tender feelings once they ironed out their differences over *Rana sevosa*, and let him into her world.

Prepared to plead his case, Hugh gazed at the obviously contented frog, sitting with its eyes closed as if contemplating the meaning of life. He gathered the shoebox, a couple of photos from his desk, the bottle of merlot he'd been saving for a special occasion, and another of exceptionally fine chocolate liqueur, and headed outside. Thinking red wine might not be her libation of choice, he prayed the dark, creamy concoction would be enough to entice Claire into seeing things from his perspective.

He smelled the pungent aroma of wood smoke mixed with the crisp scent of fresh snow, and noted the storm had gentled to a whisper. Balancing the box, bottles, and photos, he rapped on her door.

Claire heard Hugh's knock and steeled herself for the assault. She hated arguing for any reason, but she couldn't allow him to sway her, no matter how clever his powers of persuasion. She had to

turn the frog back into a man as soon as the
weather allowed. In the meantime, she'd pretend
to listen to his logic. Aunt Polly had avoided her
calls all day. Once she got the frustrating woman
on the phone, she would pass to Hugh the location of other Dusky Gopher Frogs, thus ending
her dilemma.

Stepping aside to let him in, she noted that
he'd brought gifts, as well as *Rana sevosa*. She accepted the shoebox and gave her frogman a thor-
ough inspection, then set the container on the
coffee table, pleased to see that he looked pretty
much as he had yesterday. Unfortunately for her
libido, Hugh looked even better. Instead of a
flannel shirt, he wore an oatmeal-colored sweater
that hugged his broad shoulders and tapered to a
nicely rounded backside encased in tight-fitting
jeans. Darn, but the man made her weak in the
knees, even when he had the upper hand.

He held out two bottles of what she assumed
was wine. "I thought we might celebrate your
aunt's find, before we come to terms on our mutual friend."

"That's a nice idea, but I don't drink much."
She walked through the living room into the
kitchen, and he followed. "Red wine gives me a
headache."

"Then you're in luck, because the other bottle
contains a delicious chocolate liqueur that

shouldn't have that effect. Do you have a corkscrew?"

Rummaging in a drawer, she pulled out an old-fashioned wine opener and passed it to him. Moments later, they sat side by side in front of the fire, each gazing at the frog-quarium while tasting their drinks. Hugh finished his glass of wine in a few swallows, while Claire was pleased to find her own cordial infinitely more appealing than red wine. If she weren't in this pickle, it would be so easy to lose herself in the romantic moment and allow things to develop with Hugh.

She gave him a sidelong glance, and wondered what he would do if she leaned into his arms while she ran her fingers across his mile-wide chest and raised her lips to his. Staring into the roaring blaze, she drifted with the sensual thought . . .

Hugh cleared his throat—several times—before he said, "Would you mind if I showed you exactly how I know this is *Rana sevosa*?"

Claire sighed at his patient tone. She'd expected him to bring up the frog, but not in so hesitant or benign a manner. If it were her, she'd probably be demanding and rude. Why did he have to be such a nice guy?

"I guess it can't hurt." She drained her glass. "As long as you remember who he belongs to."

Hugh handed her a series of photos. "I want

you to take a look at these and compare. I'm sure this is the Dusky Gopher Frog, but it's important you're certain, as well."

She studied the pictures while he removed the frog from the box. Cupping it in his palm, he pointed out the similarities between the specimen in the photos and the creature in his hand. After a minute, she agreed with his assessment, and he returned the amphibian to its home.

"I've been thinking about our predicament, and I'd like to suggest a compromise." He refilled her glass and handed it to her. "Will you let me *borrow* the frog?"

Claire chewed on her lower lip, then took another swallow of her drink, hoping to avoid a final answer on the question. "This is really good. I never knew alcohol could taste so—so chocolaty."

"I'm glad you like it." He inched closer to her side. "I promise I won't do anything to him without your permission. You can even come to my lab at the university and watch me run a few tests if you want. With school closed, I'd welcome your assistance."

"I don't know what to say." She finished the second glass of liquor. "Aunt Polly sent me the frog for a reason. I doubt she meant for it to be used as a—a science experiment."

"An experiment? If that's what you think, you're mistaken. I merely want to preserve the species. *Rana sevosa* will be treated royally. I plan to study him, and try to find him a mate. If you arrange for me to speak to your aunt, I'd only talk to her for a moment. It's imperative I learn where she found him."

Overwhelmed by his passionate outburst, Claire poured another glass of the decadently sweet liquid, and took a long swallow. She hadn't lied when she'd told Hugh she didn't drink much, but this stuff was yummy. Unfortunately, the effects of the alcohol went straight to her head, clouding her judgment and numbing her tongue.

"I promise to be gentle with her. You could accompany me to Louisiana, and ask the questions for me."

Had Hugh just said he wanted to go to New Orleans to visit Aunt Polly? With her? She appraised her nearly empty glass. How many drinks had she finished? The warmth creeping into her cheeks set her to quivering. The cozy fire heated her on the outside, while the liquor seared her from within. Or was it the touch of Hugh's hand on her arm, and the way his eyes bored into her, as if they could see into her very soul, that caused her to burn from somewhere deep inside?

Feeling light-headed and strangely out of control, she gazed at her imprisoned visitor. His froggy lips drew back in a grin. Then he winked one amphibious eye.

Good Lord, what was happening to her common sense?

"I—um—I'll need to think about it." *I need to think about a lot of things,* Claire lectured herself. Like how quickly Hugh Burton had come to be a part of her life. He'd been gallant and charming on yesterday's ride, then witty and kind while he'd helped package her orders. Right now, even with the problematic frog between them, she was falling under his spell. Thanks to Aunt Polly's gift, she also knew he was a dedicated scientist with an abiding concern for the world's endangered species. He was exerting pressure in a firm yet patient way, even though finding *Rana sevosa* was a high point of his career.

A girl could do a lot worse than fall in love with a guy like Hugh. He was the perfect Prince Charming.

Swiveling in her seat, she came face to face with him. Gazing at her as if she were a precious jewel, Hugh plucked the empty glass from her trembling fingers and placed it beside his on the coffee table. Slowly, ever so slowly, he leaned into her until his lips brushed hers in a soft caress. When she didn't retreat, he deepened the kiss, taking her to a wondrous place she'd never been before.

Claire felt lost when he broke away. "What—what are you doing?"

"Kissing you." His brow furrowed. "Am I doing it wrong?"

"No. Not at all."

"I can do better. I just need a bit of practice." Cupping her jaw in his hands, he bent forward. Teasing and nibbling, he devoured her mouth as if he wanted to suck the chocolate from her lips. "How was that?"

Hugh's eyes sparkled like sapphires in the firelight, and Claire realized he'd removed his glasses. She'd been so absorbed in their embrace, she'd forgotten to breathe. She tingled from head to toe, as if coming awake from a long sleep. Was this how the frogmen had felt when she kissed them?

She smiled at him. "Wonderful."

Hugh's groin tightened as he focused on Claire's mouth. More than anything, he wanted to work through this barrier between them. At first, he thought it was all about the Dusky Gopher Frog, but one taste of her tempting lips adjusted his thinking. *Rana sevosa* meant nothing if she wouldn't be in his life to share the discovery. Her aunt had somehow found this frog, which gave him hope there were more. Instead of waiting for scouts to find them, he'd take that sabbatical and invite Claire to join him. She could stay with her aunt, care for the woman in her final days, while he staked out the swamp and waited for his quarry.

He stood and drew her into his arms. "I still want to find a way to make things work with you and *Rana sevosa*, but not tonight. Right now, I can't think of anything but making love to you until morning."

She nodded and his heart soared. Clasping her hand, he led her up the stairs to her bedroom. Stopping in the doorway, he kissed her, then raised her chin with his thumbs. "I have a confession to make."

Her eyes fluttered open.

"I've watched you since you first moved in, dreamed about getting you into bed. Does that offend you?"

Claire wrapped her hands around his wrists. "You have been spying on me."

He grinned at her surprised expression. "If you call peeking out the front window every time I heard the sound of your door or listening to your laughter through the wall spying, then yes. I guess I have been. That's the reason I noticed the frogs and the men on your side of the porch."

"The men?"

The curiosity was killing him, but Hugh refused to grill her about her past affairs, if that was what they were. "I don't want to know anything more about either of them. I'll abide by your decision regarding your aunt and *Rana sevosa*, no matter what it might be."

"I never slept with any of them."

One corner of his mouth hitched in a grin. "The frogs or the men?"

She poked him in the chest with her fist. "Very funny."

He kissed her forehead. "It wouldn't matter if you had."

Arms entwined, they walked to the bed and undressed between hushed words and tender caresses. Finally, Hugh pulled back the sheet, climbed in beside Claire, and held her close. She turned in his arms and nestled a knee between his thighs.

"Is that another icicle, Dr. Burton?" she asked, wrapping her hand around his shaft.

"It's the state in which I continually find myself whenever I'm within ten feet of you. Damned embarrassing, if you ask me." He shaped a breast in his hand and leaned down to capture the nipple in his mouth.

"The last thing I want is for you to be uncomfortable." She moaned, arching against his lips. "What do you think we should do to make it melt?"

"Friction." He ran his mouth to her other breast. "And heat. Lots and lots of heat."

"Hmm. Perfect." Claire opened her legs and he covered her with his warm body, filled her with his length, encompassed her in his love.

She shuddered as he began to thrust inside of her. Moving as one, they danced in a rhythm as old as time. Hugh called her name, and she answered. He sighed and she clutched him to her breast.

An urgency built inside of Claire, until she thought she would fly off the mattress. Bucking under him, she tensed as the climax rippled through her body.

Hugh felt her release and plunged into her again, driving them on until the world faded and there was nothing in their hearts and minds but each other.

· 6 ·

Claire woke to brilliant sunshine spilling across the foot of her bed. A dusting of flurries blew past the window and she spied the tops of the trees, their bare branches glittering with ice and snow. She had no idea of the time and didn't care. She'd spent the most wonderful night of her life with a man who made her feel cared for and special.

She had dated plenty of Mr. Maybes in her twenty-nine years, and bedded enough to know the Mr. Rights were in short supply, so she'd decided not to rush headlong into any more relationships.

Last night with Hugh had changed everything. He'd been strong yet gentle, and in complete control while allowing her to lead them on a wild ride that fulfilled her every fantasy. She now knew the geeky impression he first gave was a cover for the intelligent, witty, and sensitive man she was half in love with. A man with whom she could easily imagine sharing the rest of her life.

Sighing with contentment, she nestled in the tangle of Hugh's muscular arms and raised her eyes to study him. Sound asleep, with his dark hair tousled and his breathing even, she marveled at his calm, steady exterior. They'd made love twice, and the second time had been even better than the first. He'd been a generous partner, the kind who made sure a woman's needs were met before he saw to his own.

Smug in her musings, she smiled. He'd lived up to her dream of the perfect man, and then some. She had found her Prince Charming and, contrary to Aunt Polly's meddling, had done it on her own.

She eased from his embrace, slipped into her robe, and walked across the room to peer outside. The snow had stopped and the roads looked clear. Children walked to school while cars puttered down the street, telling her the world was awake and ready to begin the day.

She took a quick shower and dressed in comfy clothes, then shut the bedroom door and headed downstairs. After starting coffee, she went to the living room. The fire had burned to embers, their empty glasses and Hugh's horn-rims were still on the table, and the makeshift aquarium holding the Dusky Gopher Frog was exactly where they'd left it.

This was the chance she'd been waiting for. She could kiss the frogman, hustle him into a cab, and send him to the bus station with enough money for a ticket to New Orleans, then phone her aunt and find out what the woman knew about *Rana sevosa*. She'd give Hugh the information over breakfast. If he asked her again to go with him to Louisiana, she'd say yes, and stay with Polly while he mounted his search.

There was just one teensy problem. If she and Hugh were to have a relationship, Claire didn't want to start the journey with a lie. She had to come up with something believable when he asked about the missing amphibian.

She mulled over her choice of answers, and realized there weren't many that made sense. She could say nothing and act surprised when he found the shoebox empty, or admit she'd set the frog free and wait for the fallout. Or she could simply tell him the truth.

Polly St. Germaine was Claire's father's great aunt from New Orleans. Her business, an eclectic mix of voodoo, hoodoo, and witchcraft, specialized in matchmaking. As an aside, she also sold charms with ready-made spells for prosperity, good health, and a few additional worldly wishes, but the ones promising a love match were by far, according to Polly, her biggest sellers.

Claire had met the woman a handful of times, but on her last visit to Louisiana, about three years ago, she and Polly had gotten along so well they'd begun to write each other with regularity. When Claire launched her handcrafted jewelry business on the Internet, Aunt P had been her first customer. Her order for necklaces, earrings, and pendants set with semiprecious stones had given Claire enough money to tide her over until sales started rolling in. Thanks to her aunt, she was on her way to a six-figure online business.

Claire was horrified when she'd learned that she was the latest victim of her aunt's matchmaking shenanigans. Cupid Aunt P was not. She envisioned her doddering relative questioning each presentable young man who came into her store to make sure they were suitable before she cast her spell. The poor chumps probably never knew what hit them.

Claire thought about her sister Marie. Wed for six years to Robert, they had two children and another on the way. They'd met through Polly, and seemed happy enough, but how could they be certain it was love when they'd been introduced by an aunt who was also a talented witch? What if it was magic that kept them together, and not a melding of their hearts?

If her parents were still alive, she'd value their

opinion on the matter, but they'd been killed in an automobile accident years ago. Claire had no one but Marie and a few shirttail relations to call on when she'd decided to study her aunt's success rate. Though everyone in her family raved about Polly's skills, they'd also confessed they had no idea if their marriage was the result of a spell or true love. She remembered telling them she had every intention of meeting the right man someday, but she was going to do it on her terms—not through magic.

And now it appeared she'd done it.

She had found Hugh without any help from Aunt P. They'd met because he'd been gallant enough to help her in the storm. Last night, before they'd slept together, he'd said she meant more to him than the Dusky Gopher Frog. If he'd been honest, he would accept whatever explanation she gave.

She had to act quickly to break the final spell. All it would take was one kiss, and she'd be free. The last thing she needed was to have Hugh skip downstairs and find a naked man in her living room. And the longer she waited, the harder it would be to keep the frog sequestered so she could get the turnabout done.

She walked to her coat closet, found the last pair of sweatpants and lone T-shirt, and carried the clothing to the sofa. Sitting in front of the shoebox, she unsnapped the lid, and removed the frog. Balancing it on her palm, she gave *Rana sevosa* a final once-over.

Staring, she cocked her head. There it was again—that odd froggy grin. And that knowing wink.

Stop it. You're letting this entire episode drive you crazy. Just do what you have to and be quick about it.

Puckering her lips, she sucked in a breath, leaned forward and placed her mouth on the frogman's head.

"Good morning."

Claire jumped a foot and the frog jumped with her. Flying from her hands, it landed with a little plop and hopped madly across the room and straight under her computer desk, taking her hopes for a fast solution along for the ride.

She placed a shaking palm on her chest; her eyes darted from Hugh to the workstation and back to him. "Oh, my God, you scared me to death." She inhaled several deep breaths. "What possessed you to sneak down the stairs and—"

"I wasn't sneaking. I made enough noise to wake the dead, or so I thought." Hugh's mouth stretched into a grin. "Were you doing what I think you were doing?"

"I don't know." She folded her arms. "What do you think I was doing?"

"Kissing *Rana sevosa*," he said with a chuckle.

She spun on her heel, sidled to her desk, and dropped to her hands and knees. "Don't be silly. I was merely . . . admiring him. Why in the world would I kiss a frog?"

Hugh trotted to the coffee table and picked up his glasses, then joined her under the computer station. "Oh, I don't know. Maybe you were hoping he'd turn into a prince?"

Claire peered into the cubbyhole to hide her expression of dismay. If only he knew. "That is ridiculous." She scooted back and let him take the lead. "Do you see him?"

"No, but he can't have gone far." He crawled out and rose on his knees to face her. "By the way, if you're in the market for a Prince Charming, I know where you can find one at a very reasonable cost."

He leaned into her and clasped her upper arms. "Last night was unbelievable, Claire. It's important I tell you how much it meant to me." Hugh tilted his head and kissed her.

She melted into the embrace and succumbed to the thrill of his touch. Arching into him, she pressed against his chest and felt his hands roam possessively over her back. His erection prodded her pelvis and she groaned, more than willing to let him take her there on the living room floor. In that moment, she knew she loved him—fully and forever—no matter what happened with the frog.

Suddenly, a croaking burble filled the air.

Hugh gazed into her eyes and smiled as if he knew what she was thinking. "I guess we'd better find him."

She blinked. "Him?"

"The Dusky Gopher Frog. The direction of his call tells me he's moved to a new location." Returning to his hands and knees, he peeked under the sofa, then crawled to the picture window and checked under the table that held her miniature, potted Christmas tree, then behind the floor-length drapes.

Claire sat on her heels, her mind racing. What the heck had happened? Not just now with Hugh, but with the frog?

She replayed the act in her mind. She'd picked it up and held it, then brushed her lips over its head, exactly as she'd done to all the others. As soon as her mouth made contact, each of the other frogs had regained human form. What was wrong with this one?

Her stomach roiled at the idea that she might have done something to ruin the spell or break the enchantment. Was there a rule she wasn't aware of, one that required she kiss the frogman within a certain time frame or doom him to amphibian servitude forever? It would be just like Aunt Polly to have sent her a frog that needed special handling, and neglect to include the instructions.

She held her hands to her temples. Hugh

crawled to the foyer and she shook her head. Only a minute ago, she'd lost focus and allowed him to distract her. No matter how much she loved him, he was a complication she didn't need right now. She had to find the frog and try again. If that didn't work, she had to get hold of her aunt.

He stood, walked to where she was kneeling, and helped her up. "He's in the house some-where. Maybe I should check the second floor. He might have hopped up the steps while we were occupied. He could be looking for water or—"

"I think you need to leave," Claire said, not meeting his eyes. "All this activity is probably frightening him."

Hugh opened and closed his mouth. "You want me to go? Now?"

"That might be best."

"But *Rana sevosa*—"

"Is mine. I dropped him, so it's my responsibil-ity to find him. Please go."

He frowned. "You're throwing me out?"

"Not exactly." She couldn't tell him she needed to find the frog, figure out what she'd done wrong, turn him into a man, and send him pack-ing, could she? "I'll call you."

Glancing around, Hugh stepped to the coffee table. "I suppose these are for me?"

"What?" Claire zeroed in on the gray sweats

and T-shirt he held in his hands. "Of course not. Why would you think that?"

"Because this is the outfit every man who's left here in the past few months has worn. I assume it's my 'parting gift' for a job well done?"

She stiffened her spine. "I told you I never had sex with those men."

He tossed the clothes on the table. "And I believed you."

"But you don't now."

"I don't know what to believe. I thought we had the beginning of something special. Something real. Now you're acting as if last night never happened and dismissing me without an explanation." He scanned the room. "Even if you're finished with me, there's *Rana sevosa* to consider."

"I can read between the lines, and I resent being called a liar." She jutted her chin. "Need I remind you, that frog is nobody's business but mine."

He arched a brow. "Give me one good reason why I can't speak with your aunt. Explain to me why she sent you an endangered frog, of all things, and tell me why I can't buy or borrow it. I don't care about the men, Claire, though I am curious as to who they were and what, if any, connection they had with those other frogs. I need the Dusky Gopher Frog, but more important, we have a relationship to consider—one I hope will be based on complete honesty and trust."

Claire had no answer for him, so she remained mute.

Hugh stuffed his hands in his pockets and headed for the foyer. "Call me when you find *Rana sevosa.* Until then, we have nothing else to discuss."

The door slammed and Claire felt the jolt all the way to her heart. Closing her eyes, she swiped at a tear. Thanks to her aunt's crazy machinations, she was in danger of losing a man she loved and admired. There had to be a way to save the frog and her relationship with Hugh.

If only she knew what to do.

Hugh had paced the day away, alternately walking to the front door to go to Claire, and checking his Web site for messages from his scouts. He'd even dialed information and tried to find a number for Polly St. Germaine, but had no luck.

Time and again he wanted to kick himself for stomping out in anger. He should have been man enough to respect her wishes and leave as she'd asked, without taking potshots at her integrity or grilling her as if she were a felon.

In truth, he'd been a jealous idiot whenever he thought about the men he'd spied on her doorstep. He'd lied when he said their presence hadn't bothered him. Now that he'd accepted the fact he was in love with Claire, he didn't want her to treat him as she had the others. He wanted her to see him as someone with whom she could share her future.

He wanted her to marry him.

He raked his hands through his hair. His sisters had often said that the true measure of a man was his ability to admit when he was wrong. And Hugh knew he was wrong, big time.

But only about Claire. Not *Rana sevosa*. He refused to reverse his stand on the frog. And if he got back in Claire's good graces, he would convince her of the same.

He tugged on his boots and grabbed his coat. It was past six, but thanks to the holiday season stores were open late. He wasn't going to get any rest until he made things right with her, so he might as well go shopping. He had a mission and he wasn't about to be deterred.

When he was determined, nothing ever stopped him.

Claire sat on her sofa and sipped her morning coffee as she stared at the frogman, who seemed happy resting in a corner of his shoebox. She'd finally found him last night, hiding in her kitchen pantry. How he'd managed to get in there was beyond her, but she swore he'd had a particularly superior grin on his face when she'd taken him out.

That's when she'd called Happily Ever After and her aunt's house, and heard the same message on both machines. The store was closed for the holidays and would reopen after the first of the year. So much for getting any guidance from Polly.

She'd kissed the frog two more times—without success—before placing him in his home and bringing the aquarium upstairs. Terrified he might have some kind of latent reaction to her kiss, she'd set the shoebox on her nightstand in case he returned to his human form and needed her.

This morning, she'd awakened to a series of cheerful sounding croaks, burbles, and snorts. After another froggy lip-lock she'd eaten breakfast, and was now waiting for Hugh to ring her bell. Though fairly certain the next time she spoke with him it would be on a strictly professional level, she knew he'd be over soon.

Sniffing, Claire glared at the frog, as if willing it to turn into a man. Darn Aunt P and her goofy ideas. And darn her for letting the woman get away with her meddling for so long. If she'd put her foot down immediately after the first frogman had appeared, she might not be in this predicament right now—teetering on the brink of losing the one man she truly loved.

The doorbell rang and she sighed. After smoothing her sweater over her hips and tucking her hair behind her ears, she walked to the door and opened it to her neighbor.

"What do you want?" she asked, knowing full well why he was there. He wanted the truth about *Rana sevosa*.

He gave her a lopsided grin. "I want to apologize."

Claire's heart did a happy little tap dance inside her chest as she stepped back to let Hugh in. "I found *Rana sevosa*," she said, just in case she hadn't heard him correctly.

"I figured you would."

"I still haven't spoken with my aunt, so I don't know if it's all right for you to borrow him." If the poor guy was cursed to forever remain an amphibian, he could at least be of some use to the world.

"Not a problem." Hugh walked to the table and glanced at the shoebox. "He looks very happy right where he is. I don't mind waiting, as long as you promise I can have him after your aunt gives her approval."

Not sure she could make that promise, she said hesitantly, "We'll see. Did I hear you say something about an apology?"

Hugh sat on the sofa and gazed at her, his puppy-dog eyes pleading. "Come sit with me. I have something to tell you, and something to ask you, and I'm not sure I can do either with you standing there looking so beautiful and untouchable."

Beautiful? Exhausted, maybe. Definitely confused. And positively curious.

She took a seat next to him. "Are you going to argue with me again?"

"Only if you refuse my apology, or say no after I've made my speech." He focused on her eyes. "I've been rehearsing all morning, so please don't interrupt."

She nodded.

He cleared his throat. "I am sorry I acted like an ass last night. I was wrong to jump to conclusions about the reason you were asking me to leave. I know this business with *Rana sevosa* has upset you, and I'm sorry for exerting pressure. My fondest desire is to come up with a plan that will save the species, and save our relationship at the same time."

Claire furrowed her brow, afraid if she smiled she would break the spell Hugh had woven with his words. "Do we still have a relationship?"

"I sincerely hope so, and you promised not to interrupt."

She nodded again, and he clasped both of her hands in his. "Now for the next part. I love you. I think I've loved you since the second I saw you, but I definitely loved you the moment I fell on you in the front yard during that snowstorm."

Her heart segued into a chest-pounding rumba. "Oh, Hugh, I love you—"

He bent forward and kissed her mouth shut. "I'm going to keep doing that until you stop interrupting, which means we'll never get to the question."

This time, she did smile.

"I know I'm being presumptuous, thinking that one night of mind-blowing sex is enough to ask this of you, but—"

"No, it's—"

He kissed her again, harder. Dazed, she sighed.

"I want to spend the rest of my life with you. Claire, will you marry me?"

Trembling from head to toe, she sniffed back a tear. "Can I talk now?"

He snuggled closer to her. "Please."

She gazed at the frogman, who seemed to be watching with interest, then centered her mind and heart on her very own Prince Charming. Hugh loved her and she loved him, which meant they could sort out anything.

"Yes."

· *Epilogue* ·

It was Christmas Eve, and that morning Hugh had proposed. Claire gazed at the sparkling, emerald-cut diamond on the fourth finger of her left hand. Except for the fact that she had yet to hear from Aunt Polly and *Rana sevosa* was still a frog, her life was pretty much a fairy tale.

Hugh came out of the kitchen with a glass of wine in one hand and a glass of chocolate liqueur in the other, and sat next to her on the sofa. "Have you reached your aunt yet?"

She took a sip of the creamy liquid, then frowned. "No, and I can't imagine where she's gone to with tomorrow being Christmas. I even called my sister, but she hasn't heard from Aunt Polly, either."

"I don't blame you for worrying, especially if the woman is as frail and unwell as you said. Maybe we should plan a trip to New Orleans, so you can look in on her and make certain she's all right?"

Claire set the glass down and snuggled into his chest, ignoring the niggle of guilt she felt for leading him to believe Polly was on her deathbed. "And while I'm visiting her, you can begin a firsthand hunt for a few of our froggy friend's relatives." She poked his stomach. "I know you're dying to get down there."

"I am." He caught her fingers and brought them to his lips. "But it would be more fun if we went together. I promised you I wouldn't hound the poor woman, and I meant it."

Claire tipped her head and kissed the underside of his jaw. She knew he wouldn't harass her aunt, even though he had dreams of finding more Dusky Gopher Frogs. "Have I told you recently how much I love you?"

"Not in the last ten minutes." He kissed her forehead. "I love you, too, more than words can express."

She gazed at *Rana sevosa*, perched placidly in his shoebox. Did the airlines have rules against taking a frog on a plane? If not, she'd cart him to Louisiana, and return him to Polly so she could figure out what had gone wrong and undo the spell.

The doorbell rang and Claire sat at attention. "It's late. Who could that be?"

Hugh grinned. "There's only one way to find out."

Claire stood, walked to the door and opened it to a diminutive older woman with stylishly cut, snow-white hair and a mischievous grin. The woman trundled inside, a large tote bag in one hand and a gaily wrapped package in the other.

"Aunt Polly? What are you doing here?" Claire scanned the street, but didn't see a cab or any means of transportation.

Aunt Polly set down her bag and *tsked*. "I keep forgetting to check the weather reports when I come north. Didn't expect this much snow." She passed the package to Hugh, who had come up behind Claire, then shrugged out of her coat and thrust it at her niece. "I know I should have called, but I was in a rush."

Claire bent to kiss her aunt's wrinkled cheek. "How did you get here? Last we'd heard the storm had closed all the airports." She hung the well-worn mink coat in the closet. "I've been trying to reach you for two days."

Instead of answering, Polly grinned at Hugh and held out her hand. "Dr. Burton, I presume?"

Hugh juggled the package and took her hand. "Yes, and you're Claire's Aunt Polly." He gave Claire a questioning half smile. "Her very frail and bedridden Aunt Polly."

Claire rolled her eyes, muttered, "What can I say? We're a family of fast healers," and trotted after Polly, who had crossed the room, plopped herself in front of the roaring fire, and fixed her gaze on the frog-quarium.

"Would you like something to drink or eat? How long are you staying?" Bending down, she hissed, "We have to talk."

"I know, dear. That's why I'm here." Polly tilted her head toward her special delivery. "Thank goodness my gift arrived in one piece. I've heard horror stories about the way those express companies handle fragile shipments. This creature led me on a merry chase, I tell you."

"I—we—need to know where you found him," said Claire.

"Why, in the swamp, of course, where I go to harvest a few of the ingredients for my shop." She smiled at Hugh, who was still holding the package. "That's for you, by the way. A sort of welcome-to-the-family present."

Hugh set the box on the table and peered at Claire. "I thought you said you hadn't reached her?"

"I hadn't."

"But how does she—"

"It's a long story."

The package went airborne for a moment. Then it croaked. Claire's stomach lurched and she held a hand to her middle. "Aunt Polly—"

"Go ahead," Polly said to Hugh. "Open it."

Claire watched as he tore into the Christmas wrap, gazed in wonder at the air holes punched in the top, and quickly removed the cover. As if one, they both sucked in a breath that was more of a gasp, and chorused, "The Dusky Gopher Frog!"

"And a lovely specimen, she is," chirped Polly. "She'll make this fellow a wonderful mate."

Hugh removed the amphibian from its nest of straw and held it in his palm. "I don't know what to say." He took off his glasses, and inspected the frog. In seconds he was totally engrossed in his gift, and paid no attention to either woman.

Claire took a seat next to her aunt and focused on *Rana sevosa.* "Then he isn't . . . you know?" she whispered.

"If I remember correctly, you were quite emphatic in our last phone conversation," responded Polly in kind. "You told me no more enchanted frogs, so I sent the next best thing."

Confused, Claire gazed at her fiancé, who had collected the shoebox and new frog, and was charging toward the door.

"I'm pretty sure I have something large enough to hold both of them. Have a nice visit," he called over his shoulder just before he disappeared from sight.

"But I don't understand," Claire said when the door slammed. Tears welled behind her closed eyelids. Now she would never know if Hugh loved her for herself, or because of magic. "If you sent the frog, then it must have something to do with the reason Hugh and I . . . we . . ."

"Here now, no tears." Aunt Polly took her hand. "Trust me when I say Dr. Burton loves you for you, dear. The frog was merely a catalyst—a way for the two of you to have something to puzzle over and talk about. If you weren't meant to be together, you wouldn't be wearing that ring right now."

Claire sniffled. "There's no spell—on the frog—or Hugh?"

"On Hugh?" She shook her head. "If there's a spell on Dr. Burton, my dear, you only have yourself to blame. True love is the greatest enchantment of all, and it comes from what you and Hugh have. Please believe me. I had nothing to do with his feelings for you, or yours for him." She patted Claire's hand. "Now, how about we pick a date for your trip? Springtime in New Orleans is perfect for a wedding—and a honeymoon."

Before Claire could answer, Hugh rushed into the foyer and walked to the sofa. "I'm sorry, I was so excited I forgot my manners."

"Not a problem," replied Polly. "I'll just settle in the guest room and go to bed. My niece and I will have time to talk tomorrow." She hoisted her tote bag and flew up the stairs, as spry as a spring lamb.

Claire stood and stepped into his arms. "Hugh, I—"

He drew her into a protective embrace and squeezed. "I don't want to know."

Sighing, Claire gazed into his eyes. "I owe you an explanation, for so many things. Aunt Polly is—unusual."

"I figured as much." He led her to the front door. "What say you spend tonight at my house? I thought you might enjoy helping me put together a bigger aquarium for your aunt's gifts. Oh, and what do you think about a spring wedding in New Orleans?" He cocked his head. "Why are you looking at me like that?"

"No reason, Prince Charming." Smiling, Claire hugged him as if she'd never let him go. "Let's go take care of our frogs."

The Thirteenth Santa

Joanne Pence

It was Christmas Eve and Homicide Inspector Rebecca Mayfield was on a case.

Garlands of silver tinsel and strings of cheery lights decorated the open parking lot of San Francisco's largest mall. In the center of it, while curious shoppers gawked and impatient drivers raged over the loss of parking spaces, yellow crime scene tape surrounded a black body bag. Homicide detectives were put in charge when a suspicious death occurred, and as soon as Rebecca arrived the concerned merchants of Stonestown descended on her, screaming their outrage over the distasteful police presence. A corpse could dampen tidings of good cheer under the best of circumstances, they protested, but to see one at high noon on the day before Christmas would cause shoppers to flee to the competition.

Frankly, surveying the crowd, it didn't appear as if anyone much cared.

Earlier, as she drove to the mall in answer to the SFPD dispatcher's call, she'd worried about the crime scene because of both the day and the location. She hoped the death would have a simple and obvious explanation—bad health, for example. Joggers, in particular, were big on dropping like flies in the damnedest locations.

Given the strange smirks on the faces of the patrol cops who guarded the body, though, she had the bad feeling that there'd be nothing at all normal about this case.

Officer Mike Hennings was a friend from the Taraval Station. Like her, he was single and therefore a prime candidate for holiday duty. They'd dated a couple of times until both realized it wasn't going to work. Maybe it was because as a homicide inspector, she was superior to him. Or maybe something else. She didn't know, and preferred not to analyze it.

"What's so funny, Mike?" She pushed back the sides of her black wool blazer, her hands on the hips of her black slacks as she surveyed the area. The air was crisp, the sky pale blue. Gulls swarmed overhead awaiting discarded food from overfed, harried shoppers. "You guys look ready to split your guts about something."

Officer Hennings's eyes darted toward his partner. His mustache twitched in his effort to keep a straight face. "There's nothing funny, Rebecca. A man's death is never amusing."

His partner sputtered and clamped a hand

over his mouth. Rebecca glared. The more he tried not to laugh, the more his shoulders shook.

"You're right, Mike." Rebecca flipped open her pocket notebook. "A man's death is a grave matter."

Hennings's partner stomped his foot, and doubled over from his struggles.

"Remove the sheet, please," she ordered.

Hennings carefully lifted it away, reversing the direction he'd placed it over the body to cause minimal disruption to any evidence.

Even being a cop, the sight jarred her at first, then calmly, she studied the victim. He lay next to a Dumpster like a bloodied, broken rag doll. Apparently, he'd only been discovered because the scavenger company had come by to remove the overflowing trash bin.

His bones were twisted at unnatural angles and his body seemed oddly squished, as if he'd fallen from a great height. She looked up and then all around. They were in an open parking lot. No buildings were near. There was nothing for him to have fallen *from*.

That was when she realized what had amused the cops. Even before Hennings spoke the words, she could predict what he was going to say. "It looks like"—he began before, like his partner, he sputtered and chuckled—"it looks like he fell off his sleigh."

"He hit the eject button by mistake," his partner blurted.

"Santa the skydiver." Hennings howled.

As the two rolled around with laughter, Rebecca made no reply. It was Christmas Eve, and Santa Claus—red suit, tasseled hat, black boots and all—lay at her feet, dead.

"What the hell! Damn! Shit! Piss!" Richie Amalfi stomped back and forth over an empty parking space, gesturing wildly and bellowing his rage. "I don't believe it!"

Wasn't it bad enough that he, a man who usually saw the light of dawn when he was going to bed, had faced it this morning when he was getting up? Now, the whole reason he'd roused himself at an ungodly hour had blown up. He should have stayed home. Bed, booze, and broads—that's what made life worth living— and his life wasn't going to be worth squat if he didn't solve this present problem.

He ran both hands through his black hair. His eyeballs bulged; his scalp felt like it was being squeezed. Christmas spirit—in a pig's eye! His Christmas spirit was going to get him a .45 through the brain.

That morning at the San Francisco airport he'd picked up his charges one by one as they arrived from different parts of the country. The first was there at seven, the last at ten. The four who'd come in from the East Coast had arrived the night before and stayed at an airport hotel.

Like some little Mary Sunshine googly-eyed social director he'd gathered them all together, waited while they put on their disguises—lifetimes of paranoia didn't die easy—and squeezed them into the twelve-passenger Ford Econoline van he'd borrowed from his *goomba* for just this purpose.

He'd barely left the airport, on 101 North, when the piece of crap van started to cough and shimmy like a TB victim. He pulled off at the nearest freeway exit. It was just a block from a gas station, so he'd told the passengers to wait while he went for help. Nothing wrong with that, was there? At least he didn't have to go far, dressed as he was in an Armani double-breasted pin-striped suit, white shirt with lots of starch in the collar the way he liked it, a red tie, and brand-new wing-tipped shoes.

He'd had to wait about twenty minutes for the station's mechanic to finish up with one customer, even though he'd tried to slip the guy a C-note to ditch the earlier job. It could have been a lot worse, though. The day before Christmas every housewife, Sunday driver, and certifiable moron who should never be allowed behind the wheel of a moving vehicle got on the road to clog it up and call for help when they couldn't figure out how to get the car out of "Park." Bah, hum-

bug! When he saw he'd have to wait for the mechanic, he'd tried AAA, but the phone line was
so jammed up he was left on hold and couldn't
even get through to an operator.

The day had not started out the way he'd expected, to put it mildly.

And it had just gotten worse.

"It's a van!" he yelled at the bored mechanic.
"A huge mother! It can't just disappear."

The mechanic leaned against the tow truck
and chewed on a toothpick. "Maybe this is the
wrong street?" His manner was so lackadaisical,
his tone so condescending that Richie was ready
to take the toothpick and shove it down his
throat.

But then he thought . . . maybe the jerk-off was
right.

Not that he forgot where he left the van, but
that his passengers might have gotten it going
again and test drove it a little way. Yeah, that was
it. Hadn't he heard Joe Zumbaglio used to be
called Joey Zoom because he was so good with
cars? Although, if he was good at fixing them or
at heisting them, he couldn't remember.

Richie rubbed his forehead, then, disgusted,
flung himself into the truck and directed the mechanic which way to go. Then he directed him
another way, and another, until they ended up
driving all over the neighborhood, up and down

side streets, checking out driveways, back alleys, even along the freeway.

Nothing. No van. No passengers. Only a snickering mechanic.

A small bead of perspiration broke out on Richie's brow. *This isn't happening to me.*

They returned to the gas station and he peeled a fifty off his roll of greenbacks for the driver, the whole time trying to figure out what the hell to do next. He checked the time on the pancake-sized platinum Rolex on his arm. It was a little after one. He had plenty of time. All day, in fact. No reason to panic.

He paced. He'd call a cab, go home and get his car. Yeah, that would work. And while he was at it, he'd make a few phone calls. Just call to say hello, right? And for sure, somebody would say to him, "Hey, Richie, you won't believe what I just saw."

It wasn't as if he could actually tell anyone what had happened, not if he wanted to see Christmas Day. San Francisco Bay was too close by, and he was allergic to concrete overshoes.

Homicide was completely, painstakingly empty. Space-vacuum kind of empty. No telephone rang. No memos to read. Not even an impersonal interoffice e-mail wishing her a "happy winter season."

A little sad, a little lonely, maybe a little sorry for herself for being stuck here at work instead of with her family for Christmas, Rebecca leaned back in her chair and put her feet up on her desk. She'd always wanted to do that. She tapped the eraser end of her pencil against her desk, and watched it bounce. Even the new man in her life, Greg Horning from Vice, had gone back to Cleveland to spend the week with his family.

She sighed. "Jingle Bell Rock" went through her head although she didn't like the song. Then a Snickers bar called her name, and she made her third trip to the candy machine. This time, she was out of change and slid in a dollar bill.

The machine burped, and the bill slithered out again. She shoved it in; the device upchucked and spat it back. The junky contraption looked as though it was sticking its tongue out at her, daring her to try once more.

Grabbing the dollar, she returned to Homicide to check her e-mail yet again to see if CSI or anyone else had contacted her. They hadn't.

Not only was Homicide a barren wind tunnel, so was the entire fourth floor of the Hall of Justice. Even the women's bathroom. Heck, she could have used the men's room if she'd wanted. No thank you.

Lieutenant Hollins, head of the division, had given everyone the day off except for Rebecca and her partner. It wasn't that Hollins was being generous; he knew nothing got done on Christmas Eve. Past years, when the staff came in, they fretted about last-minute shopping yet unfinished, then went down to the third floor to drown their sorrows with Christmas cheer in the district attorney's office. The punch was so strong, Rebecca was sure the only fruit in it was an orange dipped twice then discarded. Christmas wasn't the time of year a lot of homicides occurred anyway. That was New Year's. All of Homicide would be on duty next week.

She glanced over at her partner's empty desk. Good ol' Bill Never-Take-a-Chance Sutter. He was a snail on the slow road to retirement. With enough time in to collect a pension, he was merely hanging around until he felt "ready" to officially leave. He'd probably show up around ten o'clock today, leave at three or four. Rebecca wondered if he ever would retire. Generally, a person needed something to retire *from*.

Frankly, it didn't matter if Sutter was here or not. Except for the weird death this morning, all was quiet. Too quiet. She tried to rouse someone from the coroner's office to do the autopsy right away, before they went home or visited the DAs, but so far her calls went unanswered. If no one was willing to do the autopsy today, she'd have to wait until December 26 for the results. Not even the coroner was ghoulish enough to do such a procedure and then go home and carve up a Christmas turkey.

She riffled through the reports of the few eyewitnesses at the mall. Everyone denied seeing or hearing anything. All she could do was wait.

Wait for the fingerprints to run through the system, wait for photos of the victim, wait to use them to scan criminal records for digitized matches. She was tired of waiting, and couldn't help but wonder if the dead Santa had a family who was also waiting—waiting for him to return home.

He looked old, as though he could be someone's grandpa. What kind of Christmas would his family have once they learned he was dead?

She'd never forget the first time she had to inform a family on Christmas that the husband and father wasn't coming home again. It was horrible. She shook off the memory. She was a cop; she knew death didn't stop for holy days.

The California penal code lined the wall behind the secretary's desk in the reception area, kept there both because it was huge and also so it wouldn't get lost in the piles of papers around the inspectors' desks. The way the mall's management had pushed her to shut down the crime scene as quickly as possible had rankled badly. She'd hurried, and didn't believe she'd compromised the investigation by doing so, but she wanted to be able to quote back chapter and verse of the code if she ever again found herself in a similar situation.

Somehow, she didn't think the managers would have been so bossy if the inspector in charge had been one of the guys—Paavo Smith or Luis Calderon, in particular. Nobody told either of them what to do. Then there was Bo Benson, who would have worked out a give-and-take deal, or "Yosh" Yoshiwara, who would have found a way to get what he wanted and had the managers think it was their idea. Bill Sutter would have been a no-show. Only *she* could be pushed around. It was because she was a woman, she was sure—the first and only female homicide inspector in San Francisco.

She'd often been told that she was tough enough for the job. Well, boys, she was about to get even tougher.

Citing the penal code was one way to do it.

She sat scouring the complicated index at the empty secretary's desk when a guy she'd never seen before swaggered in. He was a couple of inches shy of six feet, a hundred-ninety-or-so pounds, and about forty years old. His hair was jet black, a little long and wavy on top, and his brown eyes heavy-lidded, down-turned, and intense.

She pegged him right away. It wasn't the designer threads, the way he carried himself as if he had no fear, or the expensive hardware like the watch that probably cost half her yearly salary. It was those eyes—dark with a certain knowledge and experience—that told her which side of the law this smooth operator walked on. Her instincts twitched and her back stiffened. Slowly, she sat up and put one hand on her lap, out of sight and closer to the 9mm Beretta in her handbag. She nudged the bag with her foot to place it exactly.

"Hey, there," he said. His hands were in his pockets, and he looked over his shoulder a couple of times. "How you doing?" His voice was as mellow and buttery as his brown leather jacket.

"Okay," she said in an even tone. His wasn't the usual greeting for someone coming to this department. "This is Homicide," she pointed out.

"Yeah, I know." He glanced over his shoulder again. "I'm looking for someone. Paavo Smith."

She wondered if it was about a case. The guy looked nervous enough to be about to confess to murder. "Inspector Smith isn't in today. Perhaps I can help you."

His leer was definitely rakish as he said, "I'm sure you can, but not in this. I need a cop. What, is he off today or just out on a case? Can you reach him?"

What an a-hole. She stood up to her full five-foot ten-inch height and looked him straight in the eye. "I'm a homicide inspector," she said coolly. "Now, what is it you want, *sir*?"

He took a step back, hands raised as if to fend off a punch. "Whoa, I didn't know death cops came like"—he waved a hand toward her then quickly dropped it—"uh, yeah. Sorry. I just need a little info but, as you said, Paavo's not in today." He stopped; hard eyes studied her, then a half-smile, half-smirk curled his mouth. "Come to think of it, you probably can help. Why not, right?"

"Right." With cool detachment, she returned the look of scrutiny with one of her own and left him in no doubt that she not only found him wanting, but pictured him in an orange coverall. "Follow me."

She headed into the bureau. "With pleasure," he murmured, his voice deep, smooth, and definitely sexy. Too bad his personality didn't match it.

If cops looked like her when he was growing up, he might have been more inclined to like them, Richie thought as he followed the woman into a big, messy room. Rows of desks were hard to see because of all the paperwork piled up around them on bookcases, file cabinets, and computers.

"You read all this stuff?" he asked as she stopped at a desk and motioned him into a folding aluminum chair.

"No. I use it to cut paper dolls." Her chair tilted, swiveled, and rolled. She leaned back in it comfortably.

He found himself grinning. So, she had a mouth that went along with the face and body. Not that she was his type. Far from it. To begin with, she was a cop. As they say on TV— *fuhgetaboutit*. Then, she was too tall. If she put on high heels, they'd be like Mutt and Jeff. And he liked women who were soft in all the right places. She didn't look the least bit soft anywhere, and way too flat-chested. Big bazoombas, that was his taste. Something a man could get his hands around, so to speak.

She was older than he thought when he first walked in and saw her with one side of her straight blond hair tucked behind an ear, the other side draped down half covering her face as she poured over some thick books. When she looked up at him, her light touch with makeup added to the youthfulness. Her face was shaped like a triangle with widely set smoky-blue eyes and prominent cheekbones tapering down to a small, pointed chin. Most women he knew would give their eyeteeth for bone structure and big eyes like hers. He was surprised she didn't doll up a little more—her white blouse, black slacks, and black boots with low one-inch heels looked like a uniform. But then he reminded himself that she was a death cop. Why bother to wow the corpses, right?

She opened a spiral notebook. "Name?" she

asked, reaching for the green pen at the corner of the desk.

He gripped the cold metal arms of the chair and shifted, trying to find a comfortable way to sit in the hard seat. "Richard Amalfi."

"Amalfi?" She stilled, a sudden question in her blue eyes. "You're related to Paavo's fiancée?"

"Yeah. Angie's a cousin."

"I see." She shut the notebook. "What can I do for you, Mr. Amalfi?"

"You can call me Richie,"—he glanced at the nameplate on her desk—"Rebecca."

"You can call me Inspector Mayfield." She twisted the top back onto the pen.

"Yes, ma'am, Inspector Mayfield, ma'am."

She regarded him like a schoolteacher with a truant.

His voice rumbled over the quiet room. "Look, I need you to help me find some, uh, friends. They're older . . . gentlemen." He wracked his brain, trying to figure out how to best explain this. "They're in a van. Here's the license number." He pulled a piece of paper from his pocket and gave it to her.

"You want me to find this van?" she asked.

What was she, stupid? "Well . . . yeah," he replied, palms upturned, open. "Why else would I be here? Call somebody and then tell me where it is. I got to go pick up the guys. They shouldn't be driving around this city all alone. It's a dangerous place, you know."

Her eyes narrowed. "How long has the van been missing?"

He slid back his sleeve and looked at his watch. "Two goddamn hours." He ran his knuckles against his jaw as he thought of what the guys could have done in that time.

"Two hours? That's not much." She slid the paper with the license number to the corner of her desk. "I'm sure they'll turn up. They're probably sightseeing or something."

"I called everybody I know." His loud voice echoed through the empty office. "Nobody said nothing about them showing up. This morning, I picked them up at the airport, and I'm supposed to see that they get someplace special this evening. That's all. But now, they're gone. And today's important."

"Because it's Christmas Eve?"

That's as good a reason as any. "Yeah, right. And it's up to me," he exclaimed, hands pressed to his chest, "to get them there." *Enough of this!* His impatience was about to boil over. He lowered his voice. "Look, Inspector, it's twelve old guys in a big Econoline." He leaned over her desk, picked up the license number and slapped it in front of her. "Call around. Maybe somebody's seen them."

She tapped the paper against the desktop. "Nobody's going to notice such a thing."

"They might."

"Why should they?"

He clamped his mouth tight. He really hadn't wanted to say, but she was right. There was no reason anyone would notice just any twelve old geezers. That wasn't the case here, though. He supposed he was going to have to tell her, much as he didn't want to. He would have told Paavo, but he trusted Paavo. Paavo was a man; he understood stuff. He didn't know if this skirt would. She acted kind of uptight, come to think of it. "Maybe I can reach Paavo at Angie's," he said, standing.

"And how is he going to help you?" She kept folding and unfolding the license number and seemed almost amused by his predicament. He was getting more pissed off by the second. "Paavo's off duty."

He sat again. She was right, damn it. He looked back over his shoulder—an old habit, and one that gave him time to think. "Just a few phone calls to some dispatchers or something," he said. "Just to ask them if they've seen the van. That's all I need, and I'll take it from there."

She seemed to think for a minute, then nodded. He figured she wasn't exactly rolling in cases. "Okay. If that's what you want. I can make a few calls, but you're just wasting your time and mine. Nobody's going to have noticed."

"Well . . . there's more to it," he admitted.

She waited.

He swallowed. "The twelve old guys I mentioned"—she nodded—"they're all dressed up like Santa Claus."

If anyone had told Rebecca Mayfield this morning that she'd end up in a black Porsche sitting next to a guy who looked and sounded like he stepped out of a bad remake of *Pulp Fiction,* she would have told him he was nuts. If he went on to say that she'd be investigating a Santa Claus corpse who looked flat as a mosquito on a car windshield and was now in hot pursuit of a van with twelve more jolly ol' Saint Nicholases, she'd have called the men in white coats for him.

She glanced at Richie Amalfi, who had just swung to the wrong side of the street to pass a cable car, nearly causing a head-on with a Gallo Wine truck, and suppressed the urge to stomp on the brake pedal—while his foot was still on it—and write him up.

Earlier, she phoned the dispatcher at Central Station and learned, to her amazement, that a report had come in from Chinatown about a van filled with Santa Clauses blocking the area around Waverly Place and causing a commotion. Waverly was a narrow side street parallel to

Grant Avenue in the heart of Chinatown, and lined with tongs—legitimate family associations, or so they told the police. The dispatcher had just sent two squad cars to get the old guys out of there before the scene erupted into another tong war.

"Sounds like your boys are in Chinatown," Rebecca said to Richie when she got off the phone.

"Holy Christ!" Richie got up and headed for the door. "Thanks."

Mrs. Mayfield hadn't raised a stupid daughter. Some guy dressed in red pajamas had gone splat on her watch, and now twelve more were careening through the city with Lucky Luciano, here, in hot pursuit. There had to be some connection. No way would she believe it was a coincidence.

"Wait up!" She grabbed her purse, jacket, and was clipping her hair into a barrette at the nape of her neck as she followed him. "I'm going with you."

"No, you aren't." He spun on his heel in the doorway, hand on the frame as if to physically block her way.

"Yes, I am," she said, nose to nose with him as she put on the jacket. "You don't know where in Chinatown they are."

"It's a huge van. How hard will it be to find it?"

Her jaw jutted as she smiled. "You'll never know, will you?"

His eyes narrowed. "Why do you want to get involved in this?"

"Civic duty?" she suggested. "Helping the elderly? I mean *you*, not the Santa boys."

"Me?" He grinned and dropped his arm. "All right, Inspector. Have it your way."

They had another argument when they reached the parking lot. She didn't like getting into cars with strangers, although him being Angie's cousin helped. He absolutely refused to ride in the rickety city-issue Ford Taurus and leave his car in the lot. Her choice was either to ride in the Porsche or to follow it—and then have to deal with parking, losing him in traffic, or having him simply take off and the Taurus be unable to keep up.

No argument. She folded her long body into the sleek little sports car, and was filled with suspicion over where and how he'd gotten it. The powerful motor hummed and darted into traffic.

"So," she said, assessing the cable-car-passing, wine-truck-menacing maniac at the wheel, "you picked up twelve old guys at the airport. Are they all friends?"

He sped up at the yellow light, hit the intersection as it turned red and cruised across. "Something like that, yeah."

"You're obviously worried about them. They might get lost, I suppose."

"They know the city."

"No need to worry, then," she offered, closely watching his reaction.

His mouth wrinkled, but he didn't answer.

"What about their families?" she pressed. "Have you notified them?"

"Look, Inspector, cut the third degree. They're missing, all right? It's Christmas Eve. There's people they want to be with. Although"—brown eyes darted her way—"maybe you don't know about that kind of stuff. Why are you working today?"

She never answered personal questions from suspects. Not that he was one. Yet. "Tell me what you were doing with the old guys. It might help us find them."

"No family here, huh?" he persisted.

"My family's in Idaho, thank you. Now, if you expect me to help you, I need some information."

"They're going to ring bells for the Salvation Army." At her sneer, he added, "I volunteered to drop them off at their pot-stands."

An eyebrow lifted. "So you're one of Santa's little helpers."

"Well . . ." He screeched to a halt behind a car that'd stopped for a pedestrian. "Just like you said. Civic duty." He lowered the window, stuck his head out and yelled, "Move it, douchebag!"

Okay, she told herself, *so he's not going to tell me what he's up to.* She hadn't exactly expected he would. His furtiveness told her that it was probably shady and likely to end up with someone dead. Someone like her victim this morning.

She directed him toward Waverly Place. Half a block before reaching it, the traffic stopped completely. A crowd of people surrounded the entrance to Waverly.

Richie threw the car into reverse and was just about to career backward when another car pulled up behind him. And right behind it was a Coca-Cola truck. "What the—!" He pounded the steering wheel.

The streets of Chinatown were narrow, often one-way, and cluttered with double-parked cars and trucks unloading food, souvenirs, and tourists. The streets around Waverly were clogged under normal circumstances, and Waverly itself was even worse. Richie couldn't go backward, forward, or down the sidewalk.

He shut off the motor, yanked out his key, jumped from the car, and ran toward Waverly.

"Hey!" Rebecca climbed out and watched his retreating figure. What the hell, she thought, and took off after him. If someone stole or towed the Porsche, it was his problem, not hers. She mentally ticked off his fifth traffic violation in as many minutes: illegal parking.

Richie marched up and down the small street, puffing and snorting. "I don't see any van," he yelled. "Why don't I see the van?" He furiously kicked a bag of refuse, knocking it over. Its loose ties fell off, and rotting contents spewed onto the sidewalk. She eyed it, then him in distaste. Public littering.

"The report," she began, "said they went into a mah-jongg parlor next to the Hop Sing Tong—"

Before she finished, Richie took off down the block. "There it is." He pointed toward a dark brown brick doorway. It was nondescript except for some Chinese writing painted on the side. She eyed it skeptically. "Don't tell me you read Chinese."

"No. Just the words"—he pointed at two characters—"mah and jongg."

With a calm swagger, Richie went inside. She'd never been in one of the Chinese gaming parlors before. They were illegal as hell, but the cops were under strict orders from the city fathers to leave them alone. You could either chalk it up to "understanding diversity" or "bribes." Take your pick. She followed.

The room was shrouded in a thick haze of smoke. Considering all the gambling going on, the city's no-smoking policy was a nonfactor. A jumble of tables with fluorescent lights over them filled the room. People sat, four to a table, looking almost like a bunch of bridge players except for the intensity of their expressions. Even now, in late afternoon, the room was nearly full. The clinking of game tiles was deafening. No one paid attention to the newcomers.

Richie strolled up to a pudgy bald-headed Chinese man at the desk and the two greeted each other like long-lost pals. They talked quietly a while before the man shook his head and pointed up the street.

"They split," Richie said, ushering her toward the door. "He thought they were going to a restaurant, or trying to shake the cops who were looking for them. . . . Though, uh, they'd have no reason to be wary of cops," he quickly added. "None at all."

"Why were they here?" she asked, knowing better than to expect an answer. She gave the mah-jongg tables one last look, then let him steer her out.

They reached the street just in time to see a large white van go by on the opposite end of Waverly Place, over on Washington Street. The van must have been double-parked or have done something people didn't like because a crowd of elderly Chinese men shook their fists and yelled after it in Cantonese. No translation needed.

"God damn!" Richie ran to Washington and watched the van lurch uphill. So did he. Rebecca sprinted up the hill with relative ease, and was surprised that he managed to stay in front of her.

The van turned at the corner onto Stockton, and by the time they reached the intersection, it was nowhere in sight. Richie bent over, hands on knees, trying to catch his breath, his face a brilliant shade of purple.

They returned to his car to find that the crowd had dispersed and his Porsche was now the only thing blocking traffic. The Coca-Cola and Toyota drivers stuck behind him had apparently decided to push it out of the way. One man stood with his hands on the back bumper while the other sat inside, foot on the clutch, ready to release the hand brake when Richie yanked open the door, lifted the guy out by the lapels of his jacket, and tossed him onto the street.

The man looked up at the outraged Richie, apparently decided he had no complaints, and scrambled back to his beat-up Camry. The Coca-Cola driver followed.

Rebecca scowled at all three. Assault and battery on Richie's part, and possibly destruction of property depending on what happened to the Porsche once the two geniuses got it rolling. She was tempted to arrest them all or go back to Homicide and use a more traditional approach to crime solving.

"You coming?" Richie asked as he got in. She hesitated, but Richie might be her only lead to the dead Santa for a long while. She jumped into the passenger seat and before she'd even shut the door, he stomped on the gas pedal.

"Why did the Santas go to the mah-jongg parlor?" she asked and fastened her seat belt.

"Is that a joke?" He zigzagged past obstructions to proceed around the block. "Like, why did the chicken cross the road?"

"Ho, ho, ho." Her fingers itched to smack him. Hard. "What did they want in there?"

"They went for old-times' sake, I guess," was his unsatisfactory response. For a man who emoted big time, he was remarkably tight-lipped, which meant he had secrets.

The Porsche disappeared into the Stockton Street tunnel, the easiest route between Chinatown and the downtown area, and popped out near Union Square.

As opposed to Chinatown, which always resembled a corner of Hong Kong in the 1950s no matter what the season, holiday or time of year, the square was lit with Christmas decorations. Up ahead was Macy's, to the right, Saks Fifth Avenue. On the opposite street, the St. Francis Hotel, one of the city's oldest and finest, took up the entire block. Smaller exclusive shops and boutiques ringed the square and nearby Maiden Lane. Rebecca couldn't afford a handkerchief in one of the lane's shops, as opposed to Angie Amalfi and—by the looks of him—her insane cousin.

Here, people rushed about doing last-minute Christmas shopping. She'd gotten all hers finished two weeks before Thanksgiving. That was when stores held truly big sales, and there were no crowds. She could shop quickly, efficiently, and save money besides. Same with wrapping the presents and sending them to her parents, her brother and his wife, and her two nephews back in Idaho. By shopping early, she could ship them in the most practical manner as well. No need to waste money on overnight or even on priority.

Her Christmas season was efficient. No hubbub; no crowds teeming with energy. None of this kind of holiday excitement filling the air and making her spine tingle.

"Damn! Look at all these people." Richie broke into her thoughts as he waited impatiently three cars back from a red light. "I still have four presents to get. Looks like I'll be short."

"The disadvantages of your profession, I suppose." Her tone was thick with sarcasm.

Something flashed across his dark eyes. "My profession? You don't know beans about my profession. Look to your own, if you ask me." A laughing, package-laden couple jaywalked in front of them. He turned almost rueful and surprised her by saying, "Not exactly normal jobs for normal people, are they?"

Maybe it was the holiday bustle, maybe it was the sudden glint of honesty she imagined had been in his eyes, maybe it was the fact that they were both alone and working on Christmas Eve, but she said quietly, "Then we wouldn't be who we are, right?"

"Right." His elbow rested on the doorframe, hand to chin, and speaking more to himself than to her, in a voice so soft his words were almost imperceptible, said, "How bad would that be?"

She had no response and for a long moment they sat there in mutual silence, spectators to a festive, holiday scene, outsiders together.

The mood was broken when Rebecca spotted a large white van turning into the underground parking garage beneath Union Square. "Is that it?" she asked.

"We got them now!" Richie punched the air as he swerved out of his lane, crossed oncoming traffic and cut in front of cars lined up waiting to enter the garage. A burly driver honked long and loud, then got out of his car and stomped toward them. Rebecca rolled down the window and held up her police badge. He backed off.

Richie roared up and down narrow parking lanes until he spotted the van. Every nook and cranny nearby was filled, often illegally, and he had to park an entire floor away. "Let's stay close to the lot." He headed for the elevator. "They should come back soon. You married?"

The question surprised her. "No," she replied, and focused back on the problem at hand. "Why not just wait near the van?"

"Hell, no." Thick concrete pillars held up the

ceiling. Above was a park with trees, grass, and winter plantings. "I'll wait till I'm dead to have dirt and people walking around on top of me. Besides, I don't do underground in earthquake country. Engaged?"

"No." Not that it was any business of his, she thought. He was like a bulldog. "Don't you know the chance of there being an earthquake while we're waiting down here is practically zero?"

The elevator bell bonged and the doors opened. "Yeah? Well, tell that to the people who died going across the Bay Bridge during the last big one. I'm going up to the square. I'll take my chances aboveground."

"But you could be trapped in an elevator," she reasoned, stepping on.

"It's faster than taking the stairs." His hands twitched, his whole body bounced with nervous energy.

"What about tall buildings?" She wasn't sure if she was intrigued or simply enjoyed making him squirm. "Do you go up in them?"

"I would, if I had business up in one." When the elevator doors opened, he catapulted off it then tugged at his jacket in a show of casual indifference. It didn't fool her. "Let's walk around the park." He forged ahead without waiting, obviously ill at ease with her questions. Behind his back, she smiled.

The area was crawling with Santa Clauses.

Everywhere they looked one or two stood, collecting money or handing out flyers. One was even playing a saxophone, the case open in front of him, collecting money. It wasn't a Christmas tune, but "My Foolish Heart." Rebecca stopped and listened. She didn't know the words to the old tune, all she remembered was something about "beware, my foolish heart." Good advice, she thought. She had the most foolish heart she knew, wasting it on a man who was engaged to another woman and probably spending a warm and joyous Christmas Eve with his fiancée.

How ironic was it that she was with that woman's scoundrel of a cousin?

They were soon out of range of the saxophonist and neared a children's choir singing about city sidewalks dressed in holiday style. Suddenly, she was glad she was out of Homicide and here, surrounded by the warmth of the holiday—even if she was with a whack job a few trucks short of a convoy and searching for old coots who sounded like Santa's elves on speed.

"There they are!" Richie grabbed her hand and pointed toward the big, main entrance to Macy's a block away. "Come on!"

He plunged into the street, pulling her with him, jaywalking between cars and buses. She was glad the traffic was all but stopped due to the crowds. She couldn't believe he'd spotted the Santas. She could scarcely make them out in the chaos, and she'd been trained in crowd surveillance.

He ran up to them. "Where's the rest of the boys?" he asked. Only about eight were there.

The Santas looked at him strangely. He returned the favor, with decided disapproval, hands on his hips. They'd been gathered around an evangelist holding a sign that read DON'T FORGET THE CHRIST IN CHRISTMAS, while offering stacks of brochures and Bibles to passersby.

Richie's face went through a series of contortions: anger, disbelief, mulishness. He reached out and tugged at one of the Santa's beards. The elastic stretched and revealed a frowning mouth. "Uh . . . sorry." Richie let go and the beard snapped back into place. He grabbed a second. He tried for a third when the Santa, who was bigger and more muscular than the others, clutched Richie's black Polo pullover.

"Don't even think about it, bud," Santa growled.

Richie backed off.

"It was a good try," Rebecca said.

"Yeah." He smoothed his shirt, then the jacket, and ran his palm, diamond pinky-ring flashing, against the sides of his hair to smooth it. The whole time his back was to the Bible-toting Santas as if he couldn't care less about them.

They walked down to Market Street, heads

swiveling from side to side, up, down, even under a time or two. "I've never seen so many goddamned Santa Clauses in my goddamned life!" Richie exclaimed. The streets swarmed with jaunty red caps and white beards mixed among the throngs of shoppers.

Rebecca spotted a group of Santa hats marching toward the Ferry Building. "Are your Santas short?" she asked.

"Yeah! Where?" He looked where she pointed, then frowned. "What the hell. It's worth a try."

They hurried after the group, but slowed down as they neared. The Santas all carried Girl Scout cookies.

Richie kicked a mailbox, making a dent in it, and uttered a string of Italian curses. She ignored him, except to tick another violation: mutilating federal property. "This is dumb," he complained. "Let's get back to the van and wait."

"Why don't you tell me why you want to find the Santas?" she asked.

"Why don't you tell me why you care?" He shot back.

"Hey, you asked for help." She sidestepped the question.

"Yeah? You're supposed to be investigating murders," he pointed out. "Nobody's dead. Just some old guys missing, yet you've glommed on like Crazy Glue. It don't fit, Inspector."

She wasn't ready to tell him about her dead Santa. Not with the way he'd been behaving.

They were in the parking elevator before she said, "Tell me why you need to find the Santas, and I'll tell you why I'm interested."

He glared at her, and they existed in a vacuum of sullen silence, a silence that thickened appallingly when they got off the elevator.

The van was gone.

"Where to now, boys?" Joe Zumbaglio, otherwise known as Joey Zoom, asked as he slowly drove the van up and down the city streets. Skinny, with sagging cheeks and gnarled hands, he was seventy-five and the only one who still had a valid California driver's license—so to speak. In case they got stopped, they didn't want to take any chances. The driver's license gave his name as Hiram Bernstein.

"I think we should'a stayed downtown." Lorenzo the Slug scratched his fake beard. He used to be called the Slug because he was so good with his fists—a slugger. Now, though, it was because he had to stop at a bathroom every thirty minutes so it took him forever, sluglike, to get from one place to another. That was also why the others let him ride shotgun next to Joey Zoom. He could get in and out of the van easily and no one had to sit next to him if they didn't

find a john in time. Nobody told Lorenzo that,
though. They let him think he was the same
strong pugilist as ever. That was the thing about
the crazy names the guys gave each other, they
were for fun, honor, and at times, a surprising
amount of affection.

"Three women handed me money," Lorenzo
continued, his brows thick with tangled white
strands. "I was just standin' there, too. Wish I'da
known how easy it was to make a buck wearin' a
Santa suit. Woulda saved me a lotta trouble."

"What? You gotta pot 'a rubble?" Frankie
Vines shouted. "What you gonna do wit' rubble?" Frankie didn't have a nickname. They tried
to call him Frankie the Ear because of his obvious
difficulties, but he thought they said Frankie the
Beer and went on a toot that lasted three years.

As usual, everyone ignored him.

"How was we supposed to know everything's
changed so much?" Lorenzo asked. "Who
woulda thought Big Leo retired? I was countin'
on him to help!"

"I told you I heard he died," Peewee Carducci
whined in a high voice. He had a long narrow
face and oversized ears that jutted out like wings
under his Santa hat. "Just like today. I told you
we shoulda used a wood chipper. That's the way
we did it in the old days."

"Naw, Big Leo didn't die," Lorenzo said confi-
dently, his scrawny Santa suit-clad chest puffed

out. "We'll find him and get him to help. He knows everything, and if he don't wanna help, we'll make sure he remembers who he's dealing with."

"He don't remember nothing if he's dead," Peewee muttered.

"Who's Fred?" Frankie shouted.

"Maybe he's got alkaselzer," Guido the Cucumber piped up. He was called that because of his love for antipasti, but he liked to brag that it was for another reason. Guido was round with a big belly, a jowly face, and thick ankles that seemed to ooze over his shoes. "You know, that memory thing. Like Ronald Reagan."

"Yeah, and maybe he thinks he's president, too," Joey Zoom remarked with a sneer. "Time's wasting. We gotta find him and take care of business. After, maybe we'll call Richie. Who's got his number?"

All were silent, but then two of the Santas were asleep, four had turned off their hearing aids, and two were too busy looking out the window to pay any attention to the conversation.

"Well, somebody's gotta have it," Joey Zoom muttered.

"At least we got ridda him," the Cucumber said, tugging on the Santa suit around his thick thighs where the material was cutting into his circulation. "And Joey Zoom still has his stuff." He high-fived the Santa next to him so hard that poor old Joe fell off the seat. Six of the Santas were named Joe, which made things confusing sometime.

"Try North Beach," the Slug said. "That's where all the *paisans* hang out. And I gotta use a bathroom. Somebody there'll know how to find Big Leo." Everyone agreed.

As they drove by St. Francis of Assisi, they saw an elderly woman dressed in black step out of the church. She appeared confused, as if she wasn't sure which way to go.

Joey Zoom slowed way down, concerned about her, when two young men walked by. One of them grabbed her purse. She hung on tight and fell to the ground, but the youth yanked it hard and ran off with his buddy.

The van roared to life. Joey bore down on the thieves.

They angled right and so did the van. Pedestrians jumped out of the way; city trash bins flew. The young men turned down a narrow side street only to discover it dead-ended. High-pitched girly screams mixed with the squeal of brakes. The van stopped just in time. Six more inches and the assailants would have been spending Christmas in purgatory.

Lorenzo jumped out, snatched the purse from the dumbfounded muggers who stared blearily at the van of Santas.

"Don't mess with little old ladies," Lorenzo

ordered as Joey backed the van out of the alley. "Or, with Santa Claus."

As Richie drove in circles, speeding, swerving and swearing, around the downtown and Mission Street areas, Rebecca wondered once more if her guess that her dead Santa was connected to the missing Santas wasn't a bad mistake. Maybe she had had a sudden glucose attack from her failure to get a Snickers. Maybe she'd let the lure of putting away a punk like Richie Amalfi seduce her.

But if, as he'd said, there really were twelve Santas out there, why? What were they planning? She'd seen enough of Richie Amalfi to believe that any plan he was involved in had nothing to do with holiday giving.

Holiday taking was a better possibility. And now, it was up to her to prevent it. Whatever "it" was. She needed a different approach. One to lull him.

"Do you spend Christmas with Angie and her family?" she asked casually.

His eyebrows jiggled with surprise before he said, "Naw. My mother cooks. My sister and little brother and their families show up. We eat. Watch a little football. Tell old family stories. I'll take home a plate of food that'll see me through the next couple of days." His gaze slid her way. "You?"

"I'm on call over the next thirty-six hours. So, I'll spend the day tomorrow basically hoping nobody gets killed. I won't see my family until January."

"What's—"

His question was cut off by the ringing of her cell phone. It was Traffic, calling with an answer to her earlier query.

She listened, then hung up and studied Richie. It was time for answers. Her voice turned hard. "Who do you know at the Stonestown Mall?"

His face registered confusion. "Why you asking about the mall? You got to do Christmas shopping? You can leave anytime, you know. You aren't doing me one damn bit of good anyway, since the cops in this city don't seem capable of noticing a van filled with Santa Clauses. Are they blind?"

"There was an accident—an auto accident—near the airport this morning."

"Yeah?"

"You picked your friends up at the airport."

"So?" He waited, and when she said nothing he swung the car into a red zone and shut off the engine. She braced herself for another explosion of temper, ready to meet it head on. Instead, he shifted in his seat to face her, his voice low, and somehow even more deadly. "You think just because I lost some old guys I'm responsible for everything that goes wrong in this town?" He sounded almost indignant. "What's with you, lady? Why are you here anyway? You can get the hell out of this car and go back to Homicide. It's not as if I'd miss your help."

She weighed her options. It'd be in the newspapers soon anyway, so it wasn't exactly a state secret. "All right," she said. "Today, around eleven, a car went off an overpass by the airport. It landed upside down and was pretty much flattened. By the time the cops and paramedics got there, though, the driver's body was gone. An hour later, a man dressed in a Santa suit was found at the mall. He was dead. His injuries made it look as if he'd fallen from a great height."

"A Santa suit?" Richie seemed dumbfounded by the story, but at the same time, his eyes darted. "What do you mean? Like he fell or jumped out of a building?"

"Maybe. The problem was, he was in the middle of the parking lot. There was nothing near he could have fallen from."

Richie blinked. "So . . . it's sort of like he fell out of—"

"Yeah," she said quickly, not wanting to hear the words she knew he was thinking.

Richie chuckled.

"It's not funny!" Rebecca stated for the umpteenth time that day.

Something about her indignation made his chuckle develop into a belly laugh. "You're wrong, Inspector. It is funny. Maybe you should do blood work and give Santa a posthumous DUI." But then he glanced at her frown and his humor died. "Okay, so what does it have to do with me? You were at a mall, for cryin' out loud. They're lousy with Santas."

He was right—it should have made sense, but it didn't. "He wasn't wearing a mall-issued suit, for one thing. Wasn't recognized, had no ID, and nobody seems to be missing any Santas but you. Are you sure you were expecting twelve Santas and not thirteen? Or maybe you only had eleven, and the dead guy is the twelfth?"

He looked startled at first, tense, then fell suspiciously quiet. "When I left the airport, I had twelve Santas," he replied, but then he asked, "What does he look like?"

"He's older, late sixties, seventies. Gray hair. A small guy. The photographer has probably e-mailed me copies of the best digital photos from the scene by now. If we go back to Homicide I can show you. Maybe you'll recognize him."

"I got a better idea." He opened the glove compartment and took out a handheld computer device that looked like an iPAQ or BlackBerry, but the writing on it was in Japanese. He turned it on and punched a few buttons then held it toward her.

"Log onto your e-mail," he said.

She shook her head. "Won't work. It's a closed, internal system, lots of security."

"Trust me."

Dubious, she took the device and used the tiny keys. In a matter of seconds, even faster than her supposedly secure terminal at work, she was into her e-mail. She didn't want to think about it.

A message from the photographer was there. He'd sent her two pictures. She opened both, then put the clearest one on the screen. "Are you squeamish about looking at dead bodies?" she asked.

"You talking to me?" Richie reached for the photo, glanced at it and blanched. Before he turned white then an anemic green, she saw recognition in his face. He handed the computer back to her. "Never saw the guy before."

"You're lying."

"I never lie." He cranked the ignition and pointed at the computer. "Keep it close. Let's get going."

"Where to?"

"I don't know. It's a small city, a big van. Something's got to show up."

"You're lying again!" Any minute now, she was going to pull her Beretta on him, no doubt about it. "You've got someplace in mind. Now, tell me where we're going."

Richie ran long fingers through wavy blue-black hair that was almost but not quite thick enough to hide the thinning spot at the back of his head. She noticed a hint of gray at the temples, a slight cragginess to the skin, and lines at the outer corners of his eyes. Normally, she liked such signs of maturity in a man. She might need to rethink that.

Richie's next comment brought her back to earth. "I said I didn't recognize the guy in the photo. But I know someone who might."

The building was shaped like a triangle. The pointed nose, on the corner of Columbus Avenue, held the front door. In the early days of the last century, LaRocca's Corner was one of the most popular mob hangouts. These days, it was mostly filled with yuppies who liked the post-Prohibition décor, and wiseguy wannabes. Rebecca never doubted, however, that a few of the real thing continued to frequent it as well.

Richie's mouth scrunched as he perused Rebecca head to toe. "I better go in alone. You wait."

She said firmly, "No."

"They'll wonder who you are. What you're doing with me."

"Tell them I'm a friend."

He tugged an earlobe, and looked uncomfortable. "Well . . ."

She glanced down at her black jacket, slacks, boots, and white shirt blouse buttoned to the collar. She'd pulled her hair back in a barrette as they'd left Homicide. He was right. She didn't look like someone a guy like him would hang around with. Which was, frankly, not a bad thing.

"Just wait a minute." She dug some lipstick out of her purse and put it on, then unfastened the barrette and shook her hair loose. Taking off the jacket, she cinched her belt tight, then rolled the sleeves of her blouse to the elbows and un-buttoned the top two . . . no, the top three . . . buttons and spread the collar wide.

"Now?" She expected the scrunched-mouth look again. Instead, he reached up and pushed a couple of strands of hair back from her eye. To her surprise, his expression softened as he gazed at her. He nodded.

They walked inside with his arm around her waist. He kept her close as they approached the bar, waving to people, calling out greetings in Italian and English, and using the kinds of nick-names she thought had been made up for shows like *The Sopranos*.

He ordered bourbon and water and quietly asked her what she wanted. She hesitated a frac-tion of a second then said, "Gin and tonic."

The understanding in his eyes was even more unsettling than the fact that she had ordered al-cohol on duty. Well, she could order it, but it didn't mean she had to drink it.

As he talked to the bartender and others, she pretended to sip her drink, listening carefully, even though little of what they said made sense. Most of it was almost in code, and sounded suspiciously like the kinds of conversations one might have with a bookie. The only difference was that this time of year they talked football, not horses. Christmas and college bowl games seemed to go better than mistletoe and holly in this little establishment.

A very drunk man staggered over and put his arm around Richie. "How's it goin', pal?" he slurred.

"Fine, Pinky. Looks like you've got a heat on. You got cab fare to get home?"

"Naw. I'm not ready to go home anyway." He eyed Rebecca suspiciously. "Say, where's Sheila?"

"She's home with the kids. Let's get you a cab."

"No need, Richie, really."

Richie sweet-talked him to the door.

Home with the kids. Interesting, she hadn't thought of Richie as being married. He didn't seem settled, and hadn't mentioned a wife and kids earlier when he talked about Christmas at his mother's. He might be divorced, but then, a lot of these hoodlum types didn't talk about their wives. The women kept the house, raised the kids, prayed in church for the ever-deteriorating souls of their husbands, but nothing more.

Given all she'd seen so far, it was interesting that Richie Amalfi was on Angie's father's side of the family. From what Paavo told her, Sal Amalfi was straight—a businessman who'd made millions on shoe stores and real estate. Angie's mother's relatives were another story. One branch of Serefina's family, headed by her uncle Bruno Bacala, also called Bruno the Tweeds because of his stylish clothes, was connected up to the armpits.

Richie tapped her arm. "You got the gizmo in your purse with the picture of the dead body?"

She handed it over and he showed the bartender.

"Sure I know him," the man said. "It's Cock-eyed Lanigan. Mean old coot."

"He's dead," Richie stated.

"No fooling? Man, the old guys are dropping like flies. Nobody's going to mourn Lanigan, though, you can count on that."

"Any idea why he'd be headed to the airport this morning?"

"Not me. The only guy who ever talked much to him was Leo Respighi. Maybe he knows."

Richie's attention was distracted from the bartender when a new customer came in laughing about some old Santas who broke up a mugging. The kids they caught not only gave up the old lady's purse, but went into the church to thank God they were still alive.

The clientele at LaRocca's Corner laughed as if it was the funniest thing they'd ever heard.

Richie was all over the newcomer finding out just where the van was, who was in it, and where it was going. The information didn't help much, but at least they knew the Santas were in the neighborhood.

By the time they left LaRocca's, it was fairly dark out, even though it was only five o'clock. "Damn!" Richie said, scowling at the sky. "It's going to be harder than ever to find them." He checked his watch. "I've only got four hours."

"Then what?" Rebecca asked. "Your Santas turn into a pumpkin?"

"No, I do."

Just then, right before their eyes, a big white Econoline van drove by on Columbus Avenue, then turned onto Mason.

"Holy shit!" Richie cried and took off after it.

The van started up a hill. Richie and Rebecca tried to catch it but were losing ground when a cable car clanged for them to get out of the way. As it went by Rebecca grabbed the pillar that went from the back guardrail to the roof. She used it to pull herself onto the bottom step on the cable car's side.

Richie was behind Rebecca and couldn't grab the same rail. Instead, he lunged for the back of the car. Both hands grabbed the top of the guardrail. He had to run faster than she thought possible to keep his footing, and then he shot up, lifting a foot onto the bottom rail and pulling the second foot up after it. Fortunately, the soles of his shoes were rubber so he didn't slide right off again. That surprised her; she'd expected he'd be the type of guy who always wore slick leather. He held on tight. "Watch out!" he shouted.

She looked up to see the back end of a UPS van jutting out into traffic, only a half-foot from the side of the cable car. She gasped. He grabbed her shoulder and swung her toward him just in time to avoid having her face—and every other part of her body—decorate the truck.

A red-faced conductor stormed out of the cabin. "What the hell is wrong with you two idiots? You want to commit suicide, you do it on somebody else's car! Now get up inside and pay like everyone else, or get the hell off!"

The cable car was halfway to the next corner when it had to stop behind a row of cars for a red light. Richie saw that the van was stopped as well.

Ignoring the conductor, he leaped off the car and ran toward the van. When Rebecca saw what he was up to, she followed, but not before mouthing "Sorry," to the outraged ticket-taker.

Violation: riding public transportation without paying fare.

"Open up!" Richie yelled, grabbing the driver's door handle and pounding on the window. "What's the matter with you guys?"

Rebecca was on the passenger side, yanking on the doors, but all were locked. She looked inside, and sure enough, just as Richie had promised, there were rows of little old Santa Clauses, dark brown eyes gaping back at her in surprise and wonder. She had to admit that until that very moment, a part of her simply hadn't wanted to believe his story was true.

She was tugging on the door handle with both hands, one foot on the frame for leverage, when the light turned green. Other cars began to move. She yelled, ordering the Santas to open up. Suddenly, the door swung open and slammed hard against her. The window hit her nose, hurtling her end over end. Black lights and bright stars exploded in her head. Luckily, she rolled in the direction of the sidewalk out of the way of the oncoming cars. The van rocketed away.

Richie's hands tucked under her armpits and lifted, helping her move onto the curb where they both sat. "You okay?" He took out a handkerchief— she didn't think anyone used them any more— and pressed it to her nose. Maybe in his line of business he needed one. When he lifted it away, she saw blood. There was no maybe about it.

The world turned as red as her blood. She'd been dragged all over town, had a drink in a bar with a nest of criminals, broke enough laws to spend a week in jail, and now she'd been hit in the nose by a van of Santas. Her breath started coming short and fast; her ears rang; everything began to tilt.

Suddenly, he grabbed the back of her head, shoved it between her knees and held it down. Her hand found his chest and she strong-armed him, then sprang back up. "What the hell are you doing?" she shrieked.

"You turned pale," he said. "You gotta take it easy."

"Take it *easy*?" Her temples pounded. "How can I take it easy around you! You moron! You dolt! You—" She grabbed the handkerchief from him as she felt blood trickling down her nose to her upper lip and covered both. "You pithant!" She lisped.

"Calm down," he ordered as if talking to a child. "You're hurt."

"I'll show you hurt!" She swung her arm and socked him in the ear, hard, then jumped to her feet.

"Ow!" He rubbed the side of his head.

"I must be crathier than you are to have wasted my time on you and your bullthit!" The thought that she was no closer to knowing why he was driving around with the Santas, what he was up to, how it was all connected to her dead guy, and the fact that she was lisping, turned her purple with rage. She lifted the handkerchief long enough for choice words to tell him exactly what she thought of his goofy ideas, his friends, and his heritage.

A car driving by stopped and a middle-aged man gawked at her, his mouth hanging open. "What's your problem?" she demanded. He sped away.

She spun back to Richie, still sitting on the curb watching her in stunned silence.

Abruptly, she stopped, stared down at him, then lifted her head and walked away, once again holding the handkerchief to her nose.

He shook his head in wonder, then got up and followed.

The twelve Santas marched single file into LaRocca's Corner wishing Merry Christmas to one and all. Half followed Lorenzo the Slug in a rush to the bathroom, while the others took over two tables, three barstools, and ordered twelve boilermakers. Earlier, they'd had lunch at the replacement for the Old Spaghetti Factory, and espresso at the replacement for the Café Trieste. Neither, they'd concurred, was as good as the "real" places they remembered.

Once they got settled, after a few words with the bartender about the Good Ol' Days, Guido the Cucumber said, "By the way, we're looking for Big Leo Respighi. Seems he's given up mah-jongg. Even closed his business. What's up? You know where we can find him?"

The bartender looked surprised. "Leo? I hadn't heard he'd closed up shop. I suspect he's home with the old lady."

"No way," Guido said. "His wife's dead."

Stricken, the bartender put down the rag he'd been wiping glasses with. "Anna Maria?"

"Hell, no!" Guido scowled. "That's Punk Leo's wife—"

"Don't call him Punk if you know what's good for you," the bartender warned.

"Who cares?" Guido said. "We're talking his father—*Big* Leo."

"Hey, fellows, I'm sorry," the bartender said. "Leo's old man died about six, seven years ago."

The other Santas were listening and they all doffed their caps in memory of Dead Leo.

"See, I told you!" Peewee muttered. "Maybe we shoulda thrown that guy offa pier this morning. It mighta been safer."

"Who's gonna appear? Morley Safer?" Frankie Vines shouted his questions, then looked at all the bowed heads. "Jeez, did he die, too?"

"Frankie, shuddup," Joey Zoom warned.

"We gotta plan." Lorenzo the Slug sat at a table and the Santas gathered around him. "I thought Big Leo would be the one to help us. He knew a lotta things money can't buy. We needed him, and now . . ."

"Poor Leo," the Cucumber muttered.

"I got an idea," Joe Pistolini, called Joe the Pistol for obvious reasons, said. "I know a woman who'll help us. Her uncle's a good friend."

"I hope so," the Cucumber said. "I'm starting to get a little tired with all this eating and drinking and gabbing. I gotta save my energy for tonight."

The others wearily concurred.

Richie was trying to figure out if he should get rid of the woman beside him. Somebody was pulling a fast one here, and he was in the middle of it. The last thing he needed was a cop on his ass. What if the extra Santa had shown up at the airport and said he was supposed to be part of the group? Richie wondered if he'd have believed him and let him join the others. Or better yet—what if he'd bumped off one of the real passengers and took his place? Would the others have known he didn't belong? In fact, what if one of them already *was* a fake? What if they'd all been kidnapped? How would he explain how he'd let *that* happen on his watch?

The thought turned him ashen.

Some insider had to have leaked out the information about the Santa costumes. Who was the snitch, and whose side was he on? Were the old boys, right now, in danger?

He doubted it. They hadn't looked the least bit scared when they tried to sucker punch him with the van's door.

He'd chuckled about the Santa costumes when they'd first been proposed. These old geezers were only "somebodies" in their own minds, he'd thought. Some had served time. Others were lucky, had never been caught, and the statute of limitations had long passed on anything they might have done.

On the other hand, considering that they were on the lam and another Santa was dead, maybe they'd been right to be paranoid.

He thought about letting someone on the inside know what was happening, but doing so meant he had to admit that he'd lost the twelve guys. Twelve! Who in the hell loses twelve men? That was more than a frigging football team!

It was embarrassing. Not to mention potentially deadly. Scratch the "potentially." Much as he hated to admit it, the inspector was his last, best hope.

The chance of the Santas being picked up by the cops was high. Frankly, he never imagined they could drive around in a van all day and not get nailed. None of them could drive a straight line, he was sure, and he doubted they could keep this up for very long now that it was dark out. Half the guys had cataracts and the other half were legally blind. No way could they continue night driving without running into something.

Once that happened, Rebecca would get the call from the dispatcher, and he'd rush with her to wherever they were, pick up the pieces, and deliver them on time.

"Your nose stop bleeding?" he asked.

"Yes." She'd put the handkerchief in her purse. She'd clean and mail it to him.

"Good. Doesn't look like you'll have a shiner for Christmas, either." He tried not to chuckle, but failed.

"Yeah, well . . ." The way she'd lost her temper irritated her. Paavo Smith would never have done anything so undignified, and she shouldn't have, either. She needed to put things back on an even keel. "Your kids must be excited about Christmas," she said. "Are any young enough to still believe in Santa Claus?"

He jumped. It wasn't the kind of question a guy liked to hear. "My *what*?"

"Kids. The ones you talked about at LaRocca's."

"I don't have any kids! None that I'll admit to, anyway," he added. An old joke. He was sure he didn't have any, though he'd lived pretty wild in his younger days.

He glanced at Rebecca. She was a quiet woman, but he liked it when she talked to him, even if she said some oddball stuff. "What made you think I had kids?"

She looked confused. "Somebody asked about Sheila, and you said your wife was home with the kids."

"Wife? No way! She's an old girlfriend. A widow. She's got kids. May her husband rest in peace, but after I dated her a while, I could see why he decided to check out so young. I don't have nothing to do with her anymore. Or . . . not much."

"No wife, no girlfriend?" she asked.

"No wife. Lots of girlfriends," he said with a grin. "None serious. You?"

She thought about Greg Horning at home in Cleveland for Christmas. "Could be," she admitted. "I'll see how it works out after the holidays."

He nodded. "Another cop?"

"Sure. Who else do most cops date?" she asked with a rueful shrug. "We're the only ones who understand us."

"That's what I figured," he said. "I warned my cousin Angie about that, but the Amalfis are all pretty stubborn."

Her eyebrows lifted. She couldn't imagine anyone having a negative thought about Paavo Smith. He was the best cop she'd ever met. Angie Amalfi, on the other hand . . . "That's funny, because all of Homicide warned Paavo about Angie."

He did a double take. "You crazy? Angie's a great catch."

Rebecca frowned. "A lot of women go for the uniform."

"Paavo's plainclothes." Richie eyed her. "Why? Who do you think is better suited for him?"

She stared straight ahead. "I have no idea."

An awkward tension descended suddenly in the small car. He eyed her firm mouth, her small pointed chin, jutting proudly. "Oh, yeah?" he asked.

She glared as if she'd gladly see him burst into flame. "That's what I said."

He drove with no more questions, and stopped at a house halfway up Telegraph Hill on Vallejo Street. "Wait here." He got out of his Porsche.

To his irritation, she simply got out of the car. Before he could open his mouth, she said coldly, "If you think I'm about to twiddle my thumbs in your car while I've got a dead body to investigate, you're wrong. If this guy knows anything, I'm going to hear it."

Although his ear was still smarting from the smack she gave him, he stuck his face in hers until they were almost nose to nose. "He won't talk to a cop," he shouted, arms spread straight out at his sides.

"He'll talk if I take him in," she pointed out.

She was going to get him bloody well killed!

"For what reason? Because I said he might know something? No. He'll say I was wrong. Look, Inspector, I need to find my twelve guys. If they know something about your dead merry old elf, you'll find out, but only after I've got them. So, back off!"

"Go to hell," she said calmly.

"Trust me," he pleaded, running out of ideas and time.

"Not on your life."

He glared. "Then keep your trap shut and don't—whatever you do—let on that you're the law."

She glared right back. "I'm not making any promises."

He grumbled and swore, but grudgingly led the way up the outside stairs to the front doors. There were three of them, in the typical style of San Francisco flats. He rang a bell and one of the doors buzzed open. Inside a narrow foyer they faced another long flight of stairs.

"Hey, *goomba*—it's me, Richie."

"Richie! *Caro mio!*" a woman's voice called down. As they reached a bend in the stairs, they looked up to see a middle-aged woman with a square face and short, black curly hair standing at the landing. She wore an apron and was wiping her hands, a diamond-and-platinum ring on each finger, then held them out to give Richie a big hug. He hugged her in return.

She stepped back and eyed Rebecca. "Who's this? A new girlfriend, Richie? She's very pretty."

He took Rebecca's hand and pulled her forward. "This is, uh, Becky May . . . Mason. Becky, meet Anna Maria Respighi." Anna Maria grabbed her hands and welcomed her. "Is Leo here?" Richie asked.

"He's in the back, watching TV. I'll go get him. Sit down in the kitchen. You hungry, Richie?" She patted his face. "You and your girlfriend, you want to eat something?"

"No, sweetheart," he said. "We're fine. Just got to talk to Leo."

"*Aspetti.* You come to my house, you eat." She gave them both a glass of red wine and made up plates of the leftover rigatoni and meatloaf still on the counter from dinner. While she zapped them in the microwave, she lit herself a cigarette and asked Richie in Italian all about his new girlfriend. He only prayed Rebecca didn't understand as he sang her praises in the bedroom and the kitchen—the only places he figured that mattered. He decided she didn't have a clue what he was saying since she neither blushed nor shot him with the gun he knew she was packing in that big black purse she lugged around everywhere. Come to think of it, she probably never blushed.

With the cigarette smoldering in an ashtray,

Anna Maria put a plate in front of Richie, and another before Rebecca. "*Mangia*," she said, then softly to Rebecca, "I hope you like it."

She said it so sweetly, Rebecca found herself murmuring, "I'm sure I will." The smell of the spicy red sauce and the hint of garlic, onion and oregano in the warming meatloaf, reminded her that she was starving. The food was delicious.

Richie, too, ate with gusto. "You're looking too skinny, Richie," Anna Maria said, adding more rigatoni to his plate as she watched the first serving disappear.

"I'm not skinny—just not so heavy anymore. I was letting myself go. The hell with that. I joined the gym. Run, box. It's good for me. I actually feel better."

"You were overweight?" Rebecca asked between bites.

"For a little while," he murmured, then stuck his head farther down toward his plate.

"A woman," Anna Maria called to Rebecca as she stood by the open back door for the last few drags. "She was no good. He's lucky to be rid of her."

"Thanks, Anna Maria," he said, washing down a swallow with wine. "That's just what I came here to listen to you talk about. Where's Leo?"

Rebecca found this conversation interesting,

however. "Was that Sheila?" she asked Anna Maria.

"Sheila? No, no, no. It was Jeannie. She was—"

"Enough already!" Richie shouted.

Anna Maria laughed, crushed the cigarette butt, and headed down the hall to find her husband.

Rebecca's eyebrows were still high on her forehead. "A lot of girlfriends, huh?"

He pushed his plate away after practically licking it clean, and said succinctly, "Women!"

She was going to take up the gauntlet when a big man wearing a brown toupee and a yellow satin robe walked into the kitchen. His bare legs looked like toothpicks below the robe, and his feet were shod in loose, floppy black patent-leather slippers. " 'Ey, Richie, how's it going?" His deep voice reverberated throughout the kitchen like a boom box. His wife followed, and she cleared the plates, then poured everyone coffee and anisette.

Leo sat down while Anna Maria cleaned the kitchen and put leftovers away, paying no attention to the group at her table. Richie introduced Leo and Rebecca, calling her his "acquaintance." Leo's brows slanted downward as he nodded. Leo's nose, lips, and ears were all oversized and blubbery. The only things small were his eyes and, it seemed, his intelligence.

"We're trying to find out who this guy is."

Richie showed him the thirteenth Santa's photo on the small computer screen.

Leo no sooner looked at it then he threw it onto the table and bellowed, "I don't know him, and I don't want to know him."

"What do you mean?"

"He's trouble. I don't have nothing to do with him. Nothing. Is that clear?"

"He's dead, Leo," Richie said starkly.

Leo's face darkened. "Dead? You show a picture of a dead guy to me? You do that in my house! Bring me seven years' bad luck!" He lunged, toppling Richie and his chair to the floor.

Anna Maria screamed. Using his arms and legs, Richie was trying to shove the big man off him. Rebecca was careful where she looked as the two scrambled on the floor and the bathrobe lifted, revealing more of Leo than she'd ever wanted to see.

She attempted to separate the men and got an elbow buried in the stomach for her trouble, doubling her over to gasp for air. The gun she had in her purse tempted her, but it would give away that she was a cop, and Richie had warned her not to. She could use some of the karate she'd learned, but she didn't like the idea of breaking anyone's bones on Christmas Eve.

Anna Maria solved her dilemma by grabbing a dust mop and shoving and shaking the head of it between the two men, bopping first Leo then

Richie in the face. Clouds of dust billowed with each smack. When the two men started coughing, she swung the mop even more forcefully, hitting their noses and foreheads, then chest and shoulders. With each swing, more dust flew, making them pant more, which meant they had to take bigger and bigger gulps of air and only managed to get even more dust in their mouths.

Finally, they let go of each other and rolled to their sides, eyes watering and choking.

Cold-cocked by a dust mop. Rebecca tried not to laugh, but as she looked at Richie gasping from his exertions, the thought struck that she was actually having fun, and that she hadn't been around such an interesting and provocative man in a long, long time. God! Where had that come from? The crack on her nose must have been harder than she'd thought.

"Cover yourself, Leo!" Anna Maria yelled. "What's wrong with you two? It's Christmas Eve! You should be ashamed!"

As Anna Maria helped Leo struggle off the floor, Rebecca held out a hand to Richie.

"You get that filth out of my house!" Leo roared, facing Richie again. "I don't know Cock-eyed Lanigan and I don't give a damn that he's dead!"

"Do you know what he was up to this morning?" Richie asked, stubborn as usual.

Leo went beefy red. "What are you, some kind

of cop? I don't know nothing! Get the hell out of here, Richie," he said. "And if you know what's good for you, you'll go home and forget about all this."

"The cops will find out what happened, Leo," Richie said, wearing a predatory, lopsided grin. "After all, the guy's dead."

"Yeah?" Leo adjusted his robe and toupee. "Then that means there really is a Santa Claus."

The Santas were standing outside the Fior d'Italia restaurant waiting to meet the woman Joe the Pistol had phoned. To their surprise, as they cheerfully wished Christmas greetings to passersby, people kept handing them money.

They took it.

Then, a little boy and girl went walking by. The boy looked about seven and the girl six. They stopped, glared at the Santas and stuck out their tongues.

As they started to walk away, Guido the Cucumber limped after them. "What's the matter with you kids?" he yelled. "Don't you know better than to treat Santa Claus that way?"

"We hate Santa," the boy said.

"Yeah, we hate you," the girl chimed, but her blue eyes filled with tears.

"Hey, what's wrong? Santa didn't do nothing to you," Guido protested.

"You aren't coming to our house," the boy

said. "Daddy's sick and can't work. We wanted bikes, but Daddy said no way. Santa doesn't give things like that to poor kids. Seems to me, the rich kids could get their parents to pay for things, it's the poor ones Santa should help."

The Cucumber nodded. "Well, your daddy may be right most of the time, but there's twelve of us Santas here, and maybe we can work something out. You tell me where you live, so I won't have trouble finding the right house, and maybe between the twelve of us, we'll be able to help you."

The kids looked wary. "I thought Santa Claus knows where everybody lives," the boy said.

"Well, yeah, but look at us, we're getting old. You know old people are forgetful sometimes."

The kids gave their address, and all the Santas wished them Merry Christmas as they left.

"What we gonna do?" one of the Joes asked.

"Think, guys. Who do we know who can help?" Guido looked from one to the other.

"Santa's dead," Peewee said remorsefully. "We know all about it."

"Where's Santa's bed?" Frankie Vines shouted. "I'm ready to lay down. All this is a lotta work!"

They ignored him, as usual.

"No problem. I know someone," Joe the Pistol said with a big smile. "We were just talking about his old man, too. Punk Leo—he sells toys and all kinds of stuff. I'm going to his house tomorrow for Christmas dinner. We can call him."

Joey Zoom stared at him, annoyed. "Did you tell him we was all coming here today? We weren't supposed to tell no one."

"What's the big deal? He's expecting me," the Pistol argued. "His wife's aunt's husband was my wife's brother-in-law, God rest his soul, so we're related. I told Leo not to worry, that we was all dressed in Santa costumes so nobody'd recognize us."

"I hope you're right," Guido said, "and I hope he knows enough to keep his mouth shut."

"Sure he does. Let's go find a pay phone. I'll call him. You'll see. Punk Leo's a nice guy, despite what everybody says about him. He'll get some bikes and deliver them. No problem."

"Hey, wait a minute," Lorenzo the Slug said, his bushy eyebrows knitted with suspicion. He'd come in late to the conversation since he was using the snazzy facilities at Fior d'Italia. "If you talked to Punk Leo, how come you didn't know Big Leo's dead?"

Joe the Pistol shrugged. "I ain't talked to Big Leo since the summer of eighty-three. We had a fight. I was gonna ask Punk Leo about him when we got together. Don't need to now."

"What was the fight about?" Lorenzo asked.

Joe looked remorseful. "Damned if I can remember."

* * *

"You were talking about Stonestown," Richie said after a long silent period punctuated only by curses as more time elapsed without a van sighting. It was nearly seven-thirty. "I remember that Leo runs an import-export business. Furniture, toys, all kinds of stuff. I think his warehouse is in Stonestown."

Rebecca's head snapped toward him. "That means he probably ships furniture around the country, or the world . . ."

"Exactly," Richie said.

The more Rebecca thought about it, the more sense it made. Wrap the body up good, pack it in a furniture crate, put on a sticker to Madagascar, and then pay a few bribes once it arrives. Who'd know? Or, even simpler, ship it to Las Vegas and pay some friends down there to create another lump out in the desert far from town. Easy. But, *why*?

And, if someone were trying to get Cockeyed Lanigan's body to Leo's shop, what if they freaked out at all the security around the mall due to Christmas, dumped the body, and took off?

"Let's go check the place out," she said.

"Why?" Richie looked at her as if she'd lost her mind. "My guys won't be at Leo's business."

"How do you know?" she retorted. "He acted more than a little suspicious. He clearly knows more than he's saying."

There was more under-the-breath muttering

about women and cops. "All right, Inspector. We'll take a quick look, then we're out of there and back to North Beach. I've got the feeling they aren't far away."

Stonestown was almost completely deserted because it closed early on Christmas Eve. They found Leo's import-export business, then drove to the loading dock area in back of the building. All the lights were out. It looked quiet and empty.

Richie parked along the side of the building, then they tried the doors, hoping to find one open and something going on in the warehouse. They didn't.

"Well, it was worth a try," Richie said, dejected. "I should give this up. I don't know where else to look, what else to do. I guess it's time for me to face the music."

"Which means what? Are you in trouble? We've spent the whole day searching, Richie, and I don't even know why."

For a moment, the way he gazed at her, she thought he might open up. He didn't. "You don't want to know. Trust me. I'm supposed to deliver them somewhere. That's all there is to it."

They started to walk back to his car. "Well, maybe they'll go there on their own," she consoled.

"They don't know where it is. It's a secret." He glanced over his shoulder a moment. "I'm sure they expect someone will help them, but I can't if I don't know where they are."

"That makes no sense," she insisted.

"It doesn't, except that they're old guys who are used to others looking out for them."

"As in, they've been in jail most of their lives?" Rebecca asked suspiciously.

"As in . . . you might be right about that. Whatever it means, I lost them, and I'll have to pay the consequences."

"You make it sound as if the consequences are dangerous." They parted and he walked toward the driver's side, she to the passenger's.

He looked upward. The stars shone brightly in the clear night sky, the moon just rising over the mountains. "I'll find out," he said.

He was maddening. It was like talking to a cipher. "Well, you might be wise to worry." She faced him over the top of the car. "A killer is out there somewhere. Maybe he's hunting down your Santas—maybe not. But he's there, and if you're involved, you could be in danger, as well."

"Me? I never do anything dangerous. I'm allergic to it."

Just then a shot rang out. Richie ducked after feeling the bullet whistle by his head. Rebecca dropped behind the Porsche. A Dumpster was behind her and she ran to it, curled between the trash bin and the wall, waving for Richie to follow. He did.

As far as she knew, Richie Amalfi wasn't armed. But she was. She slid the gun from the special pocket in her handbag where it was held down with a Velcro strap. She thumbed the safety off and waited. One more shot, and she'd see where the shooter was hiding.

"Cover me," he whispered.

"They only do that in movies," she hissed and made a grab for him.

She was too late. He sprinted off in the direction of the shooter and stood behind a telephone pole. Another building was beside the import-export loading dock, and that one also had a large parking area with pillars and ramps. Richie headed for it.

With a curse, she followed. Spotting a smashed beer can, she grabbed and tossed the can as far as she could toward her right, hoping the sound as it landed would draw fire and she'd be able to spot the gunman.

It didn't.

She scrambled after Richie. She had no idea where he'd disappeared to, only that he needed some protection . . . and she needed to catch a killer.

She heard a "thump" then an "Oomph!" followed by another "whack, thump, blam." Quickly, she followed the sounds. Two men held Richie while Leo pummeled him.

She stretched out her arms, a two-handed grip

on her gun. "Stop right now, Leo!" she shouted loud to make herself heard over the swearing, punching, and Richie's grunts of pain. "I don't miss when I shoot!"

Leo's arm was high when he looked over and saw the barrel of a powerful Beretta facing him. It wasn't some wimpy twenty-two. It was a cop's gun—city issue.

The two guys with him decided to show respect for a serious firearm. They let go of Richie and ran. She let them go. It was Leo she was after.

"So, your girlfriend's a cop," he said, his voice sneering as he faced Richie, who was sitting on the ground rubbing his ribs and stomach. "What were you thinking bringing a cop to my house? Here, to my business? I told you to keep away from me, but you wouldn't listen! This isn't over, Richie."

"Yes, it is," Rebecca said, showing her badge. "I'm bringing you in for questioning about the death of . . ."—she hesitated, but it was the only name she knew—"Cockeyed Lanigan. You're not under arrest yet, but you come quietly or you'll be charged with assault and battery."

"I didn't hurt Lanigan! I was trying to stop him from . . ." Suddenly, he shut his mouth. "I know nothing. I want to talk to my lawyer. I won't answer any more questions."

She knew enough about the law and lawyers to

know there was no way she was going to be allowed to interrogate Leo on Christmas Eve after he'd asked for a lawyer. Probably not Christmas Day, either. She didn't have enough probable cause to go after an arrest warrant. Not yet, anyway. "You'll have plenty of chance for that," she said. Let him stew a while, she thought, as she turned her attention on Richie. "Are you all right? Do you want to go to a hospital?"

"I don't need a hospital." He touched his bleeding, swollen lip. "I just need my handkerchief back. And I want Leo to tell me where the old Santas are." He faced Leo. "I know you know about them."

"Sure," Leo said eyeing the two. "I just got a couple of kid's bikes for them. That's why I'm out here and saw you two sneaking around my warehouse. Why?" Slowly the light seemed to dawn. "Is that what this is about? You're trying to find them? You're the transport, right? And you lost them." He chuckled. "I was wondering about that. Well, I'll be damned!"

"Where are they?" Richie demanded again.

Leo folded his arms. "No way, Richie. You ruin my Christmas, I'll ruin yours."

"Damn you!" Richie moved forward.

Rebecca put an arm out, stopping him.

"Eat me," Leo said with a nasty smirk.

"Cool it, you two." Rebecca put her gun in the handbag and handed Richie the handkerchief, then faced Leo. "Why did you shoot at us? Why beat up Richie?"

He looked disgusted. "The first was to scare you away, the second was to show what happens to somebody too stupid to run after being shot at. Officially, however, I thought he was a burglar."

Rebecca had to admit to a certain logic to that. "I'll let you go tonight, but stay close to home and to your phone. We can talk tomorrow—"

"But it's Christmas!"

"At eleven in the morning. Have your attorney call me." She knew the guy would call and say he and Leo wouldn't be there, but it was okay. Leo wasn't going anywhere, and her gut feeling told her he wasn't a murderer.

Stupid and crooked, yes. Murderer, no.

"What is it they call you?" she asked, directing her question at her so-so suspect. "Punk Leo? Makes sense to me. Get out of here now."

He ran to his car, casting aspersions on Richie's manhood the entire way.

Angie Amalfi looked at the clock when she heard the knock on her apartment door. It was early for Paavo and besides, the knock was too quiet for him. He had a cop's "open up or else" knock, even when coming to see her. They were going to go to dinner and then to her parents' house for Christmas Eve.

Angie was a petite woman with wavy brown

hair streaked with light auburn highlights. She'd been looking forward to this Christmas Eve for some time—the first one for her and Paavo as an engaged couple.

She opened the door, then her mouth dropped and she stared. Was this a joke? Her mother, Serefina Amalfi, stood in front of her dressed up like a vision of a very w-i-i-d-e sugarplum wearing a Christmasy red dress decorated with large white polka dots, her black coat haphazardly tossed over one arm. Springs of mistletoe formed a corsage. Serefina's cheeks were fiery red. She'd obviously been testing the eggnog.

That wasn't the whole story, though. Behind her were more little old Santa Clauses than Angie had ever seen. "What's going on, Mamma?" she asked, wide-eyed. "Did you raid the North Pole?"

"These are my good friends," Serefina's words slurred as she linked arms with two of them. Her coat fell and Angie picked it up. "We've been celebrating, talking about the good old days. And we have a favor to ask of you."

"Where's Papà?" she asked, sticking her head out the door to better see through the blaze of red.

Just then, her neighbor Stan Bonnette, probably because of all the commotion, opened his apartment door, gazed into the hall at the plethora of Christmas spirit, gawked, and then quickly shut the door again. His dead bolt clicked into place.

"Your papà is home," Serefina answered.

"He's waiting for us, the old fart. He doesn't like to go out, as you know." She lowered her voice to a stage whisper. "And he doesn't approve of all my friends." She put a finger in front of her mouth and said, "Shush."

"Mamma, I think you need some coffee," Angie said, pulling her inside.

"Your father is such an old man!" Serefina wailed. "Not like *i miei amici!*" To Angie, her mother's friends looked eighty at youngest. "So, are you going to make them stand in the hallway, or are you going to help us?"

Angie instinctively put her arms up to block the door. It was Christmas Eve and Paavo was coming over soon for their private celebration. This couldn't be happening. With brows creased, she asked suspiciously, "Help you with what, Mamma?"

After Richie's lip stopped bleeding, he looked at his watch. It was after eight. "Damn! I've got to get going."

"Drop me off at Homicide?" she asked.

"Sure."

They rode in silence except for the time he asked her what she was looking for in her purse. She told him it was her key card to get into Homicide after hours. Actually, it was one-half of a homing device that she planned to stick under the Porsche's passenger seat. The other half remained in her purse. She wasn't about to let him ride off, possibly to meet with the killer she was looking for, without doing anything about it. She could tell from the way he drove, constantly checking side and rearview mirrors, that he was far too paranoid about being followed for her to tail him the normal way.

The magnet on the homer made a little "dink" as it met the metal bars under the seat and she coughed, trying to cover the sound. He glanced her way. She patted her chest. "Sorry."

"Look, Inspector," he said, "I'm sorry about this, too. The day didn't go quite the way I'd planned. I didn't mean to put you in danger. Or myself."

"I know. For me, it goes with the territory."

He stopped just outside the Hall of Justice parking lot. Her car, a five-year-old Jeep Cherokee with four-wheel drive, a V8 engine, and a CD player, perfect for when she went up to the mountains or to some remote beach for vacation, was the only one left in the center of the lot. A couple of security-guard cars were right next to the building.

"Looks like everyone's gone home for Christmas Eve," she said.

"Yeah. Guess so," he murmured, facing her, his gaze intense. "Look, uh . . ."

She got out of the Porsche. "See you around, Richie Amalfi."

Dark eyes caught hers and he nodded. "You, too, Inspector."

She shut the door, and he drove off.

Hurrying to her car, she set up her half of the homing device on the dashboard. It whirred for a moment, not doing a thing, then began a steady, pulsating beep. Success!

She started out, heading left as she'd seen him go. She'd ridden with others as they'd used one of these devices to follow a suspect, but she'd never done it on her own and it was trickier than she'd imagined. Richie would turn a corner, and she'd go straight, only to realize her mistake when the beeps grew weak and slow. It'd be a matter of U-turning when possible, if not racing madly around a block to pick up the strong steady pulse once again.

They headed up Twin Peaks and were nearly to the top when the beeps grew fast and loud. She slowed to a crawl and when she rounded a curve in the winding road, she saw the Porsche in a driveway, Richie getting out.

She stopped and shut off the car's lights then backed up onto the side of the road. The street-light illuminated him as he walked to the front door and unlocked it. She wondered why he wanted to go home. Again, doubts about every-thing he'd told her that day surfaced.

The lights turned on, one by one, as he went through his house. The place looked like the kind of home he might have. Modern and red-wood, with a bow-shaped plate glass window in the front giving him what she imagined must be a sweeping view of the city. She waited, fairly certain he wouldn't be staying home alone all evening. She'd follow in hopes that wherever he went, she'd learn about the twelve Santas, her dead Santa, and perhaps what this day really had been about.

Twenty minutes later, the inside lights started to go off. Richie appeared in suit and tie and got back into the Porsche.

She ducked down in her SUV and waited until he was well out of sight and the homing device began its slow beeps that told her it was safe to follow.

Presidio Heights was an area filled with man-sions of the rich and famous, including politi-cians and some of the top medical specialists and lawyers in the country. She expected to go straight through it when the beeps began to grow faster and faster. He must have stopped, she thought. She pulled over. This was one of the few parts of the city with street parking readily avail-able. It was because there were few apartment dwellers vying for space, and many of the man-sions had added underground parking to keep their expensive cars safe from the elements and thieves. For a moment, she could scarcely believe she was in San Francisco.

She got out of the SUV. At the corner she stopped. Ahead was a brightly lit mansion with many cars parked near it, Richie's Porsche among them.

She phoned dispatch to find out who lived in the house. To her surprise, the answer wasn't readily available. A major search had to be performed before she got a name: Giorgio Boiardi.

"My God," she muttered. The name was familiar. Back in her SUV she turned on her Black-Berry handheld with its wireless Internet and prayed it would work in this area. It had cost her an arm and a leg, but was handy for her job.

It connected. Within seconds, Google verified her memory and added to it. Giorgio Boiardi, mobster, headed West Coast operation 1949–1978, in prison 1979–1992 when released due to old age and infirmity.

Curious, she searched for his birth date, and when she found it, looked again to make sure she was reading it right. He was born exactly ninety years ago. Today was his birthday.

This must be a birthday party. And all the old men . . . could they all have been . . . ?

She had to swallow hard. Had she stumbled upon a group of old criminals gathering in one place to celebrate his birthday with the *capo di tutti capi*? The Don? Is that what was happening?

No wonder Richie wouldn't tell her what was

going on. How many of the guys he was looking for had outstanding warrants? How many could she pull in to finally serve time for the crimes they'd committed? That was the reason for the Santa suits. Not that they were a bunch of do-gooders, but because they were wanted men! They needed to hide their faces. What better way than as Santa Claus the day before Christmas?

And Richie Amalfi was in the middle of it all.

Now what? One person who was a cop and yet understood the Amalfis came to mind—Paavo Smith. They needed to talk. She tried his cell phone, but it went straight to messaging.

Intuition sparked and she flipped through the stored addresses on her cell phone.

A cheerful, feminine voice answered the call. A few minutes of conversation yielded more than she ever imagined.

She put the light beacon on top of her car, turned on the siren, and sped across the city. The city was tiny, but between traffic jams and traffic lights, it could easily take a half hour to go a few miles. Fortunately, the streets were pretty empty.

Most people were home with their families, not racing around hoping to make a career-establishing, big-time arrest.

She left her SUV by a fire hydrant, and nearby was the white Econoline. She all but rubbed her hands in glee. She was on the right track after all.

Impatiently, she waited for the elevator to bring her up to the top floor of the building. She'd never been there before, but she'd heard talk about it often enough to know not only how to find it but exactly what it would look like inside.

The door opened. Angelina Amalfi looked prettier than ever in a red silk dress with matching shoes and gold and pearl jewelry. Rebecca had never even owned dyed-to-match shoes. She felt frumpy as she realized what her once-white blouse and crisp black slacks must look like after today's exertions. And she'd never even put the barrette back in her hair. She buttoned her jacket, hoping that might help.

"Come in," Angie said. "We've got eggnog and lots of cookies. The last batch of biscotti is still baking—and Paavo's back from the grocery now, too. We used a lot of sugar tonight."

Rebecca's gaze swept over the apartment before settling on that of her fellow inspector. The living room was much more attractive than she'd expected. The furniture was a mixture of antique and modern. She'd imagined it would be gaudy with dark wood and Victorian curlicues as far as the eye could see. Instead, it was light and peaceful, much simpler and more tasteful than she'd thought . . . or, than she'd hoped.

Paavo was standing in the dining area talking to

a heavyset older woman. He excused himself and approached, a drink in one hand, the sleeves on his white shirt rolled back, his tie slightly loosened, and with a smidgeon of flour on his brown slacks. He looked relaxed and . . . happy. Not the stern, serious man he always was at work. Her heart contracted.

"What's the problem, Rebecca?" he asked, knowing she wasn't there on a social call. "I heard you were looking for me."

Earlier, when she'd called simply to ask for Paavo to talk over all she'd learned with him, she could hardly believe what Angie told her. Now, she had a duty to perform.

Santas sat around the dining room table, on the petit-point sofa, antique Hepplewhite chair, and across the room on a pair of wingbacks. A couple of them stood in the kitchen. They still wore their suits, but their hats and beards were off. Even sitting, she could tell that most of them were little men. Perhaps once large and forceful, they now looked stooped and frail. They were *old*.

"I . . . um . . ." She looked from one Santa to the other. Canes were everywhere. At least no one used a walker. Hauling them all into jail was going to be a bit more awkward than she'd imagined. What would the AARP say about this? "I've got to question them, one by one."

"That'll take some time," Paavo said. "They're

planning to go somewhere for Christmas Eve, although I get the feeling none of them know how to get there."

"None of them are suspects," she said, "but someone might know something." She faced the group and asked for their attention, then introduced herself. "Cockeyed Lanigan was killed this morning, and I'm trying to find out if anyone here can help in my investigation of his death."

"Cockeyed just died?" Joey Zoom said, surprised. "I thought he was already dead."

"I told you! People ought to use the wood chipper, like in the good ol' days!" Peewee exclaimed.

Joe the Pistol turned to Serefina. "If I'da known you was so chummy with all these cops, I never woulda called you!"

The others told him to shush.

Rebecca knew what was going on: they'd spent a lifetime conditioned not to talk to a cop. "I know where you're supposed to be tonight," she said. "And I can take you there, but not until I learn something about Cockeyed Lanigan."

As one, they all started to put on their beards and hats.

"I don't know why I'm bothering with this getup," Lorenzo muttered. "We're already at a goddamned cop convention."

"Hold it, everyone," Paavo said. "Rebecca's okay. She just needs answers to a few questions."

"Easy for you to say," the Cucumber sneered.

"Wait! He's my son-in-law to be," Serefina protested. "You trust me, you trust Paavo."

"We trust Paavo. Just not *her*." Joey Zoom waved his thumb at Rebecca. "She comes here threatening. The hell with that!"

Rebecca realized the folly of her completely wrong approach with these men. "Look, I've just got a couple of questions."

"Tell the girl," Serefina urged. "Nobody liked Cockeyed."

The Santas eyed each other.

Finally, Joey Zoom spoke. "Cockeyed was bad. Word was, he, uh, hated a Big Somebody. Real big. Maybe he wanted to get that somebody. Thought he could follow us around, find out where the party was, and then sneak in wearing a Santa suit. Now, I ain't saying that's what happened, but it could be."

The others nodded.

Rebecca didn't buy it. "So Cockeyed was going to somehow use you guys to get to this Big Somebody, but then he just happened to get himself killed?"

The Santas all shifted nervously. "Look, we saw Cockeyed following us at the airport," Lorenzo said. "Joey Zoom took care of the van so we'd get rid of Richie, but when he pulled off the freeway, Cockeyed tried to follow. I think he made a mistake and went off the overpass instead."

At Rebecca's questioning expression, Joey the Pistol added, "Cockeyed wasn't called that for nothing. He musta got rattled, and did a swan dive."

The others agreed, some loudly.

Rebecca and Paavo traded glances. "If Cockeyed's death was an accident," she said, "how did he end up at Stonestown Mall?"

The Santas all turned expectedly to Joey Zoom. "As I see it," he said, "Punk Leo spilled the beans to Cockeyed, and then realized that if Cockeyed hurt Big Somebody, Leo'd be toast. So, he followed Cockeyed to try to stop him. He musta seen when poor Cockeyed was called by His Maker. Maybe it scared him, who knows, and he didn't want to leave the body where there might be questions about him and his Santa suit. Word gets out, you know, and Big Somebody— he's good at puttin' two and two together."

At Rebecca's nod, Joey Zoom continued. "Punk Leo probably figured out a way to get ridda the body. But with all the security guards at the mall, he got cold feet and stuffed the body someplace hoping to get it later. But he didn't hide it so good, and it got found."

"Isn't that sweet?" Serefina said, clasping her hands to her ample breasts. "Punk Leo saved the D—, I mean, Big Somebody from Cockeyed and only disturbed the accident scene because he wanted to help. *Madonna mia*, what a dear boy!"

Twelve Santa heads bobbed up and down in agreement.

Paavo looked at Rebecca and shrugged as if to say, "Could be." He was right, she thought. Punk Leo did a lot he shouldn't have, but murder probably wasn't included. Still, it'd be up to the DA and Leo's lawyers to sort it all out.

As for the old Santas, she probably could haul them into City Jail on some pretext—reckless driving, if nothing else—and see if any outstanding warrants turned up.

Her eyes strayed to the beautiful Christmas tree in one corner of the living room; her mind replayed the scene of Richie and herself in Union Square earlier that day, watching the shoppers and tourists, listening to Christmas carols. . . .

And something loosened in her heart. She looked at Paavo who was regarding her steadily, with trust, and then at Serefina's anxious face.

"One more question," she said to the group. "One thing I didn't understand. Since Richie Amalfi was your driver, why did you run off and leave him?"

"Why not?" Lorenzo the Slug wrinkled his mouth in disgust. "He was a pain in the ass, thinking he had to baby us, watch out for us, tell us to do this, do that. We've taken care of ourselves for eighty years and don't need some young punk doing it now! Besides, we wanted to get a present for a dear friend who's celebrating his birthday today. Something that money can't buy, and I think we've got it."

Angie took that opportunity to carry from the kitchen a big Italian hand-painted pasta bowl filled with just-from-the-oven biscotti, amaretti, and honey-dipped cookies. The whole thing was wrapped in green cellophane, gathered at the top to form a flowery design, and tied with an enormous green ribbon. "Here it is!" she cried.

The old men who were still awake cheered. The others woke from the noise and cheered as well, eventually.

Rebecca knew what she had to do.

She waited for what seemed like a century on the doorstep after speaking with an immaculate butler.

The door reopened and Richie appeared, his gaze questioning.

"I have a present for you," she said and stepped aside.

His expression was indescribable as he saw the twelve Santas, the cookies, and Rebecca. Then his face spread into a wide, toothy smile. "Come on in, guys. Everybody's waiting for you." He stood back, and the Santas entered, single file, to loud greetings and cheers.

He and Rebecca remained alone in the doorway. "Where'd you find them?" he asked.

She grinned. "They were baking cookies."

Dark eyes met hers. "You've saved my life! Do you realize what the reaction would have been if I told the birthday boy I'd lost his twelve best friends?" He shuddered.

She chuckled. "Glad to be of service."

Laughter from the party erupted. In the background, Sinatra sang "Winter Wonderland."

"Rebecca," Richie said, pointedly not using Inspector Mayfield, "come on inside with me. It's Christmas Eve. Join the party."

He took her hand. His was warm, hard, and masculine. Thoughts of their crazy adventure filled her, running up and down the streets of Chinatown, him sitting on a curb as she ranted at him, him fighting with Punk Leo in the kitchen.

The air was cool and crisp, the night a velvet canvas filled with stars. Inside were warm lights and happy sounds of the party.

She pulled her hand away. "I don't think so." Once done with work, she'd phone her family in Boise. She wanted to hear and talk to them on this holiest of all nights, a night for families and old, dear friends. She started to turn.

"Maybe some other time?" His eyes were too dark, too difficult for her to read or understand.

"No." She walked down the steps to the sidewalk.

"Merry Christmas, Rebecca," he called.

She glanced back at him with a surprising stab of regret as she waved good-bye, and suddenly, the strong feeling hit that she hadn't seen the last of Richie Amalfi. "Merry Christmas," she said, unable to hide the warmth in her voice.

She had a job to do, but as she walked to her car, she thought about Santa falling out of his sleigh.

And despite herself, she laughed.

With a pinch of pernicious and a dash of dastardly,

JOANNE PENCE

**cooks up a scrumptious banquet of murderous fun
in the Angie Amalfi mysteries**

Coming soon

COURTING DISASTER
0-06-050291-6/$6.99 US/$9.99 Can
There's already too much on the
bride-to-be's plate . . .
and much of it is murderous.

And don't miss these titles, available now

TWO COOKS A-KILLING
0-06-009216-5/$6.99 US/$9.99 Can
Nothing could drag Angie away from San Francisco—except
for a job preparing the banquet for her all-time favorite soap
opera characters during a Christmas Reunion Special.

IF COOKS COULD KILL
0-06-054821-5/$6.99 US/$9.99 Can
When Angie's friend Connie Rogers' would-be boyfriend
is sought by the police in connection with a brutal
robbery/homicide, the two friends set out to find the real killer.

BELL, COOK, AND CANDLE
0-06-103084-8/$6.99 US/$9.99 Can
When Angie is called upon to deliver a humorous confection
to an after-hours goth club, she finds herself
up to her neck in the demonic business.